65 West 55th Street

65 West 55th Street

Gagan Suri

iUniverse, Inc.
Bloomington

65 West 55th Street

Copyright © 2012 by Gagan Suri

All rights reserved. No part of this book may be used or reproduced by any means, graphic, electronic, or mechanical, including photocopying, recording, taping or by any information storage retrieval system without the written permission of the publisher except in the case of brief quotations embodied in critical articles and reviews.

This is a work of fiction. All of the characters, names, incidents, organizations, and dialogue in this novel are either the products of the author's imagination or are used fictitiously.

iUniverse books may be ordered through booksellers or by contacting:

iUniverse
1663 Liberty Drive
Bloomington, IN 47403
www.iuniverse.com
1-800-Authors (1-800-288-4677)

Because of the dynamic nature of the Internet, any web addresses or links contained in this book may have changed since publication and may no longer be valid. The views expressed in this work are solely those of the author and do not necessarily reflect the views of the publisher, and the publisher hereby disclaims any responsibility for them.

Any people depicted in stock imagery provided by Thinkstock are models, and such images are being used for illustrative purposes only.

Certain stock imagery © Thinkstock.

ISBN: 978-1-4759-6218-5 (sc)
ISBN: 978-1-4759-6220-8 (hc)
ISBN: 978-1-4759-6219-2 (e)

Library of Congress Control Number: 2012921568

Printed in the United States of America

iUniverse rev. date: 12/10/2012

Message from the Author:

Love goes beyond boundaries. To all those who go against convention and dare to love someone of a different religion, culture, or country, believe in yourself, and stay firm in your belief. All forces against you will gradually wither away, and what will remain is true love.

Dedicated to my wife, my best friend, my soul mate

I am grateful to all my family and friends who over the years have provided me support and encouragement to write this novel. A special thanks to Charles Boebel for helping edit this novel and to Gaurav Shivpuri for literally putting the pen in my hand.

Prologue

1971, India–Bangladesh (East Pakistan) border

A bullet zips past Major Dev's left ear, tearing his earlobe, and hits Lieutenant Ravi in his chest. Ravi dies in Major Dev's arms. With blood on his hands and tears in his eyes, he signals the soldier carrying the wireless in his backpack.

"Call General Bhatia."

A minute later, General Bhatia comes on the air.

"Sir, I need permission to deploy heavy artillery. We are under intense attack from the Pakistani army. I have lost ten men in the last few minutes, including Lieutenant Ravi; over and out."

After a pause, the wireless comes alive. "You have permission. Jai Hind [Victory to India]; over and out."

The Pakistani battalion had no idea what was headed their way. Their intelligence had grossly underestimated the firepower of the Indian army.

The Indian army fired flares that lit the night sky and revealed Pakistani positions. A few minutes later a slew of shells wiped out most of the Pakistani forces at the border.

Two hours later, at dawn, Indian soldiers inspected the battlefield to round up the injured Pakistani soldiers. They witnessed the gruesome sight of human limbs hanging on trees and acres of blood-soaked land. They captured twenty-two injured Pakistani soldiers. The ones who could not stand either sat or lay on the ground until medical help arrived. Subaydaar Major Bheem prepared a list of the ranks, names, and ID numbers of the prisoners of war.

Major Dev walked past the line of dead Indian and Pakistani soldiers and the prisoners. He brushed past Major Atif, who was badly injured but still standing proud. They looked into each other's eyes with deep hate and anger.

1. Unchained Melody

Twenty-seven years later, 1998, New York City...

"Get moving!" shouted JJ Valaya's nasty, pencil-thin fashion show coordinator. "Next batch of guys in the lineup, like, *now*! JJ didn't bring you to New York for a holiday. Boys and girls, you're here to work."

She barked orders left, right, and center, music blaring, spotlights dancing on the catwalk, and models zipping by every minute.

"She needs to eat; maybe then she wouldn't be as nasty. She looks like a bamboo stick," whispered Zeina to Shiraz as they worked with costumes on hangers.

"I think she needs to get laid. I can almost sense her frustration," replied Shiraz in her thick Israeli accent, smirking and sneering at the show's coordinator.

The two girls were working as part-time dressing models to make a few extra bucks. Both had recently graduated from Parsons School of Design and were working on freelance assignments in Manhattan.

After the show, the two of them went out with the models and coordinators to a party at a nearby club. Everyone enjoyed happy hour at the club, after which Zeina and a few others were invited to a private after-party. At that party, one of the hot-body Indian models, Sukhvinder, a.k.a. Sukhi, a "cut-surd," which is a casual way of referring to a Sikh man with cut hair, and a chubby Indian Punjabi designer, Rahul, started flirting with her. They got into a "pissing contest" to see who could flirt more and came on to her pretty strong.

"Hi there! What is that you are drinking? Let me get you another drink," said Rahul, getting a bit too close to Zeina.

"Hey, Rahul, can you give us some space, please? Can't you see I was talking to her?" Sukhi said. He gave Rahul a slight nudge, indicating that he should back off.

When Punjabis get into such contests, it is usually about *tandoori* chicken, beer, or a woman, in that order. The outcome of such contests can be unpredictable, but most of the time, it is hilariously violent.

Sukhi didn't want to get into a punching match that night, so he cut Rahul out of the conversation and rescued Zeina by offering her a ride home. She was glad to leave with him because she was not enjoying the extra attention and the aggressive, predatory environment.

He hailed a cab and gave the cab driver two addresses, the first stop being the hotel he was staying at. During the cab ride, he made a move on Zeina and kissed her. When the cab arrived at the hotel, he invited her for a drink. One thing led to another, and she ended up indulging physically more than she normally would have with someone she had known for just a few hours.

Later that week, Sukhi had plans to go meet his high school friend Karan, who lived in Knoxville, Tennessee. He had a week in the States and had no other plans.

Later that night, Zeina went back to her apartment, located at 65 West 55th Street. It was an awkward good-bye. Sukhi asked her for her telephone number, using an excuse that he needed advice on freelance modeling options in New York. Out of politeness, thinking that he might be a half-decent guy, she gave her home telephone number.

Sukhi called Zeina from Knoxville two days later, but she didn't answer her phone. She returned his call later that evening. The caller ID displayed a 212 number. Karan was busy tuning his guitar, so Sukhi answered.

"Hi, thanks for calling back. I've been busy catching up with my buddy here. Listen, I'll be in New York for two days this coming Sunday and Monday. If you are free, I'd like to take you and your Israeli friend out for coffee or drinks."

"Hey, is someone playing a guitar around you, or is that recorded music?" Zeina cut him off. She could hear the soothing sound of a Spanish guitar and someone humming or singing.

"Oh that, yes, it's the guy I am here to see. He's practicing some boring country music stuff that I just don't get. Excuse me, but I really need to use the loo. Can you speak to him? I'll be right back." He handed the phone over to Karan without waiting for her to say anything.

A melodious voice accompanied by a Spanish guitar echoed in her ears. "Oh my love, my darling, I hunger for your love ..." That was the first time she heard his voice. She was a bit taken aback because she was on the phone with a stranger who began his hello with a song!

Karan could hear the giggle and almost sense the blush on her face over the phone. The unexpected harmonious strumming of six strings and the soothing melody were rather magical.

"Oh, that sounded amazing," she said, as he finished singing "Unchained Melody."

The song had neither sounded like the original Righteous Brothers version, nor did it have the same feel as it did in the movie *Ghost*, starring Patrick Swayze and Demi Moore, but there was something special about it. This incidence of Karan on the phone singing to Zeina felt like it had been created and orchestrated, as if someone or something had made it happen.

"Hi! My name is Karan, not Karen, as many folks call me. I'm usually not that flirtatious, but I had the guitar in one hand and a girl on the phone in the other hand, so I carried on with the song I just learned," he said, lying through his teeth, because just before he was handed the phone, he had been practicing "Country Roads," a song by John Denver. He had become flirtatious after living in the States for a few years.

"Yeah, sure, Karan not Karen, I believe you. Well, my name is Zeina, and ordinarily, I would not speak to strangers who burst into a song as an introduction, but I liked your voice and your song, so I'll give you a few minutes of my precious time," she responded in a regal tone. She carried on with a slightly cute attitude. "So, you, like, live in some 'ville' in some southern state?"

"Actually, the name of the 'some ville' is 'Knoxville,' and it's in the state of Tennessee, which is really nowhere as hillbilly a place as you make it out to be. Knoxville has a young population, forty-five thousand of those just at the University of Tennessee. The city is surrounded by the beautiful Smoky Mountains." He spoke as if he worked for the Tennessee Tourism Bureau.

He continued, "Well, generally Knoxville has friendly folks, with the exception of some parts of Knox County. I've been advised never to venture into those areas by the HR director of the hotel I work at. She told me that I may get arrested by a local redneck cop for just being in those areas. Apparently, any color other than white is unacceptable. I'm somewhere between white and black. Some folks here call people like me a 'sand nigger,' which means a free pass to a night in jail, which I am not too keen on. The last year here has been all right. I have not been in any jail, and my tenure has almost come to an end. I'm off to work in Washington, DC, in a few weeks." He sounded excited.

"Ah ha, that sounds lovely. So you'll be moving closer to civilization. You know DC is just a short distance from Manhattan. Have you ever been to the city?"

Strumming "The Sound of Silence," by Simon and Garfunkel, he answered, "I have indeed been to the city a few times. How could I ever forget my first visit! Here is my first visual of the city: I flew in for the first time to the US on the Fourth of July in '94 and saw Manhattan all lit up against the night sky from the aircraft at about five thousand feet. As the plane was landing at JFK, I thought the beautiful fireworks that lit up the night sky were to welcome the likes of me, arriving in the States for the first time. It was beautiful to see the fireworks from the plane against the New York City skyline. I can never forget that sight. But the magical welcome turned into a nightmare because a distant relative who was supposed to meet me never showed up at the airport! I called my elder brother, Varun, who lived in Springfield, Illinois, at the time. He told me that our uncle, who was to pick me up, had a family emergency. He instructed me to go to the domestic terminal, buy a ticket to DC at the American Airlines counter, and spend a week with another set of relatives there. Before flying to New York, I had never been on an airplane before, and had never been outside of India. So you can well imagine what I went through the first day in a new country. That was how I saw the Big Apple for the first time. I have been there many times since then." He realized that was a long answer to a short question.

"Oh gosh, that sounds awful. How interesting that you came here the same year I did. However, my mother came to settle me in at Parsons. Anyway, so other than your guitar and probably line dancing, what does one do in Brownsville?" she asked, thinking that he sounded a bit "fresh off the boat" and maybe not interesting enough to carry on the conversation with much further. After all, he had never been on a plane until recently and had lived in India for the first twenty-plus years of his life.

"First of all, it's Knoxville and not Brownsville. And really, it's a cool city. I wish you city folks could see some of this beautiful suburban

America. There are great pubs, bars, and clubs here. I spend my spare time hiking, doing photography, reading, and I do watch a lot of movies," he responded, sensing that she was losing interest in the conversation.

"Movies, eh? Seen any interesting ones recently?" She posed her final question in haste to end the conversation politely. Talking to this guy was now eating into her precious going-out time of the evening.

"I have indeed. I watched *Like Water for Chocolate* just last week, and I loved it. It's an incredible film. Watch it if you get a chance, and let me know what you think of it. It seems to me that Sukhi is doing the big job in the toilet. I can have him call you later." He sensed that she wanted to get off the phone.

"No need. I've got to go for now. Good chatting with you. Ciao!" She hung up.

Sukhi came out after sitting on the throne for almost half an hour, stinking up the bathroom with cigarette smoke and other toxic gases. The apartment was small, the exhaust fan was not effective, and the stink had nowhere to go. Karan opened all the windows and the apartment door to cross-ventilate, sprayed air freshener, and burned a few incense sticks.

"Dude, what the hell did you eat?"

"I didn't eat much, but I had a lot to drink the last few days. I have a bad stomach now. She hung up? I met her at the fashion show, and we had some fun together. She has a hot Israeli friend, I forget her name. I wanted to fuck her so badly. Maybe on my way back I'll get lucky," he announced proudly with a sly and evil grin on his face.

Sukhi's mannerism disgusted Karan. Then he asked Karan if it could be arranged for him to have sex with a white woman, paid or unpaid; anything would do. Sukhi confessed that he had never been laid by a Caucasian before. Karan absolutely refused to help in this matter. Irritable and red in the face, Karan told Sukhi that he was not a pimp. He was convinced that Sukhi didn't have an ounce of decency and remained a pig, after all the years he had known him. His mind raced back to the first time they met.

Over a decade ago, just when Karan had moved to Jodhpur, Sukhi—at that time a tall and lanky Sikh boy with a turban and a baby beard consisting of a handful of awkwardly placed hair—knocked on his door one evening. He introduced himself and offered his hand in friendship. Little did he know that meeting was meant to be; there was a greater plan linked to that meeting by the *Painter Man,* Karan's term for God. He had picked up the term from Abba's song. Sukhi was simply a stepping-stone, an aid that life used to bring him to his soul mate.

He had spent a lot of time with Sukhi in high school. Sukhi was considered bad news by most of the neighborhood. He was rebellious; he cut his hair and shaved his beard against his family's wishes. He was rather dumb and made it through high school only after several attempts. His mental airplane needed at least two runways to take off. After graduating from high school, he started a correspondence course and did odd jobs to make money, including insurance frauds. He joined a "jim" (as he spelled "gym") to keep his energy controlled. Then someone at the *jim* gave him the idea of becoming a fashion model, which worked out in his favor.

Sukhi introduced porn, alcohol, and drugs to his school cohorts. He had the balls to rent porn videos, also known as "blue films," at local video stores in Jodhpur and then arrange for viewing sessions at the homes of kids whose parents were out of town. Back in those days, porn was not easy to find or rent in India. The video stores kept them under the service clerks' desk with innocuous labels on them, such as *"Ramayan: Episode 1"* [Name of a religious scripture], to hoodwink local cops. Once when Sukhi visited Karan in Delhi, he announced that in spite of his "cool dude" image, he was actually a virgin at the age of twenty-one. Sukhi coerced Karan into accompanying him to G. B. Road, the red-light district of old Delhi, where he lost his virginity for fifty rupees, about one dollar, with an ugly Bihari prostitute with *paan* [Betel leaf]-stained teeth. Karan was so repulsed by the place that he swore never to be a part of any such "entertainment" ever again for anyone. He was dating a woman at the time and was not so desperate for sex as to stoop to that level.

The next day, Sukhi took a Greyhound bus back to New York. Karan was appalled by who Sukhi had become over the years. He realized that they had become far too different as human beings to remain friends anymore. People change over time—some for the better and others for the worse. He was far too busy to think anything more about it. He thought about Zeina, though, and hoped that she was safe because this guy could be a walking package of diseases. He felt concerned for her, but there was nothing he could do. He didn't want to interfere in anyone's personal affairs. He felt like warning Zeina about this guy visiting her again but did not act on it.

While vacuuming his apartment, Karan found Sukhi's pocket address book behind the bedside table. Thinking that he still might be in New York, Karan called Zeina on her mobile number, which was on his home phone's caller ID memory. She picked up the phone, recognizing the Knoxville area code.

She answered in a shaky voice, "Hello."

"Hi, Zeina, this is me, Karan not Karen, you remember? You don't sound well. Is everything all right? I hope this is not a bad time."

Upon hearing his gentle voice, she burst into sobs. There was an awkward silence and then she vented, yelling and cussing, "Your buddy is such a fucking asshole. I was tipsy, impressed by his 'sweep off the feet routine.' I got carried away and fooled around with him before he came to see you. I'm sure he boasted all about it to you. He walked through my door yesterday and kept asking me where my friend Shiraz was and if he could meet her. So I invited her, and we went out for drinks. All he did the entire time at the pub was hit on her. I realized that he didn't care about me. He was just using me to get to her. Everyone here has casual flings. I never had a fling ever before, and the one time I did, I ended up with such a scumbag!"

She continued, "I threw him out of my apartment, but since yesterday I can't stop feeling terrible. I feel violated and stupid. I have taken like a dozen showers but still feel his creepiness around me. I should never have invited him back. It was just a rotten, dumb decision." Zeina spoke in one breath. She had to vent her emotions and anger. She knew no one in whom she could confide something so personal, so somehow she opened up to a complete stranger.

He listened to her patiently and felt her pain. He himself had had one-night stands, but they were meant to be so; real names and numbers were not exchanged in such cases, and no one stayed for breakfast. She had broken the rules and unfortunately had not chosen well, which was the risk in the game.

"Please calm down. It's all right. You didn't know what you know now. This can happen to anyone. I'm sorry that you had to go through it. He's indeed a jerk. After what I saw of him recently, I am done with him. Listen, it's over, and it's behind you. All of us go through such experiences to learn lifelong lessons. It's just a part of life, no harm done. You just need to move on. Take a deep breath and stop being sad. He's not worth it."

"I just can't seem to stop feeling angry, more so at myself," she said even more hysterically.

Thinking quickly, he said, "The guy is just a sick surd. You know what people call surds in India? People call them 'bandaged brains.' Everyone in India makes fun of them," he joked to cheer her up. He was completely without prejudice and didn't mean a word of it.

"Here is a surd joke: two surds go to see their two other surd friends off at the Amritsar railway station. As the four of them reach the platform, they notice that the train has already started moving. Panicking, all of them start running and chasing the train, jumping over other waiting passengers on the platform, hopping over luggage, stumbling and falling all over the place. The entire platform, packed with passengers, witnessed this drama, including the passengers on the moving train. Finally, two surds managed to climb onto the last boogie, and two got left behind. Huffing and puffing, the two surds on the train gave each other a high five and started laughing uncontrollably! One of the passengers on the train asked them why the two of them were laughing, especially since they had left two of their buddies behind. One of the surds said that it was pretty funny that they had come to drop their friends off at the station, and now they were on the train, and those who had to be on the train got left behind."

Luckily, that did the trick. He heard a small laugh through tears and a stuffy nose on the other end. That was the turning point in the conversation. She seemed to have found the consolation she was looking for. She came across as a strong person. Although Karan didn't know it, she had been through plenty of ups and downs in her life. She was a fighter and was not about to give up easily on the small, sharp turns of life. The two of them spoke for a while about his upcoming move and made some small talk for almost an hour.

"Call me anytime you need someone to speak to, and keep your chin up."

She thanked him for his kind support and for patiently listening to her. She hung up after saying good-bye.

Karan left his garden-style studio apartment to catch some fresh air. It was early autumn, his favorite season. He went out for a drive in his pearl-green, two-door Honda Civic, which his older brother had gifted him on his graduation a few years ago.

The Blue Ridge Mountains, also known as the Smoky Mountains, are ablaze with stunning colors in autumn. The season starts off with the entire Tennessee valley turning into bright yellows and rusts, and as the season progresses, the colors change into flaming orange and deep hues of reds and vibrant purples. Slowly, the leaves start falling, leaving the trees bare for the winter.

One of Karan's favorite places to be in Knoxville was the Tennessee Valley Authority Dam on Douglas Lake. He drove there often with a few beers, his guitar, a novel, and his camera to enjoy what he called the best of America. That meant freedom to be whoever and whatever he wanted to be. Once again he soaked in the warmth of the evening sunlight and enjoyed a beautiful sunset while he planned his relocation. He wondered what life had in store for him.

When Zeina got off the phone, she dressed to go out. She had plans to meet her Greek friends for cocktails at Whiskey Park, next to one of her favorite places in the whole world—Central Park. She lived in a small, shared two-bedroom Manhattan apartment with Julia, her brother's ex-girlfriend, who had a beautifully decorated apartment and kept it in immaculate condition.

Zeina caught a glimpse of the same sunset that Karan was watching, but it was a reflection on a tall building's shiny glass a few blocks away. Sunset to New Yorkers simply meant that the night and fun had just begun.

Zeina was a fashion icon, always perfectly dressed and accessorized. As with most New Yorkers, her favorite color was black. This particular evening, she wore a sexy, black, fitted, knee-length dress from Banana Republic, a simple pearl necklace, pearl earrings, and tall, black boots. She grabbed her favorite black Ferragamo handbag and darted out the door, went down the small dingy elevator, and brushed past the doorman, who could never stop staring at her. She made a left on the street and walked down two blocks at a brisk pace. She didn't want to be late to meet her friends. She stopped suddenly at the end of the second block and realized she'd actually had to turn right from her building. She knew the city like the back of her hand; it was not like her to make such a mistake. She was about to turn around when she noticed that she was standing outside the video rental store to which she had a membership. The video cassette cover in the window display caught her attention instantly; it was the cover for *Like Water for Chocolate*, the same movie that Karan had mentioned to her in their first conversation. She zipped inside, rented the video, and hopped in a cab to get to Whiskey Park, where a chilled Cosmopolitan, her favorite martini, was awaiting her.

2. Like Water for Chocolate

Karan was bored of sitting in the tiny cubicle of the sales office at the Hyatt Regency in Knoxville. He shared his space with a female sales manager who yapped on the phone all day long about her personal life. He was fed up with selling hotel rooms and catering services to small businesses and local brides. He couldn't wait to get to the slightly more sophisticated government market of DC. He had graduated from Mercyhurst College in Pennsylvania with a BA and a major in hospitality. His first job was at the glamorous Hyatt Regency at Seaport Village in San Diego, where the corporate office had sent him as a corporate sales trainee for a year. He had a blast there, and who wouldn't have? San Diego has 360 days of sunny weather every year, beautiful beaches, and gorgeous women.

After a year of the trainee program, he was offered two options: either serve as a sales manager at a smaller property like the Hyatt in Knoxville, which would guarantee a fast track to a senior sales manager in a tier-1 city such as Chicago, or move directly to a tier-1 city as a junior sales manager and drag out his career. Karan felt that a fast track in life with a small sacrifice of a year was worth it. He chose to move to Knoxville and had made the most of his stay. He made great friends, dated a few interesting southern women, enjoyed hiking in the nearby mountains, and learned to play the guitar better. Apparently, every second person in the state of Tennessee knows how to play the guitar.

One aspect of work he did not enjoy was catering to the wedding market and dealing with brides. It was routine for brides to approach the catering office and behave like angels and act all sweet. They all came to him to help them plan their dream wedding. Their "dream" was his "nightmare"! All of them lost their angel wings early in the planning process and grew horns as they got closer to their weddings. He had just had too many weddings in the first year and couldn't take it anymore.

Lately, other than the bridal stress at work, he felt a void of companionship in his life, and he had been trying to fill the emptiness with the wrong women. He was looking forward to a fresh start at work and was seeking a companion for a meaningful relationship. As he contemplated the possibility of new friends, his thoughts drifted toward Zeina. He debated whether he should call to check on her or wait till he moved. He couldn't decide.

He picked up the phone to speak to his classmate Bobby in Columbia, Maryland, a city halfway between Baltimore and DC.

"Hi, Bobby. I've good news for you. I've been transferred to Crystal City Hyatt. I'll be moving in a few weeks."

"I'm so happy to hear that. You'll be so near, we can hang out often. Do you have a place to live yet?"

"No, but the hotel will host me for two weeks while I look for an apartment."

"Hey, I have an idea. I want to change my apartment as well. How about we rent a townhouse in Columbia and live together instead of living in apartments? I can drive to Baltimore, and you can drive to DC."

It sounded like a good proposition. Karan agreed, and the decision was made on the spot. He had now solved his accommodation situation and felt relieved.

Zeina was working at Tommy Hilfiger's design office that month, making the most of her one-year work permit. She came back from work, opened a bottle of Merlot, poured half a glass, lit candles, put on the radio, and sat down to relax and unwind. Her home was her sanctuary. It was beautifully decorated and had a calming ambience. She fetched her bathrobe from the closet, which was stuffed with shoes, handbags, and clothes, in that order of priority. The video cassette she had rented a week ago fell out of a handbag. She had not used that handbag since the day she went to Whiskey Park. She had completely forgotten about the video. The Bangladeshi owner of the video rental shop was sticky about the five-bucks-a-day late charge. This was NYC; nothing came cheap! She freed up her evening to watch the movie and return it that night. Julia was away for the evening, so it was perfect timing for her to watch the movie uninterrupted. She fluffed the cushions on the couch, made herself comfortable, threw a soft blanket on her legs, and started watching *Like Water for Chocolate*.

The film is a Mexican love story mixed with family drama and the main character's passion for cooking, baking, and putting her love into the food she prepares. There are many scenes with chocolate.

After the movie ended, Zeina was overcome by a strong craving for chocolate. She walked to the French patisserie at the end of the block after returning the movie and brought a thick slice of German chocolate cake and a skim milk latte back to her apartment. She changed into a nightgown, devoured the cake, and picked up the phone to dial Karan's number to discuss the movie. She hesitated for a second and thought that she had already hung up, but the one-click dial feature on her phone had dialed the number already. Half a ring later, he picked up the phone, recognizing a 212 area code.

"Hi, Zeina."

"Oh, hi! Hope I'm not calling you too late."

"I'm glad to hear from you. I have an early morning, but work comes every day. Your call is more important. How have you been?"

"Oh, I'm well, been busy working away, and getting things ready for my mother's arrival. She's coming from Islamabad day after tomorrow."

"It never occurred to me you were from Pakistan. What's your last name?"

"My last name is Zaman, Zeina Zaman—always the last one on the roll call, whether the list is arranged by first or last name," she replied with a giggle. "You have an unusual name. What does your name mean?"

"Karan was a character in *Mahabharata*, one of the ancient Indian epics. It's a popular name you get to hear in Bollywood movies."

"I love Bollywood. Mom and I love visiting Delhi; it's the best city for *desi* food and shopping. All our South Asian sort of stuff; you know what I mean? My mother simply goes crazy eating and shopping in the local bazaars. I love the spicy *chaats* [appetizers] of Bengali market and she loves those rice crepes, *dosas* at Sona Rupa. We both can't get enough of the vibrancy of Delhi."

"I love it there as well; I miss home. You know I've been back only once since I left for college. Somehow life here is pretty complex. There is never enough time. I find it rewarding, but rather lonely. My life has turned into a big rat race, but that is what my American Dream has become—one big rat race. The best opportunities are here, which keep me here," he said with a tinge of sadness.

"You sound down today. I think you need a drink and some fun. I personally love living here. In fact, I love being in the city. I don't think I could live anywhere else ever again. Speaking of a drink, I tried a really nice Australian Merlot this evening that just hit the market; you should try it; it's called Yellow Tail. The label is yellow with a kangaroo on it." After a pause, she added in a whisper, as if a telephone operator was hearing their conversation, "I also watched *Like Water for Chocolate* today. The movie is like an aphrodisiac! I really liked the film. I had to go out and get some chocolate. Thanks for the recommendation."

Awed by her candidness, he said, "I'm glad you liked it. I had similar sensations after watching that movie. I recall going to the Kroger by the house and getting a bag of brownies. I like such films; I have a lot of time in the evenings and often watch off-beat movies. Believe it or not, I love watching the American Movie Classic channel; they air classic black-and-white movies. I watched a Christmas movie I liked a lot last night called *It's a Wonderful Life* starring Jimmy Stewart. Have you seen it?"

"I love that movie; it's one my all-time favorites. I like most of the movies from that era. Have you seen *Breakfast at Tiffany's*?"

"Oh yeah, Audrey was at her best in that film; that's a classic for sure."

"I have a funny story about that movie: my brother Zoheb's roommate from Brown, Asad, visited a few days ago with his sister from Islamabad. Get this, he has never lived in England but has this heavy, fake British accent he thinks makes him sound cool. My brother and I are very close, and while he was an investment banker working here, we used to hang out a lot together. I was telling Asad that my brother treated me to an amazing champagne breakfast. He simply interrupted me and spoke out loud to his sister, announcing that he would like to take her for breakfast at Tiffany's the next morning! I burst out laughing.

"The following morning, I told my Greek friend, Kristos, who, of course, rubbed it in when he met Asad a few days later. Next time I met Asad, he made sure he told me that there is no breakfast served at Tiffany's, and that Tiffany's was a store. And my response was that I knew that very well, and it was obvious that he didn't. Anyway, the guy is hilariously jealous of my brother. I tend to keep an arm's length distance from him." She laughed, enjoying telling him the story and relishing the conversation.

"That's too funny. What an ass!"

"What is that music you are listening to? That sounds like one of my favorite *ghazals*."

"Yes, it is the *ghazal 'Aaj jaane ki zid na karo,'* sung by Farida Khanum." He cranked up the volume and sang the whole song along with Khanum.

Zeina was just blown away by his voice. She loved that song and so did her mother. She couldn't believe what a beautiful voice he had and how good it sounded as he sang. Yet again, he plucked another string in her heart. Usually she did not like classical Indian music, but this one was her favorite; it is sung by a lover: "Please don't insist on leaving, not tonight."

"So, who all is in your family?" she asked, wanting to know more about him.

"I have two brothers: Varun, who is four years older than me. He is more like a father figure for me. He is an ER physician and married to Simran, who is from a Sikh family; she is also an ER physician. Both of them work at St. John hospital in Detroit. Arjun, my other brother, is four years younger than me. He just came here to study for a master's degree in Vermont. Arjun has an undergraduate degree in hospitality from India like me. My father, Colonel Dev, is a retired Indian army officer. Aarti, my mother, is a retired school teacher. They live in our family home in Delhi. Both of them are touring the States with my brother and his wife in an RV these days. My father called me today from somewhere in the vicinity of the Grand Canyon. My parents spent a few weeks with me last month. I took them on a tour of the southern states. We visited Atlanta, Miami, the Florida Keys, Orlando, and Tampa. I get discounted and sometimes complimentary hotel rooms with the hotel chain I work for. We also went to Disney and enjoyed snorkeling and deep-sea fishing off of the coast of Florida. It was a fabulous vacation. My parents loved their time with me."

"That road trip with your parents sounds so cool. I've got to tell you a secret: I *love* Disney. I could go there for vacation every year. I first went to Disney World when I was six years old and have been there a few times since. Each time I go there, I revert back to being a six-year-old girl; it's so magical. I haven't been back for a while, but I'd love another trip soon. I still enjoy that ride 'It's a Small, Small World.' All the Disney characters, the props, the lights, the shows, the music—all of that takes me into my imaginative world where everything is picture perfect," she remarked.

She discarded her initial opinion of him as being "fresh off the boat." He was interesting, talented, well traveled, and a total charmer.

He thought that she was so chatty, bubbly, and energetic that he could hear her voice for hours. It didn't seem that the call was for any other reason than just to speak to him. The movie discussion felt as though it were merely an excuse to initiate a conversation. He didn't have to say much to keep the call going. He just acknowledged that he was on the phone with an occasional "yes" and a "hmm." He listened to her voice with a smile on his face; it was a cheerful feeling for him to hear her chatter away.

After about an hour, Karan interrupted, "You know it's almost one in the morning, and I have to wake up at six to leave for work, so I have to get off the phone soon."

"Oh, I'm sorry to keep you up. I'm not used to going to bed early," she said and, after a pause, continued, "I enjoyed chatting with you, really. So when are you planning your move and by the way, what is it that you do exactly for Hyatt?"

"My move is coming up in just another week. I work as a corporate sales manager. I'll soon be working at the Hyatt in Crystal City as a senior sales manager."

"You know, my brother lives in Annapolis, which is half an hour from Crystal City. I often go to meet him; perhaps we can meet on my next visit? *Hasta la vista* for now. Hey, listen, before you hang up, do you have a mobile number?"

"Sorry, I don't have a mobile. Frankly, I find them rather bulky and unaffordable. I do like to write. Do you have e-mail? We can correspond via e-mail."

"I do have e-mail but rarely ever use it. Call me when you have your local numbers at your new place. I'm going to be busy with my mother for a few weeks. In case we don't speak before you leave, all the best with your move."

Those were the days in the '90s when e-mail had just started to take over communication, and mobile phones were the size of a thick dictionary. A long-distance domestic call cost more than a meal at Taco Bell. Personal computers were mainly used for word processing or creating and managing databases, and not many people owned laptops. The World Wide Web had just started to gain the attention of the world.

Karan turned the bedside lamp off and summarized the conversation with Zeina in his mind. He felt comfortable speaking to her. He could be himself and not pretentious. He liked Zeina, and he liked her energy. He wondered whether she was attractive. In his heart, he hoped she was. Just recently, he had interacted with another girl in Atlanta, who sounded perfect on e-mail and wrote eloquently, but then they exchanged photographs. She had cut up a photo of herself in a jigsaw puzzle format and sent it to him in parts via snail mail over the course of a few weeks. Of course, her best feature was delivered first, which was her massive cleavage! He liked what he saw. Then, a week later, came one eye, with a letter, followed by a few other pieces. After finally putting the whole picture together, he was a bit shocked by the final result. She was a nice person to interact with, but after all the pieces of the picture had arrived, it was apparent that he would not be trying anything romantic with her.

Every human being deserves love, no matter how you look at it: "Beauty is in the eye of the beholder, and looks are only skin deep." He knew all that. But he also believed that a certain level of attraction had to be present in a relationship. For him, attraction started with the personality, then looks, and then character traits. If the physical chemistry was not present, a long-term relationship just couldn't work for him. Thoughts of women and relationships carried him into a deep sleep. Shortly after, he was snoring like a roaring lion.

Zeina had similar thoughts after the conversation that evening. She was comfortable and happy to speak to Karan about just nothing. She didn't feel that she was speaking to someone she had just come to know on the phone a few weeks ago. She also wondered how he appeared in person. He sounded sweet on the phone; he was kind and compassionate. She also strongly believed that physical chemistry was important to sustain a serious, long-term relationship. In her beautiful, perfect, imaginary world, she had painted a picture of Mr. Perfect, who looked more like Brad Pitt, and there was not much of a chance that Karan looked like Brad.

She had kissed enough frogs while looking for her prince. Most recently she had broken up with an Indian who had become a complete pest. Her mother had come to know that she was dating a short, unattractive Indian Hindu, and she had absolutely lost it. Her mom had many Indian friends; she didn't have issues with anyone's religion, nationality, and culture, as long as they stayed away from her daughter. She had a particular vision of a husband for her daughter: he had to be a well-educated Pakistani Muslim and must also be tall and handsome.

While New York is full of life and entertainment, it can be a lonely place for young singles, especially for women. Living and working there is a double-edged sword. Young people can have rewarding careers and make a lot of money, but their personal life often sucks. Relationships are usually superficial; one-night stands and multiple sex partners are common, and dating is mostly about casual sex. Meaningful relationships are difficult to come by; finding love is tough; finding true love is almost impossible. Most young men and women work long hours and then party hard in order to forget how hard they work. It's a complex cycle.

It is really odd and funny, but many New Yorkers date people geographically! Manhattan residents do not like to date Brooklyn residents because the train to Brooklyn on weekends and evenings is too slow and runs infrequently. People on the west side of the park do not date people on the east side of the park because getting across the park is cumbersome. Life indeed is shallow and relentlessly complicated.

Zeina knew what the city had to offer. She had been a student and managed on a dollar a day for entertainment at the Metropolitan Museum of Art. She had also dated bankers who spent a thousand dollars on cocktails and champagne in one evening. She was also friends with her brother's investment banking colleagues, who had a different perception of life than most people. Investment bankers thrive on a false sense of security and often harbor a superiority complex that comes from the excessive amount of money they have accumulated at a young age, in a short period of time.

Of the many friends Zeina had, Shiraz was closest to her heart. She felt blessed to have Shiraz in her life. She enjoyed some of those one-dollar days and three a.m. coffees in the West Village with her. Shiraz and Zeina were in the same boat; Shiraz was living in the city after graduation, seeking permanent work, and she was obsessed with finding an Israeli Jewish guy to marry.

Zeina was exhausted that evening after a long day at work. She dimmed the lights, turned the radio low to classical music, which went on all night long, and dozed off.

Karan started wrapping up in Knoxville. There were a few farewell parties he had to attend given by colleagues and friends. The GM of the hotel gave a flattering speech at the farewell lunch. The head of HR presented a photo of the hotel, framed with white matting and signed by the hotel staff.

Farewells were an emotional time for him, despite having moved frequently all his life. He had lived in twelve cities in twelve years of education in India. Transfers happened often for his father, even in the middle of the school year. He studied at *Kendriya Vidyalayas*, Indian government schools, where the curriculum was consistent throughout India at all times of the year. He had no permanent friends; the definition of a "best friend" for him was someone who was a good friend for the next one year.

It is indeed amazing that children of armed forces employees come out normal, with all the movement in their lives. In fact, in most cases they come out better in terms of overall personality, education, and social awareness, given the amount of physical and emotional strengthening they go through. However, deep within, Karan faced fears of leaving familiarity and moving toward the unknown. He had some accumulated fear left over from every move he had ever made. He knew he would survive wherever he moved; adjusting to new places and people was now second nature, but those few unnerving moments of good-byes with people with whom he had shared his life and gotten close were still not easy to handle.

After the last day of work came the last day of clubbing. One of his local buddies, Charles, gave him a large, personally autographed poster of some local Tennessee college football player named Peyton Manning.

Drunk as hell, Charles told him, "Dude, I know I dragged you to many games. I know that you never enjoyed any of them, but you came just to hang out with us. This poster is a memento of our times together. Peyton is on his way to becoming someone big in football. Save his poster."

Those were touching words, but there was no way he was going to frame a college footballer's poster and hang it on his walls. Nevertheless, he accepted the gift graciously. Then, there were Tiffany and Debra from the front desk, who indulged in tearful good-byes. They gave him some girly farewell gifts. After lots of hugs, kisses, and good-byes, he made his way to his apartment.

He had rented a ten-foot U-Haul truck and was going to drive with his belongings and tow his car behind. It took him just about five hours to pack up the apartment. He loaded the truck with the help of his neighbors and friends.

Karan was cleaning his apartment for the handover to the property manager, just when his home phone rang. It was Zeina! He was thrilled to receive this surprise call, as he hadn't been expecting to speak to her for at least another week.

"I just called to wish you good luck with your move," she said, cheerfully and encouragingly.

"I'm happy to hear from you. The drive will take almost ten hours. I have a week before I start work. It'll take me a few days to settle in."

"Call me when you are settled. Drive safely. I'll speak to you soon."

He completed the handover of the apartment. He was ecstatic that she had called. It was a positive start for his journey. He felt a good vibe about his relocation.

The drive turned out to be much longer than ten hours. He had never driven a truck while towing a car and it was by no means easy. U-Haul, in order to avoid speeding tickets and accidents, had locked the speed at fifty-five miles per hour. It was annoying to see old farts on the road overtake him and at the same time give him dirty stares for driving too slowly, as if it was only their right to drive below the speed limit. He felt like purchasing and displaying a large poster board saying, "This darn truck only does fifty-five miles per hour."

He made frequent stops for gas, coffee, and restrooms. Country music was blaring on the radio. The drive was scenic. Most of Tennessee and Virginia consists of mountains, rivers, and beautiful valleys. The sky was saturated with deep-blue hues, and the air felt crisp and clean. He was going to miss his life in Knoxville. He had never thought he would feel that way about the place. He had made friends who genuinely cared for him. He had learned to understand and deal with the southern accent and southern culture. He had even picked up some hillbilly accent himself, which had to be undone now that he was moving to a more cultured city.

He had ample time to reminisce while driving. Life was complicated in the United States compared to his simple upbringing in India. He had lived a sheltered life in army cantonments. His father didn't have much disposable income, but there were so many fringe benefits that they never lacked anything. In fact, now that he lived in the United States and saw how the middle class lived, he cherished memories of his wholesome lifestyle as a child. Those memories and times with his family were priceless.

During the school year, life was down to a routine, which included attending the army or government school, playing squash in the evenings, swimming three times a week, playing tennis on weekends, lots of book reading from the army library, listening to music, and a limited half hour of TV at night. On weekends there were "Tambola nights," which are minilottery games, children's dance parties called "jam sessions" at the officers' club, a movie at the open-air army cinema, hunting, camping, nature walks, picnics with yummy homemade food, and horseback riding.

It was only when he left home for his undergraduate study that he realized the harsh ways of the real world and how competitive and materialistic life really was. He had his brother to stay with and was saved from staying at the boys' hostel. Varun was completing his medical degree and had his own room. Karan was able to stay with him in the dormitory. Most of the staff at the hostel thought that Karan was a medical student as well.

Karan enjoyed his days of hotel management at Indian Institute of Hotel Management (IIHM) but didn't like the working environment of hotels in India. It was in his second year that he made up his mind to go to the States after graduation. That year, he completed a required internship at the Taj Man Singh, where he was treated badly by some of the hotel staff, especially the kitchen staff. The banquet chef was a prick. He would give all the male interns huge bags of potatoes to peel or a sack of onions to chop, and he would call all the female interns and say to them, "Come, sweetie, let me show you how to make *butter chicken*."

Then there was this asshole, the executive chef at the Chinese restaurant, House of Ming, who kept sending female interns into the walk-in freezer to look for Chinese mushrooms or frozen baby corn, well knowing that there were none in the freezer. All he wanted to see was how much their nipples would have swelled up from the cold freezer when they came out. He proudly called it switching on the interns' headlights. He actually had a rating from one to ten for how big the girls' nipples would perk up from the cold. The list of such incidents was endless. Karan decided to leave India for sure after graduation—by hook or by crook.

The straw that broke the camel's back was when one day, coming back after a sumptuous meal at Lal Dhaba, a restaurant near the hostel, Karan and his brother accidentally touched the rear of an Atlas bicycle, ridden by a couple, with the front mud guard of their Bajaj scooter. The woman was most likely a street sweeper, because she had a long, bamboo broom with her. She rather looked like a witch, with a big, black mole on her nose and three strands of long hair bursting out of it. The couple lost their balance and fell on the road. She got up from the road, took off her dirty, worn-out *bata chappal* [slipper], and started beating the brothers. Varun, who was wearing his white lab coat, tried to tell her that he was a doctor at the college and that it was just an accident. But the woman would not stop beating them. She cussed them out in foul Hindi and would not stop lashing them with her slipper.

She said, "*Maaderchaud dactar, takkar maar ke giraa diya, haayee, gaand toard dee maade,*" which meant, "Motherfucker doctor, you rear-ended us, made us fall, and broke my ass." She gathered about fifty onlookers in two minutes. People in India have a lot of time for such free street entertainment. In desperation, Varun paid one hundred rupees to the sweeper and her husband or lover and drove away from the scene.

At that moment, not only Karan but his brother as well decided to relocate to another civilized country.

Karan had made one failed attempt to move to the States just after he had graduated from high school. He had been awarded a full-tuition scholarship to Hobart and William Smith College in Geneva, New York, but his family couldn't afford to pay for the room and board. Surinder *Chacha*, his uncle in Toronto, wasn't supportive, not even on a loan basis. *Chacha* discouraged the family from sending him to the States at such a young age. After graduating from IIHM, he again managed a full tuition scholarship to Mercyhurst College, and this time he was not going to let anyone get in his way. His only fear was a denied student visa. Keeping his fingers crossed, he took his I-20 along with all supporting documents to the US embassy in Delhi. Lo and behold, he was given a student visa for four years.

Looking back, he realized this was again one of life's special moments orchestrated by the *Painter Man*. His move to the States was destined. He was meant to move there to unite with his soul mate. The probability of an Indian army officer's son going to the States is the same as that of winning a million-dollar lottery.

The visa consular asked him whether he planned to return to India after studying. He gave him the standard bullshit answer about family ties and how much he loved Mother India. The visa consular had a silly grin on his face when he stamped the visa approval. He had heard that answer a million times.

The visa consular said, "I don't see you coming back. You'll get married to a blonde and live there forever."

At that comment, he politely smiled back at the visa counselor and told him that he could almost guarantee that he would not marry a blonde, although he did have plans to sleep with a few for sure. He was young, naive, and far too *desi* at heart to be open to settling down with a *gori*, a foreign white woman.

Securing that visa was one of the most memorable moments of his life. He couldn't contain his happiness. He knew that now he had to make something of himself. His parents bought him an airline ticket and gave him $500 to start his new life; that was all they could spare at the time. They had just spent half their life savings so that Varun could go to the States just a few months before; there was not much left in the pot. Karan was off to start a new life with the support of his brother, who at that time was a struggling medical resident himself.

Right around sunset, Karan stopped for a restroom break. As he was about to enter the truck, he noticed a red phone booth. He had a strong urge to call Zeina. He called her but couldn't reach her. It was her principle never to answer unknown numbers.

He left her a voice mail saying, "Hi, Zeina, just wanted to touch base with you. I have been driving for over six hours and was thinking about you. I'll speak to you soon."

Strangely, he felt a deep connection with her; she was getting closer to his heart with each contact they had.

It was past midnight when he reached Columbia. He had dinner with Bobby and then, exhausted from the journey, he fell asleep in seconds. He woke up and examined the townhouse properly the next day. He was beyond disappointed at his friend's taste and the quality of the townhouse. It was a run-down home from the '70s with shaggy, long-thread carpets, ugly bathrooms, and an ultralow-budget kitchen. His bedroom was small and dingy, with a badly stained beige carpet. It was a mistake to have agreed to live with Bobby, but alas, it was too late. He had already paid the rent for the next six months. It was later that he discovered that the home belonged to Bobby's *Gujju* [Gujarati] friend.

Bobby's heart was in the right place, but he had not put enough thought into selecting the location. The other issue was that the driving distance to Crystal City was more than one hour.

Karan liked the surroundings of the townhouse. It was right off highway I-95 and conveniently located in a decent residential neighborhood, with lots of green spaces and numerous stores and restaurants within a short driving distance. There was a South Indian restaurant just five minutes from the house, which was the most exciting thing he discovered. He loved food, especially spicy South Indian food.

He had a theory about *desis* living in North America. All *desis* should choose a home based on a test he called the "*dhaniya* and *hari mirchi* test," which is the "coriander and green chili test." That meant that *desi* homes should be within a five-minute drive from a store where they could buy green chillies and coriander leaves, the two ingredients used in almost all food that *desis* cooked, except desserts. Well, this damn townhouse at least passed that test. He felt it was worth giving the townhouse a try, and if it didn't work out, he would try an apartment closer to work.

He put away all his belongings and made his first phone call to Zeina. To his disappointment, he got her voice mail again, so he left her a message with his new home telephone number. Then he called his uncle in Potomac and a few other old friends in the area, and finally the HR director, who requested that he start work earlier rather than later. His employer agreed to adjust leftover moving days as extra vacation days for that year.

Karan didn't know that that was the day when Zeina's mother was arriving for two weeks to stay with Zeina, after which she was to go and meet her relatives in Chicago.

Zeina was at the airport and had no reception on her mobile phone when he called. She couldn't wait to see her mom. She had not seen her for a while. They met at arrivals with lots of hugs and kisses and took a limo back to midtown. Her mom always traveled with three or four huge, heavy bags, half of which were filled with gifts for her children and relatives. Although she was tired from her long journey, she was excited to be with her daughter, whom she fondly called *Butya*, derived from *beti*, meaning "daughter" in Urdu.

Barely had her mother settled in the apartment when she started unpacking all the gifts she had brought. Among them were delicately embroidered cushions, colorful Afghan glass decorations, a small silk carpet, and fashionable traditional clothes. She always brought Zeina jewelry, either a set with aquamarine, which was her birthstone, or emeralds, which were her favorite gemstone.

Zeina's mom had amazing energy. After a short two-hour rest, she wanted to go straight to Mandarin Court in Chinatown to eat at her favorite dim-sum restaurant before it ran out for the day. She loved food. "Some people eat to live, and others live to eat"; no doubt, she lived to eat. Not only was she fond of eating, she was also fond of cooking. She was an incredible cook.

In her excitement about being with her mother, Zeina forgot to check her voice mail all day. Finally, after her mom went to sleep that night, she retrieved her voice-mail messages, including Karan's, and she immediately called him. They discussed his move, the ugly townhouse, and his new neighborhood.

She told him all about her day. "Amma and I had such a great time today. The dim-sum was so good. You have to try it when you come here next time."

"You sound excited about Amma's visit, if I may call her by that name."

"Of course you can call her Amma. All my close friends call her that. She doesn't like being called Aunty Sahar. It's so impersonal. I'm so excited to have her with me. She is everything to me, and it feels complete to have her around."

3. Rendezvous in NYC

Karan started work a few days later. The first day, he realized that the commute on I-95 and the beltway was a bitch. Driving a stick shift in stop-and-go traffic was painful. He ran into Roberta, a colleague at work who lived in Columbia as well. They agreed to carpool to ease the pain of daily driving. Colleagues at work were generally welcoming. The director of sales assigned Karan a small segment of the local government market and a handful of corporate accounts for business development. After a few days at work, he started prospecting and meeting new clients and exploring the area around the hotel.

Karan missed Zeina a great deal. It was a week since they had last spoken. One afternoon, after a sales visit near the White House, while he was roaming around the Washington Monument, he bought a postcard from a street hawker and sent her a note: "I miss speaking to you. Hope all is well and you are enjoying your time with your mother. Call me when you can."

He mailed the postcard, and two days later, late at night, she called him.

"Hi!"

"Hello, Zeina, how are you?"

"Gosh, you sound so formal. I'm fine; I have been busy at work during the day, and spending time with my mother in the evenings. I usually love cuddling and sleeping with her, but she has been coughing a lot, and when she does not cough, she snores. We both sleep in the same bed in my room, and as a result, I have not been sleeping too well. Last night, I had to go sleep on the futon in the living room. She is leaving next week to meet her cousin in Chicago, and then she will go to see my brother in Annapolis."

She sounded happy, bubbly, and energetic, as usual. He was delighted to hear her voice.

"Thanks for the nice surprise; I loved the postcard. I'll reply to it. I miss talking to you too. You need to get a mobile so we can have quick chats more often. I don't like to disturb you during the day at work. I have to wait till you get home to speak to you, and by that time I usually can't really talk with Amma around. How are you settling in?"

"I'm managing the change well. I hate the commute, but I can't do much about it for now. My work is also better than it was in Knoxville. I've got to go to Detroit for a Canadian immigration interview next week. The weekend after, I've got to go to Penn State for a friend's graduation."

"Are you moving to Canada? Why?" she asked, a bit surprised. Canada sounded far away.

He explained the reasons for his potential move. He had been working in the States for over three years, and there was no sign of his employer's willingness to convert his H1b visa into a green card. He wanted permanency in North America and also wanted to move on with his professional career and perhaps enroll in business school. One fine day, a brilliant idea had come to him; he thought about immigrating to Canada. He figured that by the time he had completed an MBA and worked for a few years, he could become a Canadian citizen and move anywhere in the world. He had applied for immigration three months ago and had already been called for an interview.

"Hmm, that's interesting. You and Amma think alike on this matter. About six months ago, she got me the immigration forms. I've the same issue as you do about long-term stay in the States. By the way, I do have a few close relatives in Toronto. I have loads of freelance work, but none of the companies here are willing to sponsor me for an H1b, let alone a green card. I've the Canadian forms in some closet. I never looked at them. I can't imagine leaving the city. I'll find a way to stick around here."

"You're just being silly about it. Fill out the forms; it's good to have a backup plan. As my father says, 'One must always have a second line of defense, and one foot on the ground at all times.' You could get the immigration in three to six months with your qualifications, and then you have one year to decide to move to Canada. I believe you can even extend the actual relocation if you need to. Once your work permit runs out, what will you do? Marry someone for a green card? I hope not!"

"Yup, that is what I'll do. I have a few marriage proposals lined up: the Bangladeshi fruit vendor, the video shop *Unclejee*, and there is the Syrian taxi driver who is usually in the neighborhood. Anyone of those guys can get me permanent residency." After a pause she laughed and said, "I'm just kidding. I'm not getting married anytime soon, certainly never for a green card. Anyway, I'll think about the forms, but for now, my backup plan is that after the work permit expires, I'll enroll at Fashion Institute of Technology (FIT)."

It was obvious that Zeina lived in the present. She came across as a free spirit who gently flowed with the wind and let nature take its course. On the other hand, Karan had been trained by his father to plan ahead, lead a disciplined, organized life, save for the future, and always have short-term and long-term goals. He noticed how different his way of thinking was from hers.

"I take it you chose Detroit for the interview because your brother lives there?"

"That's right. It'll give me a chance to see him. I've not seen him since his wedding in India. He's just bought his first home, along with his sister-in-law, who is also a physician. She lives in the basement of the house with two cats."

"When did you say you're going to Penn State?"

"I'll be there the week after. If I recall, my friend's graduation is on that Friday."

"Is Penn State not a short drive from Manhattan? Why don't you come and see me as well?" she suggested impulsively.

"Is that an invitation?"

"Sure, consider it an invite if you like," she replied.

"We've been speaking for some weeks now. It'll actually be great to meet up. I can come after the graduation and meet you for dinner and then head back."

"Won't you be exhausted with all that driving in one day? Amma is leaving that afternoon. If you like, you're welcome to stay over Friday. We have a comfortable futon in the living room for guests. Spend Saturday here. I'll show you the city, Zeina-style."

"That sounds like a great offer. Done! I'll see you then. I have to call my brother back. I can see on call waiting that he has called three times."

Just like that, they set up their first meeting.

"Hi, Varun *Bhaiya* [Brother]."

"*Bhai mere* [Dear brother], I called you a few times. Where have you been?"

"I was on the phone. Is everything okay? Anything urgent you have to speak about?"

"Nothing urgent. I was going into the ER for an extended fourteen-hour shift; I thought I'd touch base with you and see how you are settling in. Who were you talking to for so long? Let me guess—another girl?"

"Just someone I have come to know and enjoy speaking to."

Karan told his brother about Zeina and how he had come in contact with her. Varun was rather silent on the phone and did not say anything. He had to go to his shift, so he got off the phone quickly. Karan was a bit taken aback by his brother's silence. He wondered whether he had disclosed more information than necessary. But their lives were an open book to each other. They had never hidden anything from one another, not even the most intimate details of their relationships with women.

After the phone call, Karan's thoughts shifted back to Zeina. He pondered how she would find him in person, and he wondered whether she was attractive. What if he didn't like the way she looked? He figured that she had been a good person to talk to so far and why expect anything more? In his heart, he was hoping that there would be some chemistry between the two of them. He couldn't wait for the suspense to end and had wanted to make his position clear to her ever since they had started mildly flirting on the phone.

In an attempt to act like a gentleman, he wrote a short letter to her and sent a photograph of himself, desperately hoping that she would send one in return before the much-anticipated meeting. He shuffled through all his albums for an hour. First he shortlisted ten photos and then took another hour analyzing each one of them from every angle before selecting the one that was worthy of sending. The photograph he chose was the one most of his friends liked. He looked like a *desi* Tom Cruise. His hair was gelled back, and he was wearing a US Navy blazer and dark shades. The golden glow of the evening sun shone perfectly on his face.

The letter read:

Dear Zeina,
Hope this short note can bring a smile to your face. I have been hesitant in writing this note, but in anticipation of our meeting shortly, I'm sending you a photograph of me for a few reasons: first, so that you can recognize me when we meet and second, because I just wanted to.

Actually, the real reason is that it has been great connecting with you over the phone in the last few weeks, and I am wishing that we like each other more than just two people who like speaking to each other. At the risk of sounding blunt, the truth is that the only way our friendship will move any further is if we feel attracted to each other. I confess, I love talking to you and cannot wait for our telephone conversations every day. There is so much peace in your voice. I feel happy and energized after talking to you.

I am indeed looking forward to seeing you. I am hopeful that there is some chemistry between us, but just in case that spark is absent when we meet; I am also hopeful that we can remain acquaintances because I love speaking to you. I just wanted to make myself clear so that we don't hurt what we have developed so far.

Sincerely,
Karan

Zeina received the letter two days later and was thrilled to receive mail from him. She opened the letter, and the photograph fell to the ground, landing facedown. She lifted it and flipped it around; her eyes opened wide in amazement. She liked what she saw. Karan was a good-looking guy with broad shoulders and sharp features. Then she read the letter and couldn't stop smiling.

Amma saw from the corner of her eye a letter in Zeina's hand and the smile on her face. She was a sharp woman and instantly asked, "*Butya*, what's so amusing? Can I see as well?"

"No, of course not! Please get ready for the movie quickly. We are already running late," Zeina snapped back rather defensively.

As affectionate as Amma was, she was like an FBI agent and often would inspect her daughter's closets to make sure there was no guy in her life she didn't know about. They say parents' hearts are linked to their children's hearts. Amma knew that her daughter was up to something. Zeina's smile was a dead giveaway. But Amma didn't want to meddle in her affairs that evening. She had brought her daughter up to make her own decisions wisely, and she trusted Zeina to do the right thing.

It's not common for a single Pakistani woman to leave her daughter alone in a foreign country, but Amma knew that education, exposure to the world, and the strength to stand on her own feet were important for Zeina. Her daughter would never have learned any of that sitting at home in Islamabad. Amma didn't want her daughter to face dependency on a husband, something she had had to face after her own husband passed away. Her goal in life was to educate her children and make them independent so that no one ever dictated terms to them or told them how to live their lives.

They took a yellow cab to the Cineplex on Lexington Avenue to watch Karan Johar's latest production, *Kuch Kuch Hota Hai* [*Something Happens*], starring Shahrukh Khan, Kajol, Rani Mukerjee, and Salman Khan—all famous Bollywood movie actors. This movie was a superhit across the world. Both of them loved the film. They came out of the theater holding hands and singing the theme song.

They both came up with the same idea about what to do next. They wanted to go to Little India near Twenty-Sixth and Lexington, eat spicy *chaat* and kebabs, and buy the music cassette of the movie. Zeina hailed a cab. They had a great meal together. Then they bought some glass bangles, and Amma ate *paan*, which was her favorite after-meal thing to do. They came back home and heard the songs on the cassette player five times.

After Amma went to sleep, Zeina called her friend. Shiraz knew who Karan was but didn't know that Zeina had been speaking to him regularly for several weeks. She told Shiraz all about the phone calls, postcards, his letter, and the photograph. Those were the days of the early '90s; social media was nonexistent.

"So, are you going to send him your photograph? He sent you one, and I'm sure he expects one from you."

"Nope, let the suspense remain," she answered naughtily.

Later that night she called him, "Oh shit, sorry, I didn't realize it was past midnight again. Sorry to have woken you up."

"No worries, it feels like almost time for me to wake up. I'm to leave before sunrise, and I come back after dark. Life is a mess these days. I'm glad you called. Did you get my letter? I hope the letter was not offensive in any way."

She cut him off. "I'm so deeply offended. How you could send a letter like that and assume so much?"

Then she laughed. "I'm just kidding. I loved the letter. It was adorable, too cute. And you are a handsome man. Thanks for the photo. It was a good idea, but I'm not going to send you mine. You'll have to find me in the crowd."

"Oh, come on! Are you serious? At least tell me what you look like. How will I find you?"

"I'll see you outside 65 West 55th Street, right outside my apartment. I'll make it a bit easy for you. Amma just brought me a plain black *salwar kameez* [South Asian outfit]. I'll wear that. I'm almost sure there will be no other woman on that street who will be wearing the same clothes."

"That helps, but it's a bit unfair that you are not sending me your photograph." After a pause he said, "Depending on the traffic, I plan to be there by early evening." He sounded rather disappointed now that his plan had failed to get him her photograph.

"So, what'd ya do today?" he asked.

"I had so much fun with Amma. We saw *Kuch Kuch Hota Hai* on screen, and had *chaat* and *paan* after that. We bought these beautiful aqua glass bangles from Little India."

"*Tum pass aaye …*" He started singing the first few lines of the song from the movie.

"I love that song. I've been hearing it on the local *desi* FM channel. I plan to watch the film this weekend with some friends."

She heard him sing for the third time and this time a Bollywood song. He sang so beautifully that she felt a deep pull within her heart.

"Good night, my dear. I better get some sleep so I don't fall asleep at the wheel while driving tomorrow."

Not only did he wake up early on weekdays, he did that on weekends as well. Early in the morning, he would go work out, take a stroll, wash his car, eat breakfast, and run an errand or two. Then in the afternoon, after lunch, he would take a nap. He loved his afternoon naps on weekends.

Zeina, on the other hand, went out late on weekends, went to bed just before dawn, woke up after lunch, ran around all day once she was up, and was ready to go out again at midnight.

They had a lot in common, and yet they led different lives. They didn't even notice the small differences, like their weekend routines.

That Saturday morning, after he had finished washing his car, eating his breakfast, and showering, he called Zeina.

A groggy voice answered the phone, "Is that you, Karan? What time is it?"

"It's time to rise and shine. Early bird catches the worm. It's a beautiful day outside. The sun is shining, and the air is crisp. By the way, it's 9:00 a.m., to answer your question."

"Even Amma is not up yet. It's too early to be sounding so chirpy. Are you always like this? Anything urgent you need to speak about?"

She was clearly not a morning person. Some people's souls come alive at dawn, but most New Yorkers' souls come alive at dusk. She had become a true New Yorker.

"Well, nothing in particular. I was just missing you this beautiful morning, so I called to say hello since we didn't speak yesterday."

"Well, good morning to you too. I'm glad you were thinking of me and happy to hear your voice, even if it's this early. By the way, what is that strange music you are listening to in the background?" she asked, very sweetly.

"Oh, that's *Hanuman Chalisa*—you know, Hindu Monkey God music as the Americans call it. I like listening to *bhajans*, religious Hindu music in the mornings."

There was silence on the phone for a few seconds. It hit her for the first time that he was a practicing Hindu.

"I know what *bhajans* are, silly. I like many of them, but the one you are listening to doesn't sound nice. Listen, Amma seems to be bothered about my being on the phone, she is tossing and turning. I'll call you later today when the world wakes up. Bye."

After the rendezvous was put on the calendar, each day seemed to crawl. He spoke to her every day. With each day, their level of candidness and comfort increased. The countdown was painful as he anticipated meeting her. They anxiously wanted to see each other but didn't want to show it.

Halfway through the week, Karan called Zeina in the morning, but she didn't answer her mobile. He left her a message, and after he didn't hear from her for another half hour, he called her again. She didn't pick up her phone the second time, either. Since he did not hear back from her, he got worried, and after his lunch break he called yet another time. To his disappointment, she did not answer. He figured he'd call her home number to see whether her roommate was home and find out whether Zeina was all right.

Amma picked up the phone! He courteously introduced himself and told her that he was her daughter's friend calling from Washington. Amma was in a chatty mood. She told him that Zeina had forgotten her mobile phone and that she was going to meet her that evening and would give her the phone then. They spoke for a while. She didn't ask nosy questions. He told her that he was from Delhi. Amma became engrossed in her stories and experiences of Delhi. After they hung up, he breathed a sigh of relief. He had been a bit nervous on the call. He addressed her formally as "Aunty" during the conversation. He was relieved to find out that Zeina was all right. It occurred to him that not being able to reach her had been painful. He had started caring for her.

They spoke every day that week for hours each night. They spoke about art, music, culture, religion, movies, and told their childhood stories. There was not enough time in the evening for them to have a silent minute between them. The conversation always flowed, and both had a lot to say.

Amma began preparing for her departure. She bought several pounds of meat from the local halal shop. She made special complicated dishes like *shami kebabs*, *nihari*, and *haleem* and froze them. The small, eight-hundred-square-foot apartment smelled like a Pakistani restaurant; clothing and carpet all smelled of *masala*s. A common problem with apartments in the States is that the drywalls and the carpets are porous and absorb smells; exhaust fans in the kitchens and bathrooms are usually not externally ventilated. They are mostly underpowered and make more noise than they do any practical ventilation. After her mother's cooking was done, Zeina had to air out the apartment and burn a few packs of incense sticks. It was only after a few bottles of air freshener that the apartment finally smelled normal.

Thankfully, Julia didn't mind the food smell, as long as Amma kept feeding her fresh *kebabs*. Julia loved everything *desi*, including men, food, music, and the culture. She used to dance around in the apartment singing Bollywood songs that even most Indians would refuse to sing aloud—songs made for *rickshaw and tangawallas*. The music videos of such songs usually depict a half-naked Indian heroine surrounded by a dozen drooling unshaved and dirty men.

Zeina forgot that she had to speak to Julia about Karan coming over without raising her curiosity and asking too many questions. She approached Julia cautiously, as she was moody. It appeared that she had forgotten to take her *kushi kee dawai*—happiness pills—or Prozac kind of stuff, and she was way out of it that morning. No one ever quite figured out what was wrong with her, but the general diagnosis was that she had a bipolar disorder combined with severe clinical depression. She used to fall head over heels in love in every relationship, and after each breakup she went into freaky attacks of depression. It looked like she had just broken up again with someone the night before.

Zeina played it well with Julia; she casually informed her that a guest would be visiting for a night. Julia had no issues with occasional guests staying over. She had had plenty of guests over the years. They had a good understanding on this subject.

The city is a tricky place for single people who live in central areas. The first problem is boyfriends, girlfriends, and random dates staying over. Then you have some friend or other who is laid off and wants to stay over for a week or so, which can sometimes turn into a few months. Finally, summer comes along, and relatives and people who barely know you try to come and use the apartment as a hotel, since Manhattan hotels can be rather steep. She had been in those situations many times and was getting better at handling such guests.

Julia had an interesting sign on her bedroom door that said, "All our guests bring us happiness and joy, some by coming and others by leaving."

Friday finally arrived. Karan started his journey before dawn to be able to get to Pennsylvania before noon. The weather was getting cold already. The chill in the morning air felt colder than usual. He was driving against the flow of traffic. Driving through Baltimore, he saw a gorgeous sunrise. The sky lit up out of darkness into a beautiful golden hue; the clouds vanished and out came a bright, clear, blue sky. Nothing was as pleasing to him as to observe the ordinary miracles of nature.

He stopped at a rest area to capture a photo of the sunrise and buy coffee and breakfast. He noticed a pay phone and walked toward it; he looked at his watch, and it was only 6:00 a.m. He dared not call Zeina so early. He grinned at himself and started driving again.

He reached Penn State and located his friend near the graduation hall. His friend was surrounded by family and friends. She looked ecstatic to be graduating. Karan was her key supporter and had been instrumental in pushing her to come to the States. If it had been up to her parents, soon after she had graduated from IIHM in Delhi, she would have been getting married to a nice *banya* [trader] or a *Gujju* boy. She was a petite girl, four feet tall, fragile, with a heart of gold. She had a unique, uncorrectable vision issue and couldn't see too well at certain distances. She had to keep reading material two times closer than normal people.

After the graduation ceremony, an outdoor lunch was catered. The midday sun was shining, the food was great, the beer was on tap, and everyone was happy. After the party, everyone started packing up. Some friends had planned to stay overnight, but Karan had to leave. He handed his friend an envelope with some money as a graduation gift and walked over to the on-campus store to buy something for Zeina. He purchased a red coffee mug for her. Then he called and left her a voice mail. Apparently she was at the airport with her mother and didn't have any reception.

The drive to the city felt like it was taking far too long. He just wanted to get there. The traffic congestion in Pennsylvania and New Jersey was heavy; some accidents and roadwork made things worse. It was early evening, and he was still stuck on the Garden State Parkway. He stopped to get some gas near Paramus Mall in New Jersey and called her again. To his frustration, he got her voice mail; he left a message letting her know that he would be arriving close to 6:00 p.m.

As he drove past Jersey City, he saw the outline of Manhattan with the majestic Twin Towers and the Empire State Building; no doubt there was something special about Manhattan's skyline. The last time he was there had been about a year and half ago during the Christmas holidays when he worked as a waiter at a distant relative's Italian restaurant near Madison Square Garden.

He had never driven into the city before, although he had flown into JFK and taken a bus or train to Manhattan many times. He was not sure which was the best way to enter Manhattan. He didn't know about the Holland or the Lincoln tunnel, so he foolishly entered Manhattan the only way he knew, which was the George Washington Bridge, north of Manhattan. That route added half an hour to his journey. He finally got to the bridge and started driving down the FDR Drive toward midtown. It was now getting close to 6:00 p.m., and the sun was setting. Both vehicular and pedestrian traffic in the city were insane at that time of the day.

Zeina retrieved both voice mails. She had taken her mother to the airport. Shiraz had driven them in her Jeep. She was running late herself, and the traffic back from the airport was not helping her. She was afraid that Karan would reach her street before she did. She was getting nervous and requested that Shiraz step on the gas—but carefully, without risking a traffic ticket. It was almost 6:00 p.m. They were two avenues away, and traffic in midtown was inching along. She asked Shiraz to drop her off, and she ran across two avenues.

Zeina wanted to be alone with Karan when she met him, but she just couldn't say no to Shiraz. She opened the door of the Jeep at the traffic light and dashed out, sprinting in her delicate heels toward her apartment building. Her heart was beating fast, and she was breathless with excitement and nervousness.

"I'll find parking and come say hello to him," yelled Shiraz at Zeina as she was sprinting away.

After circling the block three times, Karan finally found a parking spot on the street almost opposite Zeina's apartment building. He could see the green awning of a typical New York apartment building, which read 65 West 55th Street.

He was wearing a white polo shirt, beige khakis, and black leather shoes. He had his blue blazer in the backseat but didn't feel like wearing it. The sunset was reflected in a fiery glow off the gold-tinted windows of the tall city skyscrapers. Yes, it smelled and sounded like New York City. The air was filled with the aromas of hotdog stands, roasted nut stands, and steam from the subway vents. The chaotic mixture of horns, screaming sirens of police cars, and the screeching of brakes was overwhelming. It was hard to focus and look for Zeina in all that chaos.

As he searched intently for Zeina, he noticed an angel-like figure appear across the street: glowing complexion, shiny, dark-brown hair, wearing a black *salwar kameez*. It was she! Zeina glided toward him with a beaming smile, her black, transparent *dupatta* [scarf] gently flowing in the breeze. As she approached, he noticed that she wore a single strand of iridescent white pearls, earrings to match, with a single pearl drop in each, black glass bangles on one wrist, and a thin gold *kad*a [bracelet] on the other.

65 West 55th Street

Too many cabs were on his side of the street, so she crossed the street toward him. As she drew closer to him, he could see her features better. She was about five foot five, her large, brown eyes sparkled under perfectly arched eyebrows, her skin was flawless, and her features were delicate, especially the dimple on her chin. Her hair shimmered with highlights from the setting sun.

Their eyes met for the first time, five feet away from each other. She saw a tall, handsome man with broad shoulders—the man in the photograph. She was instantly taken by the warmth in his eyes and his kind, soft smile.

He extended his hand, expecting her to offer hers, but she approached him with a cheek-to-cheek kiss instead; and in that confusion their greeting was a mix of a handshake and an incomplete kiss that missed his cheek by a few inches. She accidentally landed her red, glossy lips on his white collar.

The wind blew a strand of her hair against his face. Her scent was heavenly; the touch of her hands was warm and silky. Upon their first touch, he felt the world pause and all chaos vanish; it was just the two of them and the city—nothing between them and no one around them. All he could see was the beautiful woman in front of him. His heart was thumping at a hundred beats per minute; he had the giddiest feeling in his stomach.

When she smiled, he felt an instant bolt of lightning strike his heart. He fell in love with her in that very moment. If she gave him the chance, he could see himself being with her forever.

She was just as stunned by that magical moment. She knew she would be meeting a special person that evening, but she never imagined she would be meeting the man she had been waiting for all her life. In one look, she recognized his soul through his eyes, and in one touch, she knew that was the touch she wanted to hold on to forever.

With a single stroke, the Painter Man had painted their destiny for them.

"Take her home!" shouted an angry Yellow Cab driver, honking at them to get off the road. She held his hand and whisked him across the street like a little boy, while showing her middle finger to the cabby with her other hand.

"I'm so glad you could make it. Sorry about the lipstick stain on your collar. I have some stain remover upstairs; it'll take care of that right away," she said breathlessly. She was excited yet extremely nervous.

"I'm glad to be here; and please, no worries about the shirt," he replied, with an ear-to-ear grin.

"So, what's the plan?" he asked when they were safely across the street.

"How about we park your car, get you settled in, and then plan the evening?" she suggested.

She sat in the passenger seat and guided him to an underground parking lot. They parked the car, removed his luggage, and came back to her apartment building. The doorman scowled because he didn't like to see good-looking women tenants walking in with guys. They took the tiny, two-person elevator up to her apartment on the tenth floor.

She unlocked the door to a beautiful, ethnically decorated apartment. Shiraz walked in a few minutes later. Zeina introduced him to Shiraz as her best friend. Shiraz gave him a warm hug and a cheek-to-cheek kiss. He found her to be a pretty woman.

The apartment was small yet organized, clean, and freshly scented. One corner of the living room served as a dining area with a table setting for four. A red vase full of fresh white lilies adorned the mahogany table. Adjacent to the dining area was a black leather love seat with a matching single seater and a futon, which was supposed to be his bed for the night. It did not look comfortable.

A gorgeous rosewood trunk with brass inlay work served as a coffee table. Under it was an ethnic rug, in rust and black; that covered up a fair bit of the apartment's ugly beige carpet. The walls were decorated with perfectly aligned Mughal miniature paintings. The room was dimly lit by various amber lanterns and red table lamps. Her apartment had the tiniest kitchen he had ever seen; next to it were storage closets and a long, narrow bathroom.

Her bedroom expressed a regal theme in shades of brown. In the middle of the room was a queen-size, wrought-iron bed with a headboard displaying beautiful scrollwork. The bed was covered with a hand-embroidered brown throw with small decorative mirrors stitched on it along with cushions and pillows to match. All around the room, there were hand-blown Afghan vases and candleholders in amber tones. She sure had a lot of stuff in that small apartment, but nothing seemed to be out of place. The bedroom window was slightly open to let in fresh air, and a local FM station was playing on the radio near the windowsill.

When he went to the bathroom to freshen up, he noticed a clean bathroom, with scented candles and fresh towels. His grin got bigger. He couldn't believe that she could be this beautiful and refined and also keep a clean, well-decorated home. He came out of the bathroom with the silliest grin.

Zeina couldn't resist asking, "Everything all right? What's making you grin so much?" She was not able to figure out what he was thinking and feeling. Was he smiling because he was genuinely happy or was he smiling because he was wondering what the heck he had gotten himself into?

He mumbled a response that she didn't understand. He seemed nervous and speechless. She left him alone to breathe and settle in.

"Are you hungry? Can I offer you something to eat or drink? I have fresh *shami kebabs* that my mother made yesterday. I can make you a sandwich before we go out. I had planned to take you to a martini bar just across the street," she said and then looked at Shiraz and added, "she'll join us for a drink."

"Sure, I'd love a sandwich and some cold water, please."

She asked him to sit and chat with Shiraz, and she fetched him a tall glass of cold tap water.

"Very nice to meet you in person. Zeina speaks of you fondly," said Shiraz, shyly and awkwardly.

"She speaks highly of you as well. She is lucky to have a friend like you. I believe you attended university together?"

"Yes, we did. We took a lot of classes together."

"You live in the city as well?"

"I live on the Upper East Side with my sister, who is attending NYU. It's our family's apartment. My parents own a home on Long Island. I have to go there to return my father's Jeep later tonight."

They chatted for a few minutes while Zeina prepared and presented a professional-looking jumbo club sandwich, with perfectly toasted bread, freshly fried kebabs, lettuce, tomatoes, a fried egg, ketchup, and spicy mint chutney. The sandwich was neatly cut into two triangles with a toothpick in the middle of each to hold the fixings together. It was the best sandwich Karan had ever eaten; the taste was sensational. His grin became too big for his face, and he looked goofy.

Now he thought, *Not only is this woman stunning to look at, she is well educated, she keeps a great home, and she is an awesome cook!* There was no way he was letting her go. The question was whether she liked him enough to consider dating him. He felt that a beautiful and talented woman like her could get any good guy in the city. Why would she bother attempting a long-distance relationship with him?

"I love this sandwich. Last time I ate a *shami kebab* was in Lucknow at a *Mohammadin* friend's home. I spent a weekend with his family during college winter break. That kebab was nothing compared to this. This is delicious. Can you make me another one, if it's possible?"

"Of course I can make you another one."

She was glad to see him enjoying her quick fix. She realized that he knew little about Pakistani Muslims just by his calling Muslims *Mohammadin*, which is typical Indian nomenclature. She made him another sandwich, and he devoured it. The entire time he was speaking to Shiraz and eating his sandwich, he couldn't take his eyes off Zeina. He was admiring her and noticing how beautiful she was; he was glad to be close to her. He loved the warmth in her apartment; he wanted his own home to have the same ambience. She was exactly what he wanted in his life. He had to look away quickly each time she looked at him in order not to give away his thoughts and feelings. But it was easy to read him; he carried his heart on his sleeve and his thoughts on his face. She sensed that he liked her. She liked his presence in her home. There was something special about his aura that made her comfortable. She cleaned up the kitchen and sat down with them.

"I got you a small gift from Penn State."

"Thanks, red is my favorite color," she said, admiring the lovely mug.

"Would you like to change or shower before we go out?"

"No, I'm good to go."

It was dark when they hit the street. The city lights had taken over the skyline. They walked down to the martini bar, which was dimly lit. Hip lounge music played softly in the background. The three of them sat at a small table; both girls sat opposite to him, and all of them ordered Cosmopolitans.

Shiraz was a heavy smoker, while Zeina was an occasional smoker. Shiraz lit up and Zeina joined her, asking him whether it was okay with him if they smoked at the table. He was a nonsmoker and didn't like to be around smokers. He had never dated a smoker, but this time, his mind was far too occupied with positive thoughts to consider smoking as a deal breaker.

She sensed that he didn't like her smoking, and she quietly put her cigarette out after a few quick puffs.

He sat there trying to figure out when the third wheel of the bicycle, Shiraz, would leave, so he could pour his heart out to Zeina. After an hour, two drinks, and several jokes, Zeina also felt the need to be alone with him. She gave Shiraz subtle hints to leave, but Shiraz was too naive to catch on. As Shiraz was about to order her third drink, Zeina kicked her under the table, and that was when Shiraz finally understood that it was time. She excused herself and kissed them both good night.

Barely had Shiraz gone when Karan did something extremely bold. He gently touched her hands, looked straight into her big, brown eyes, leaned forward, and kissed her softly on her lips. Their eyes slowly closed before their lips sealed; that was their first kiss. He squeezed her hand to show that he was on top of the world to be with her. Their lips and faces withdrew from each other, and smiles returned, along with a red blush on her face, making it glow more than before. They didn't say anything to each other for a few moments and looked at each other shyly. They had already had two Cosmos each and had a good buzz going.

"Wow!" she whispered.

"I couldn't resist. You're absolutely beautiful. I can't take my eyes off you. I didn't make you uncomfortable, did I?"

"On the contrary, I loved your kiss, and you're not so bad-looking yourself," she remarked with a wink.

"As much as I liked meeting Shiraz, I just couldn't wait for her to leave."

"Sorry about that. She is a gem of a person, but very naive; she was not getting the hint until I kicked her under the table. Let's get some fresh air and go somewhere fun. How about we go for a drive?"

"Excellent idea!"

They walked out of the bar holding hands with their fingers intertwined. They walked a few blocks and bought coffee to sober up before driving. After half hour or so, he took his car out of the garage and started driving on the less crowded streets of Manhattan, admiring the beautifully lit buildings. He rolled the windows down. The air was cool, and the night was young.

She pointed out the landmark buildings in midtown and told him about various neighborhoods—which block was famous for flower shops, which for bakeries, and which for the pubs and restaurants. He thought the city was like no place else on earth and must be an awesome place to work and live. As he drove near the Brooklyn Bridge, she suggested that they park the car and walk on the boardwalk of the bridge to admire the view.

He found a convenient and safe spot to park the car, and as they walked toward the bridge, she narrated, providing interesting information about City Hall and major landmarks. He was engrossed, enjoying just holding her hand and loving the beautiful night. He was not focusing much on what she was saying.

They reached the bridge and walked about fifty yards toward the upper deck. There were no other pedestrians on the boardwalk; it was just the two of them. Brooklyn was on one side and Manhattan on the other, and the entire skyline was shimmering with millions of lights. A soft breeze was blowing on their faces; cars and trucks were zipping below them on the lower level; the tires of the vehicles on the rough surface of the road were making an awful amount of periodic noise. They exchanged a glance and extended their arms in a warm embrace. They were comfortable with each other already and held each other tightly for a few minutes, not saying anything at all.

She initiated a kiss this time; it was much more passionate than the first time at the bar. The second kiss lasted a few minutes.

"Not only are you a good-looking man, but you are a good kisser too! I like you," she said shyly. She was deeply in love with him already. Their feelings were apparent on their faces; it was just taking a bit of time for them to express them verbally.

"I like you too."

They held each other for a bit longer; then they took a short walk, hand in hand, soaking in the precious moments together. After that they returned to the car and drove away to explore some more of the city.

The streets of New York had come alive by that time of the night; it was a weekend, and there were already long lines outside night clubs. Fashionably dressed men and women waited to get into the popular clubs and restaurants. Men were trying to flash twenty-dollar bills to the bouncers to let them in. Women in line seemed already to be targeting the good-looking, rich men in the line.

"What would you like to do? Would you like to go to a club or a lounge?"

"Frankly, I've had a long day and have a long drive ahead of me tomorrow. Can we go home, enjoy wine, and chill?"

She agreed, and they drove back to her apartment. He wanted to take a shower, so she gave him a towel. She lit a few candles, put on classical music, and started putting together a cheese and fruit platter to accompany the wine. While she was busy in her little kitchen, he walked up to her, put his arms around her waist affectionately, his chest snuggled up to her back, and his head on her right shoulder. He breathed in the sweet perfume from her hair and neck. She sighed and cuddled right into him. He held her for a minute and then tightened his grip on her waist and said something least expected: "How about a bubble bath with me?"

He could feel the shiver that ran through her body as she smiled shyly. She turned around flushed and breathless; they kissed again. Still kissing, they walked into the bathroom and locked the door so that Julia couldn't walk in, started a warm bubble bath, and turned off the lights. They glanced at each other briefly; he moved closer to her, kissed her lips, nose, eyes, ears, and slowly moved his hand to her back to unzip her shirt; she giggled softly. Her shirt slipped to her shoulders to reveal a delicate, lacy black bra. He was really turned on. She helped him undress, while gently placing soft kisses on his neck and chest. He unhooked her bra, and as it dropped to the floor, she pressed herself into his chest, feeling too shy even to look at him. He held her in that position, gently caressing her until she was comfortable enough to slip into the bathtub with him. They settled naturally into each other's arms, into a perfect fit that felt neither strange nor new. The bathroom became completely silent, so silent that all they could hear were the bubbles popping in the bathtub.

He was not about to risk messing things up with her by moving too fast, and although she felt the same, neither one of them wanted to say anything. Both felt just right in each other's arms in the tub. She got out to pour some wine and came back into the tub more confidently this time. As the water turned cold, she drained the tub. They took a hot shower together and moved into the bedroom. The two of them lay intertwined, wrapped in one big towel, just staring into each other's eyes, trying to read each other's thoughts. They couldn't believe this was really happening.

He gently massaged her with lavender oil, marveling at every contour and the silkiness of her skin. It felt like the room was on fire, each touch started to feel like an electric pulse, and both their hearts were beating like drums.

She cupped his face with both her hands and whispered, "Make love to me."

"There is nothing more that I want, but I want you! All of you, not just your physical body. We need to make a sensible decision; I don't want this to be a one-night stand. I'm afraid that if we make love tonight, it might be too early, and I don't want to lose you."

"Do you really see us walking away from each other tomorrow?" she asked, pulling him closer.

They looked at each other in silence. Their eyes and their touch were more expressive than their words; their souls had connected and already spoken to each other. The love they felt was far deeper than their mortal bodies.

After the brief interruption, they started making out again. Before moving any further, she asked, "You have a condom?"

"I don't. I didn't plan for this. I was supposed to sleep on the futon tonight, remember? Does your apartment mate have any?"

"There is no way I'm asking her for one. Can you please buy some from the corner shop downstairs or the pharmacy at the end of the street? I'm so sorry for sending you out like this."

What an anticlimax that was!

"I'll be right back," he said, flustered.

"I'll be right here, waiting for you. Sorry you have to go out."

He wiggled into his pants, rushed into his shirt, and struggled to locate his wallet in the dimly candle-lit room. He rushed out and came back in record time with a pack of six condoms. They started all over again. They made love for the first time that night. It was the most passionate experience of their lives. The ultimate connection had been made between them. Both of them had a high libido. It was important for him to be with someone whom he could satisfy, be satisfied with, and with whom he could sleep a million times and not get bored. She felt the same way. Finally, both of them were tired and they drifted into sleep, hugging each other under the soft, goose-down comforter.

After the candles died, he got up and turned the radio off. The nocturnal noises of the city grew louder as the music from the radio disappeared.

A determined young man, he made up his mind that, no matter what, he was not going to let her go.

She had already given him her heart and was hoping and praying that he would never break it.

The following morning was interesting: he woke up before she did. He was so pleased to see her next to him that he softly kissed her to wake her up, and no sooner had her eyes opened than he announced to her, "I love you."

She was still only half-awake, engrossed in sweet, early morning dreams. She smiled as she heard what he had just said and softly responded in a groggy voice, "I love you too."

They made love. That woke them up. She laid her head comfortably on his chest, and they watched *Good Morning America*. Then he looked over her family albums. She told him about her family and friends and about little things in her room and how each of them related to her life.

He had a sudden urge to express himself, so he turned the volume of the TV down and said, "I need to tell you a few things about myself. I can't express enough how sincerely I feel about a relationship with you. It may sound like a story, but I really did come to the States with a few hundred dollars just a few years ago. I am who I am because of my upbringing, which I owe to my parents, my own hard work, and my elder brother's support. I don't have much savings. I'm not happy with what I do professionally. I don't have permanent residency here and, as you know, I plan to move to Canada. I hope to enroll in a good business school and change my career path. I'm aware that I have tremendous potential, and I want to capitalize on it. I'll get to where I want to be soon in life, but I want you to be with me during this transition." He went on and on. She tuned him out and just smiled at him and gazed at him admiringly.

She finally put her hand on his mouth and said, "Hush, you talk, worry, and plan too much. I'll be there for you every step of the way. I don't care what you earn, where you come from, and where you are headed. I want to make this 'our' journey together. We'll see what happens, okay? How about I make coffee?"

He insisted that she rest in bed and that he get Starbucks from the next block. He left the apartment to get her a tall skim milk latte, biscotti, and muffins. The morning sunshine felt warm; the streets were relatively empty; the citizens who went to bed at sunrise would not be waking up for another few hours. He remembered that it was a weekend; most shops would not open until 10:00 a.m. He could hear the chirping of tiny birds; he heard the church bells strike seven times.

Numerous thoughts came to his mind during that one-block walk. He wondered how to move along his relationship with Zeina. His original plan was to leave on Saturday afternoon, but now he wanted to stay until Sunday and spend as much time with her as possible. He brought the coffee and baked goods back to the apartment. She was still comfortably lying in bed.

Sitting on the small sofa in the bedroom, sipping his coffee, he said, "I was thinking that, if it's all right with you, I'd like to stay another day with you and leave tomorrow. That way we get to spend some more time together."

"I'd love that, *Jaani*!" she said, and there it was—her term of endearment for him. She had decided to call him *Jaani*, which meant "my life."

She wanted to treat him to a homemade breakfast. While he shaved and showered, she took out frozen *purees,* bread ready to be fried, and quickly prepared a spicy *aloo chana masala*, potatoes and garbanzo beans in a spicy curry sauce. She had caught on to his taste buds quickly. He liked his food saucy and spicy; it was also obvious to her that his favorite food was *desi*. She was far less *desi* in her food choices and liked a wider range of international foods. Her weaknesses were cheeses, breads, and sweets, but all those went against her metabolism and her desire to stay thin. She didn't eat raw onions or tomatoes; she had a particular aversion to the aroma of raw onions. Most *desi* food is onion- and garlic-based, and to top it all off, nonvegetarian curries taste better served with raw or pickled onions. Unfortunately for her, like all Punjabis, Karan loved his onion salads.

He loved the breakfast she had put together efficiently, with almost no mess in the kitchen. He couldn't thank his lucky stars enough to have Zeina in his life.

She had the day already planned out. She quickly packed a picnic lunch of sandwiches and chilled white wine. He made the bed and cleaned up the room.

4. Lake Sherando— Shenandoah National Park

The day began with a kiss on the doorstep of 65 West 55th Street. Zeina was expressive about her feelings; she did not hold anything back. Karan, on the other hand, was a bit reserved. His family was not big on hugs and kisses; love and affection were conveyed in nonphysical ways. He touched his parents' feet each time he met them after a long time, a gesture followed by a hug. His brothers occasionally exchanged hugs; it was through kind and loving actions that they showed their love for each other. He was aware how different she was in her expression of love and affection. It was not often that the words "I love you" were exchanged within his family, but then love doesn't always have to be communicated physically and verbally. There are other ways of showing it. He respected his own family's ways of showing love, but he liked her way a lot.

He had brought his camera bag and photography equipment with him.

"That's a serious camera."

"I guess we never spoke about it; I enjoy photography. If I had a lot of disposable income and didn't have to earn a living, I would have chosen to be a musician or a photographer. This is an entry-level camera; it's a Nikon 3000 SLR. I have a few specialized lenses that make all the difference in the photographs. I learned photography in college. One way for me to earn a tuition scholarship was by working as editor for the college weekly newspaper. To save departmental costs, I had to cover all major events personally, take my own photos, develop the photos in black-and-white, write the story, and edit it. In that process, I learned a lot, including taking good photos."

"Man of many talents. You know it's never too late. You said you want to change your career path; why not take the creative route?"

"If there weren't enough starving artists and musicians in this world, I would have. I'm not that good, not formally trained, and I am not a risk taker. I come from a background where we are used to seeing a paycheck each month; so we have been conditioned that way. We're taught that each risk must come with not one but two mitigating factors. For the time being, I'll have to take up a job with a steady and higher income and keep my talents as hobbies," he said, sounding a bit sad.

It was a magnificent day. As they conversed and walked, they heard the church bells strike ten times. The streets were just starting to get busy; retail stores were opening their shutters, and tourists were coming out of hotels.

The first stop for the day was the Disney store. As they entered, he noticed excitement in Zeina. It was as if, with the first step into the store, she had become a six-year-old child. The next hour, she went through the entire store explaining the toys, stories, and characters. She disclosed a secret to him: every person has a happy place where they transport their minds to relax. Her happy place was a Disney sort of magical world where she was a character herself; it was a place that not even Disney had illustrated. Her dream was one day to create a children's storybook with illustrations that would depict her magical world. He enjoyed her company and enthusiasm so much that he didn't mind all the kiddy stuff around him. He liked Disney and thought that their stuff was extremely creative, but he had only seen most of the cartoons while flipping channels.

"Maybe we can go Disney together someday," she suggested, laughing in excitement.

"I'd sure love that," he replied, with a doubtful look on his face.

They walked through the high-end fashion stores, admiring the window displays. She explained the new trends and identified the designers. He knew little about fashion. In fact, for him, high-end fashion meant going to Macy's or Dillard's at the local mall and picking up clothes by Nautica or Polo. She loved looking at the windows of Bergdorf Goodman and spent five minutes on each window.

He finally had to ask, "Sorry for my ignorance, but what exactly does a fashion designer do? When I think of fashion design, I think of actors from *The Bold and the Beautiful*, where good-looking men and women just paint pretty sketches."

"You watch *The Bold and the Beautiful*? No way!" she squealed.

"Well, I don't watch it regularly, but flipping through channels, I've glanced at it a few times. Anyway, even if I see one show in six months, I can follow the story. It's usually one day of events that is shown over six months," he laughed.

"I know what you mean. Amma and I have been following that show for decades now. Pretty messed-up family relationships in that show. That's the only show I know of where the same woman has potential to be a man's wife, cousin, stepmother, stepsister, sister-in-law, and stepdaughter in the same lifetime."

She explained further, "Fashion design, *Jaani*, is far more than just 'pretty sketches.' I work with garments, draping, fabric painting, pattern making, sewing, marketing, pricing, and merchandizing. Fashion illustration, which you called 'pretty sketches,' is just a small part of being a fashion designer. I'll show you some of my work and some garments I have designed when we get back to the apartment later today. Hey, look, we are here at Central Park, my favorite place."

They entered through the Fifth Avenue entrance by the Plaza Hotel, making their way toward the pond and then walking along cobblestone walkways toward the main lake. She narrated interesting facts about the park—for example, that most of the huge boulders were brought there from far-off places at a time when there were no cranes or heavy, earth-moving equipment. She knew a lot about the trees, shrubs, and flowers, and the events that took place each year in the park. It was obvious that she had spent a lot of time there. They made frequent stops to observe the flowers, caricature artists, older couples walking toward the benches, roller skaters, bicyclists zooming by on the bike path, children and dogs playing with families.

"For New Yorkers, Central Park is their backyard. The city would not be complete without it," said Zeina.

He couldn't stop taking photos of her. She looked stunning, wearing a black tank top with slim-fitting black jeans. She carried a tote that matched her metallic blue slip-on sandals. Her makeup and accessories all matched her accent color of metallic blue. Her gold *kada* was the only constant; the rest of her accessories changed daily. She tied her hair back with a blue hair clip. Her face was glowing with life. She was wearing Ferragamo perfume, which he found simply intoxicating. He could admire her all day! Every minute with her was precious; with every minute he felt closer to her.

They took a short boat ride on the lake and then settled on the sprawling lush green lawn under a huge maple tree, robust with bright yellow leaves. She laid out the picnic of sandwiches and chilled white wine. She leaned against the tree, and he laid his head in her lap, gazing at her face against the deep-blue sky. The noises of the city even in the middle of the park were loud.

"How often do you get out of this hustle-bustle? I mean, do you venture outside of the city much?"

"Not really. I don't have the time. I visit my brother in Annapolis whenever he is there and sometimes go with Amma to meet relatives in Chicago. I've seen a few other places in the States and Canada, but life is mainly here."

"Have you ever been camping?"

"Back in Islamabad, during my high school days, yes, I went camping, but not here. I'm not too excited about roughing it. I like to have shower facilities at the minimum to feel comfortable."

"Camping here is nothing like camping in our part of the world, my dear princess. Camping in the States is comfortable and luxurious. There are actually designated campgrounds with proper toilets and hot showers."

"You're kidding me. I had no idea. I love being outdoors. I could go camping like that."

"Would you like to go for a camping trip with me before it gets too cold?"

"Sure, when and where would you like to go? The weather is already getting cold."

"I'm actually thinking that if you are free next weekend, you could take a train down to Baltimore. I'll research a campsite in Virginia that we can drive to. I doubt the campgrounds will be busy at this time of the year. I'll make a reservation. If you can make it a long weekend, that'll be even better. That way, we can spend an extra day together."

She called her brother to see whether he was in Annapolis the following weekend. She couldn't imagine going to the DC area and not seeing or staying with him. The call was forwarded to his secretary, who told her that he was on his way to Dhaka and was not going to be back for another ten days.

"My brother is not in Annapolis. I have no pressure or guilt. I'll come on Thursday night after work. Camping with you sounds like fun, *Jaani*. What do I need to bring?"

"I'll send you a list in case I need you to bring anything. Most of the camping equipment I'll take care of."

His mind was already meticulously planning how to make the weekend special for her.

Sunday was a lazy morning. They had brunch at a local café, enjoyed coffee, and then walked a few blocks window-shopping. Soon it was afternoon. As the time to say good-bye approached, their hearts sank, just thinking of the separation. He greatly enjoyed and quickly got used to a spontaneous hug or a peck on the cheek from her while walking or waiting at a crosswalk for the traffic light to turn green. They leisurely strolled back to her apartment.

She made tea while he gathered his belongings. After tea, she packed two sandwiches and water for him. While he was packing his snacks, she came up to him with teary eyes and hugged him. He almost had tears in his eyes too. This was their first farewell; it was not an easy good-bye. As he held her a bit longer, his sad eyes caught a glimpse of a cute pink teddy bear on the shelf. The bear looked cuddly, one felt like snuggling with it. That was it; the word "*Snuggle*" became his term of endearment for her.

He looked into her eyes and said, "Hey, *Snuggle*, we'll meet next week, which is just five days away, and if you come a day early, that is just four days away."

Her eyes lit up, tears soaked back into her eyes, and with a grin, she asked, "*Snuggle*? Where did you come up with that?"

"That big cuddly pink teddy bear over there. It's a perfect name for you, and it totally describes how I feel about you," he responded, pointing at the shelf.

"I love it," she smiled shyly. At the same time she was relieved that he had not come up with a typical Punjabi pet name like *Dolly, Bubbly,* or *Pinky*.

He had to leave. It was getting dark, and the drive on the weekend on I-95, across the Delaware Bridge through three toll stops could easily extend his five-hour drive to seven or even eight hours. They walked to the parking garage. He paid the "extortion fee," as he called the parking fee in the city. He dropped her at the apartment building's doorstep, kissed her good-bye with a heavy heart, and started driving through the Holland Tunnel into New Jersey.

The drive back felt long. The traffic, as expected, was stop-and-go all through the New Jersey Turnpike, and all the toll stops were backed up for miles. Throughout the drive, all he could visualize was Zeina's face. He was so in love with her, he couldn't see anything beyond her. He did not for a second think about her being Pakistani or a Muslim.

India, Pakistan, and Bangladesh were all one until 1947. When the British liberated the Indian continent, they managed to divide the mighty Indian nation into three countries, as they stand today. The partition was bloody and messy, leaving scars among the Hindus, Muslims, and Sikhs. Karan and Zeina's grandparents and parents suffered those scars as well. Karan's grandfather's brother was brutally stabbed and killed while trying to get on the last train leaving Pakistan for India. Hundreds of people lost family members and their homes during the partition. Zeina's own mother had lived in Delhi in 1947. Her father noticed a cross on his door which meant that at night their home was to be attacked and burned. A Hindu friend helped them move out in a matter of hours, get them across the police checkpoint, and secure them a seat on the last flight leaving from Delhi for Lahore. The partition was followed by three gory wars between the two countries, mostly over the territory of Kashmir, and later East Pakistan (Bangladesh) liberation. The wars were recent, and Karan's and Zeina's parents and siblings had them fresh in their hearts and minds. Some of the land in northern Kashmir still remains disputed; every now and then the tension results in skirmishes between the Indian and Pakistani armies. Even today, India and Pakistan are known enemies, but, unfortunately, for no good reason. They are the same people with the same genetic pool, same culture, food, and traditions. There are more Muslims living in India than the total population in Pakistan.

Karan couldn't wait to see Zeina the following weekend. He was already planning her visit and where to take her camping. He stopped for a gas, restroom, and coffee break. He ate his sandwich and then drove nonstop toward home, which he reached in six hours despite the traffic. He called her right away to tell her that he had arrived safely. She was awake, waiting for his call.

Zeina had a pleasant evening. She kept thinking about the weekend and smiling at how differently it had turned out, compared with what she had expected. When you see a person smiling and humming while they are alone, it's almost a sure sign that they are either in love or have gone loony. Of course, as soon as he left, she called Shiraz to tell her about the weekend, minus some of the PG16-censored events. Shiraz was happy for her friend. She desired someone like Karan for herself, but the person simply had to be an Israeli Jew.

The remainder of the week crawled. Karan and Zeina spoke every day, sometimes a few times a day at work and several times in the evening. He was engrossed in planning the weekend. He didn't want to give her details of the trip and kept the weekend full of surprises. He asked her to just bring herself, walking shoes, and a light jacket.

"I feel I'm not doing much for this trip. What else can I bring or help with?"

"I'll take care of everything else for the trip. I have all the gear, including a tent, sleeping bags, gas burner, and outdoor pots and pans."

He had researched and picked a perfect campground in Virginia. The campground was located next to a freshwater lake inside Shenandoah National Park. He booked a campsite for a two-night stay. He had made sure he picked a campground that had hot showers and toilets. He had his standard camping list ready in his PalmPilot, groceries already bought for the trip, and maps ordered and ready to be picked up at the AAA office in Columbia.

Zeina took Friday off and made an advance purchase of a train ticket to Baltimore for Thursday evening. It was just Tuesday, and the week was not moving along fast enough. All of a sudden, she realized that her world had shrunk to thinking about her next meeting with Karan. She was not interested in meeting anyone other than Shiraz that week. She planned her weekend clothes meticulously. She was particular about her looks; everything had to coordinate: the clothes, accessories, and makeup. She made sure that her waxing was done and eyebrows shaped. She got a French manicure and pedicure. She had to look perfect for him. She had high self-confidence, and a lot of it came from the way she carried and presented herself.

On Thursday afternoon, she called to let him know that she would board the afternoon train, which was scheduled to arrive at the Baltimore train station at 7:00 p.m. If the train were to be late, she would call him. He left work an hour early so he could reach home in time to prepare for her arrival. His home was clean; bathrooms and kitchen were scrubbed. His roommate, Bobby, was told to limit his presence in the house.

Karan went home and double-checked everything. He figured that Zeina would be hungry when she arrived. So why not pack a warm dinner and have a picnic at the park near the train station? He quickly prepared a Punjabi meal. On the menu were *veg-biryani, khatte aloo* [sour and spicy potatoes] and *rajmah masala* [red beans]. He placed one hundred tea lights all over the townhouse and requested that when he called, Bobby should light the candles, turn on the CD player, and then leave the house for the night.

He stopped by a florist and bought a dozen red roses for her, along with a greeting card. It was his first card for her. He laid down fresh sheets on the bed, put out fresh towels for her, sprayed room freshener, and lit lavender-scented candles. Once he was done, he waited nervously for her call. The home phone rang at six o'clock.

"Hi, *Jaani*. The train is on time. See you soon."

His spirits lifted upon hearing her voice. He warmed up the food, packed a hot case, put soft drinks and beer in a cooler, sprayed on CK1 and darted out the door. He was at the train station right as the train pulled up. He waited outside the station. It was not that busy, but a cop was circling, shooing away illegal parkers. Just as the cop was about to reach his car, she appeared. He popped his trunk open. Looking at the cop, he pointed toward her. The cop drove away, leaving them alone for a few minutes.

She looked as gorgeous as ever. She was wearing a black skirt, brown turtleneck, and all gold accessories. She wore tall, dark-brown boots and carried a light-brown leather handbag. He gave her a tight hug, and as they were about to smooch, the annoying cop came back, signalizing them to vacate the passenger pickup area. They drove to the downtown park, which had over a hundred fountains, lots of trees, and an expansive green space.

"I figured you must be hungry, so I packed a picnic dinner."

"I'm starving! I had a coffee and biscotti for breakfast and then an apple at noon. I rushed home to pick up my bags, and here I am. So what's for dinner?"

"I prepared a typical Punjabi vegetarian meal—*rajmah, veg-biryani,* and these sour and spicy potatoes called *khatte aloo*. It's *bhabhijee's*—my grandma's—special recipe."

"Wow, that sounds awesome. Does *bhabhi* not mean sister-in-law? So how is your grandma your sister-in-law? This is not a *desi Bold and Beautiful* story, is it?" she asked inquisitively.

"Not at all. This is an amusing story. I was close to my grandmother. While my father was stationed in high-altitude areas, also known as field areas, where families were not allowed, we used to live in Delhi with my grandmother. At that time her brother-in-law also lived in the same house. All day long he called out to her asking for things. We kids were just learning to talk, and we were like parrots. We heard her being addressed as *bhabhijee* so many times a day that we started calling her that. Lo and behold, all her other grandchildren started calling her that. A few years later, her own children also called her by that name. Over time it just became her name. Come to think of it, she had a beautiful and Bollywood movie type of name. Most of her grandchildren may not even know her real name, which was Veerawali. She was such a wonderful human being. She passed away a few years ago." As Karan finished narrating the story, he made a right turn into the parking lot.

He got the picnic basket out of the car, picked a grassy spot by the fountain, and spread a picnic cloth to sit on. He had brought plastic plates, glasses, and cutlery, which lots of Americans like to call "silverware"! He opened the hot case. The aroma of Indian spices made her mouth water. He placed rice in a small bowl, gently pressed it, and then turned it upside down on the plate, leaving a neat, round shape of rice on the plate. Then, he carefully arranged the *rajmah*, dribbling just a little bit of the red gravy on the rice, and finally he delicately placed the potatoes at a six o'clock position on the plate. It was his training in hospitality, which was coming in handy in making an impression.

He was taught that a full culinary experience was a combination of three senses working together. If even one was missing, the experience couldn't be complete. Eyes approve first, then the nose gets the senses warmed up, and the taste buds do the rest.

She watched this professional plate presentation process in amusement, admiring the fact that her man not only cooked but knew how to serve as well.

"You know I have never had *rajmah* like this before. I love it. We cook it with beef in Pakistan. And the potatoes are delicious as well. Thanks for all this effort, *Jaani*. I've also never had a hot meal at a picnic before. We usually pack sandwiches."

"*Rajmah* with beef? That's interesting; I've heard Pakistanis spare no vegetable and everything has to be cooked with some sort of meat. Is that true?"

"Come to think of it, yes, that's true. I can't think of a vegetable not made with chicken or lamb."

"I'll open a new world of vegetarianism to you. Most vegetables have such great flavors by themselves that they don't even need any chicken or meat stock," he explained.

He was delighted to have Zeina with him. He was happy to see her enjoying the picnic dinner. She poured herself a Gatorade, and opened a can of Heineken for him. They sat by the fountain for a while after dinner, enjoying the sound of the splashing water under the dim yellow light of the streetlamp. Downtown Baltimore was quieter than New York, although there was the occasional sound of a siren from a police car or a fire truck.

"Can I borrow your mobile for a quick call, please?" he requested.

He called Bobby to give him the signal. Meanwhile, she cleaned up the picnic mess and packed the picnic basket. They disposed of the garbage, loaded the car, and drove to Columbia. As the car pulled into the driveway, he put on the handbrake and presented a greeting card to her. The envelope read, "To My Dearest *Snuggle*, Welcome Home."

She giggled and said, "Hey, it looks like the postman left your mail with me." She extracted a greeting card for him. The envelope was addressed, "To my one and only *Jaani*."

They read their cards quietly, exchanged a passionate kiss, and exited the car. He unlocked and opened the front door. She almost fell back at the magnificent sight of the hundred tea lights glowing in the townhouse. Starting from the doorstep, going up the staircase, she could see that all of the living room was glowing with candlelight. Jazz was playing in the background. She was stunned by such a grand and affectionate welcome.

She was about to say something, but he put his hand on her lips and said, "Wait, there is more." He led her by the hand upstairs toward his bedroom.

The hallway going toward the bedroom and bathroom was lined with tea lights. A dozen red roses awaited her on the bedside.

"Welcome Home, *Snuggle*."

"No one has ever welcomed me into their life like you have," she said, hugging him.

They began the evening by sipping frozen margaritas and lounging on the black leather couch watching *Life Is Beautiful*. They enjoyed a romantic evening together.

The following morning, he woke up with a grin on his face, just looking at her lying next to him. He kissed her to wake her and said, "Good morning, *Snuggle*." It was becoming his standard way of waking her up in the morning. He made tea and brought hot tea and biscuits to bed for her. He had figured out that she loved having her tea in bed in the morning. Both of them took their own time getting out of bed and getting dressed. Then they drove to a nearby South Indian restaurant for brunch. She was not big on spicy food—and certainly not for breakfast—but being a good sport, she did her best to accommodate him. She had figured out what he enjoyed most in food. They were getting to know where to give in, how much to give in, and how to adapt to each other.

When they arrived back at the house, Bobby had returned from his girlfriend's apartment, where he had spent the night. He couldn't stop staring at Zeina, admiring her. Karan had to nudge him to signal him to lower his gaze. Then the goofball addressed her as *bhabhi*, and Karan almost kicked him for that. She went a bit red in the face and excused herself from the living room to fix her makeup and get ready for the drive to the campground.

"Dude, are you out of your mind? Why are you being so cheeky with her?"

"I was just kidding, *yaar* [buddy]."

"It was a poor choice of a joke. Please don't embarrass me like that again," Karan exclaimed angrily. He went upstairs to check on her.

Bobby was a great guy, but rough around the edges. Indians are well-known to finger each other, pass judgments, come up with corny jokes, comment on other people if they look fat or sad—just anything to get a reaction. Their concept of personal space is different from that in the Western world, where unless you know someone really well, it's not acceptable to comment on a person's looks, especially if your comments are such things as: "You have put on weight," or "Did you already have a baby?" That sort of stuff just does not cut it in the Western world.

Thankfully, Zeina was not upset or offended. She had just ignored the comment and was happily packing for the trip. He took out his typed checklist, which he had made on a spreadsheet, and started gathering stuff.

"Did you type that in a spreadsheet? That is so hilarious. Wow, it has the camping list and agenda for our whole weekend by the hour. Is that normal, Karan? Should I be worried?" she asked, rather amused.

He became a little embarrassed but admitted, "Yes, I do have a bit of a problem. I keep my life organized, and I am obsessed with my PalmPilot, but this is an exceptionally well-planned weekend with lots of minor details, which had to be organized. You know what I mean?"

She got her hands on his PalmPilot and started flipping through the calendar and found interesting reminders, such as "weekly nail cut," "garbage day," and birthday reminders for friends and family. She learned something new about him. His life ran on his PalmPilot. She liked it because her life just ran by itself. Unless absolutely necessary, she planned for nothing. She was a free spirit and lived each day at a time. She had missed many friends' birthdays and social events because she didn't plan and organize, but life still went on okay for her. She still had friends and got errands done. She liked the fact that she was with a man who could balance her unplanned life.

"Goodness gracious! You also have a reminder to call me. Now is that one really necessary? I call you all the time with no reminders," she teased.

He avoided that question and ran downstairs to get the ice box ready for the trip.

"You're funny and amusing," she said in a loud voice, well knowing that he had gone downstairs to avoid further discussion.

She made tea. They sat in the living room looking over his photo albums. He proudly pointed out the who's who of his family. Then she picked up a red album that he should have hidden because it was full of women he had dated, but it had never occurred to him that he should have done that.

"Who is this?" she asked, looking at a blonde woman whose most obvious feature was her generous cleavage.

"Just a friend," he answered, a bit red in the face.

"This one a friend too?" she questioned, looking at another short brunette with Native American looks and, again, big boobs.

"Hmm, yes. Let's put this album aside and see the other one from my trip to Alaska."

"No, let's finish this one. I find these photographs intriguing," she said, sounding a bit irked. Then she posed the toughest question, one that he was hoping she would never ask. "So, how many women have you been with, Karan?"

He noticed that no "*Jaani*" came with that sentence.

Thinking quickly, as usual, he responded, "Just you, *Snuggle*, and never again with anyone else. We've got to get going; otherwise we'll get to our campsite after dark, which won't be good." He whisked the album away from her and created a sense of urgency to get going.

He made a note to get rid of all photos of ex-girlfriends as soon as he got back from the camping trip.

They gathered all their gear, cross-checked the list, and started loading the car.

They crossed DC and entered Virginia. As they drove toward the mountains, the scenery became picturesque. The Skyline Drive was spectacular. The whole valley was glowing with autumn colors and dewdrops from the previous night's rain. Sunshine was sparkling and reflecting through the water droplets, making the valley appear as if all the trees were decorated with pearls.

After about two hours of driving, he took the exit for Shenandoah. The sun was beginning to set. It was important to reach the campground and set up the tent before nightfall. He drove a few miles on a country road and fortunately, without getting lost, arrived at the entrance to the campground.

He paid the campground fee at the reception, bought firewood, and maneuvered his way to their campsite using the map that the receptionist provided. Luckily, their camping spot was adjacent to the lake, the restrooms, and the showers. She was pleasantly surprised.

"This is awesome. It's so clean and organized. The air smells fresh. It feels great to be here," she remarked, sounding excited to be near trees, mountains, and a beautiful lake.

He parked the car and unloaded all the camping gear. The first thing they did was set up the blue and red tent, which took less than ten minutes.

"I bought this tent with my brother a few years ago when we drove across America; it has witnessed campgrounds in many states."

He told her more about Mount Rushmore, the Badlands, the Grand Tetons, Bryce Canyon, the Grand Canyon, Yellowstone National Park, and all the other places where he had traveled and camped with his brother and his friends over the years. He placed the food and stove neatly on the wooden picnic bench and organized the firewood in the designated fire pit, ready to ignite after dusk. No alcohol is allowed in state parks, but he had sneaked in some wine, just as most of the campers do.

The sun was now setting. They took a walk toward the lake, which had a small, man-made sand beach. The lake water was a bit cold, but not freezing. They lay on the sand watching the sun go down and the colors of the sky change from blue to orange, orange to red, and then to dark purple.

Then both of them did something crazy. They saw a dog and a small kid swimming in the lake. They were inspired and jumped in the lake with their clothes on. It was an incredibly refreshing swim. They came out of the water, ran toward the facilities to take a hot shower, and changed into dry clothes. While she changed her clothes in the tent, he snapped some tastefully composed topless photos of her through the mosquito net from outside the tent, creating a mesh layer effect of her silhouette. She posed for him, but only under one condition: no one would ever get to see those photos.

As it got darker, the night sky lit up with millions of stars.

"There's the North Star, that's the Unicorn, that's the …" She knew so much about stars. She admitted that when she was young, she had desired to be an astronaut, but she was never good enough at science and math to do anything about it other than develop star gazing as a hobby.

"I've never seen so many stars ever in my life, not even in Islamabad."

He lit the fire, wrapped the half-baked potatoes in double foil, punched small holes in them to allow smoke to infuse, and gently placed them in the ambers. Then he grilled premarinated boneless chicken in *tandoori* paste and tossed a precut crisp salad with homemade mango vinaigrette dressing. By the time they ate the salad, the chicken on the grill and the potatoes in the fire were ready. He took the potatoes out of the fire, opened the foil, cut them half-open, gently mashed the center with a fork and added butter, salt, and pepper. What a delicious meal that was! They ate next to the yellow glow and warmth of the fire under a starlit and moonlit sky. He poured red wine; they sipped it and sat quietly on reclining chairs, gazing at the sky and the fire.

For dessert, he had brought marshmallows and wafers. They made s'mores on the campfire and devoured them with hot chocolate. It was getting a bit cold; they had to put on fleece jackets. After dinner cleanup, he brought out his guitar and mouth organ and they sang campfire songs for an hour. Finally, he sang "Unchained Melody," the same song that she had heard him sing the first time she heard his voice.

If it's possible to fall in love once again with someone you are already in love with, that is what happened to the two of them that night.

It got colder as the fire died down. He had to go looking for half-burned firewood from other campfire pits to keep the fire going. They spoke softly and chatted for a while, listening to the hissing and crackling of the fire, a few crickets deep in the forest, and music from another camper's boom box in the background. A park ranger came around to remind all campers to dispose of their garbage safely and turn down music and lights. Everyone fell asleep shortly, and there were just a few sounds of nature in the background that continued through the night—among them, the occasional call of a fox, which sounded scary and eerie.

The sounds of chirping birds and light from the morning sun woke them up. He put on his shoes, started a fresh fire, brewed instant coffee, and made farm-fresh fried eggs and smoked toast on the open fire for breakfast.

"These are the best fried eggs I've ever had. So, what's the plan, Stan?"

"We're going to hit the road, Jack. We'll take a drive and check out some more of the Skyline Drive today. Help me clean up. We can shower and then we can first go on a short trek nearby; then I thought we could have lunch at a local inn. On our way back, I was planning to buy premarinated steak and make dirty mashed potatoes. I mean 'dirty' as in, potatoes mashed with their skins. We can grill vegetables with balsamic vinaigrette. Do you like steaks? If not, we can make something else."

"I like a well-done steak and yes, I do love mashed potatoes, but you have to make them with gravy. We can buy premade gravy from the grocery store. I'll make that for you."

They drove past little villages and then started climbing up to the Skyline Drive. The name itself said it all; the drive really was like driving next to the clouds in the sky. Most of the road embraces the tops of hills and mountains; all around one could see mountain peaks with a bluish tinge, surrounded by mist and clouds. It was a breathtaking sight. He played the latest Bollywood songs in the car, and they quietly soaked in all that natural beauty around them. He stopped at various lookout points to take pictures. After about an hour of driving, he pulled over at a hiking trail, which was just one mile long. The trail led to a picturesque waterfall. He had done his research well; he knew it was an easy trail. They changed into hiking shoes and made their way to the falls. The trek downhill was easy. It was a small waterfall, but majestic as it fell from the crest of the mountain almost fifty feet down, spraying fine mist all around. There were other hikers on the trail, including small children.

"You like children?" she asked.

"What? Hold on, you're going a bit too fast for me; children? I'm almost a child myself!" he said jokingly, knowing well what she was asking.

"You silly boy, I'm just asking a general question. I like kids, but in short doses. I took care of my cousins when they were little. I enjoyed their love, affection, and innocence."

"I spent a fair bit of time with my young cousins, whom I took care of as well. I've also babysat many kids here. I like well-mannered kids. I do like little girls and would love to have my own daughter some day. In fact, I have a name for her already; it's going to be Zoia," he said with a laugh.

He told her that he took care of kids when he was in college. It was an interesting story: one day, when Karan was working in the college restaurant, a middle-aged Jewish woman, who was having lunch, approached him and started asking questions about him. The following day, Sister Lisa, who was the foreign student counselor, called Karan and informed him that a local family wanted to offer him room and board for the remainder of his college stay. In exchange, all the family wanted was for him to babysit their children occasionally and live with them like family. Essentially, they were adopting a foreign student. The family liked hosting foreign students. Although the family usually welcomed girls, because they had two sons and a daughter, they had taken a liking to Karan and wanted to give him a try. Karan was indeed surprised at the offer. It sounded too good to be true. It meant that he didn't have to work four campus jobs to pay for his boarding costs. He had a tuition scholarship and could focus on studies. The family was well-known and respected. The head of the family was a urologist, and his wife was a social worker. Finally, Sister Lisa told him the name of the family; it was Dr. and Mrs. "Lauda," which means "penis" in Hindi, and that too in an abusive way and not as a clinical medical term.

Zeina just couldn't stop laughing at the story. She laughed for a good two minutes and almost fell off the trail into a deep ravine.

"I also had to control my laughter, but it was too good a chance to pass up just because of their family name. Sister Lisa gave me the campus ministry car, and I went to meet the Laudas. Both husband and wife were wonderful people. They gave me their old Audi for commuting to college, my own room, and access to the bathroom in the attic. All I had to do was some yard work and help with the kids. Dr. Lauda was a sailor as well; he took me sailing on Lake Erie on weekends. They also took me on their family vacations. Whenever I babysat their kids, Mrs. Lauda used to pay me extra money. I'm indebted to the Laudas for life for what they did for me. They loved me, and frankly, I fell in love with the family as well. Mrs. Lauda called herself my 'American mother.' I hope you get a chance to meet them someday.

"Anyway, I was telling you about kids. I spent a lot of time with their younger son and daughter. I used to feed them, swim with them, go biking and rollerblading with them, and help them with their homework. All three of them were good children. Their elder son didn't need me as much; he was a big boy, both in age and size, and he was more like a friend." As Karan finished the story, they reached the parking lot.

"That's such a sweet story and a unique experience," said Zeina, totally out of breath from the uphill trek.

"So, let us say, you and I have kids, what religion would they be?"

"They can be whoever they want to be! I would like my children to be exposed to all religions and let them decide what they believe in. In the end if they do not wish to follow any religion at all, that is okay as well. All I want them to be is good human beings, know right from wrong, and love and respect others, no matter how different someone is. Make sense?" He laughed.

She nodded in agreement.

Zeina needed to go to the restroom. There was a vending machine nearby for water and soda, next to the blue portable toilet that she refused to use.

"I'd rather suffer a bladder infection than suffocate in one of those stinky things."

"All right, princess, but I need to go pee."

Those toilets were indeed nasty, so they drove on to find the nearest rest stop, which fortunately was just two miles down the road. As they approached the rest stop, Karan pointed to the sign of Cracker Barrel, a country food restaurant he loved.

"That's where we are getting our lunch. Have you ever eaten at a Cracker Barrel?"

"Of course not, this is the first time I'm even seeing such rural parts of the States. I'm almost sure there is no Cracker Barrel anywhere near the city."

"There is food for the body and then there is food for the soul. This place feeds the soul.

"This place serves the best biscuits and gravy you have ever had. I love their fried okra, which reminds me of the *desi* crispy fried *bhindi*. They also serve roast beef, roasted chicken, corn, sweet potatoes, shepherd's pie, and macaroni and cheese. Yes, I do have their menu almost memorized," he said, looking directly at her with a silly grin.

Both of them were famished after the trek, and all that food talk was making their stomachs growl. She couldn't get over how cute the porch of the restaurant was, with old folks sitting on the wooden rocking chairs, enjoying the sun. They walked into the lobby, which was essentially a store connected to the restaurant. The dining area had two large fireplaces; the walls and shelves had unique things like old rackets and barn equipment, which looked as if they were from the '40s and '50s. One section of the store had themes; a section of old Coke advertising products, and another with candles. There were other sections with cards, gifts, Christmas decorations, toys, soaps, candies, and musical instruments. Zeina used the restroom, and then they sat at a table near the fireplace; the warmth from the fireplace felt good.

He ordered a roast beef sandwich with a side order of okra and corn on the cob. She ordered grilled chicken with a side of biscuits, gravy, and mashed sweet potatoes. They could barely move after all that food in their stomachs and dragged themselves next door to the farmers' shop. Karan snapped more pictures of Zeina with the horses, buggies, and stacks of hay. Although they didn't want to think about food at that time, he bought two premarinated pepper steaks for dinner. She bought a jar of local honey and strawberry preserves, along with some trinkets. Karan bought a Native American dream catcher for her.

"Let's drive back to the campsite before it gets dark."

The temperature dropped fast as the sun went down. It was much colder the second night. There was no way they could have gone for a swim. In fact, some of the campers had left. He gathered extra wood and made a bigger fire. The steak dinner with mashed potatoes came out perfect. After they cleaned up, they cuddled by the fire. She told him more about her childhood, life in Islamabad, and about family and friends.

"Islamabad used to be a peaceful and beautiful place. It was safe enough that even as girls we could ride our bikes up and down Margala Road, but now with all the political instability and terrorism, the city has gone to the dogs."

That was yet another memorable day together. They were totally lost in each other. The two of them didn't care about anyone or anything in the world. They had spent the last two days in the wilderness as if it were only the two of them who existed on earth.

She looked deep into his eyes totally in admiration of him. She could see the reflection of the dancing fire in them. With all her heart said, "I love you, *Jaani*."

"I love you too," he whispered, and they sealed the declaration of their love with a kiss.

It got bitterly cold that night, and they had to dress in layers to keep warm. They were lucky to have had two decent days of good weather and one decent night. The following morning they woke up all stiff.

"Forget making breakfast today. Let's pack up and get going. We can eat breakfast at a restaurant and get home by lunchtime."

"Good idea, *Jaani*. I'm so cold and achy."

He packed up the tent and equipment in half an hour with her help, and they got on the road heading back to Columbia. On their way they stopped at an International House of Pancakes (I-Hop) and ate a sumptuous breakfast.

"One of I-Hop's meals could be eaten by at least five Somalians over five days," he said, looking in amazement at the amount of food that was served. Karan thought that it was sickening to see how much food was served for $4.99, and how much of that food people wasted.

They reached home, took hot showers, got a batch of laundry going, and put away the camping gear. Karan listened to voice mails on his home phone. One was a voice mail from Varun informing him that his parents were reaching him that week on Wednesday. They were to stay the weekend with him and then fly out from JFK the following weekend. The message sent a brainwave through his head.

He asked Zeina after she was ready and cozy in her PJs, "*Snuggle*, my parents will be here with me next weekend. They will go back to Delhi the following weekend. I think you should meet them. I mean, that it would be good for you to meet them as my friend, not my girlfriend. Unfortunately, in the last one year they have not gathered the best impression of me because I introduced them to far too many women who I thought could be marriage candidates, but it turned out otherwise. It would be great for them to at least see you and feel comfortable that I'm seeing someone decent."

"So, sounds to me like you goofed up with your folks, and now you want to use me to fix it for you," she replied. "If you are really sure it's a good idea, I'll be glad to meet them. I can come here on Friday; that way I can meet my brother as well. He is back on Wednesday and leaves on Saturday. I'll stay in Annapolis on Friday with my brother, with you on Saturday, and return on Sunday. But isn't it too early for me to meet your folks? And who are all these women you are talking about? I want to know more about that first." She sounded a bit annoyed and worried.

After a moment's pause, he said, "Yes, I'm sure that it's important for you to meet them before they return to India. They will not be back for another year, and it will be great for them to meet you." Once again, he conveniently bypassed details of the other women to whom he had referred.

She boarded the evening train back to New York, leaving a void in his life for the coming week. He was uneasy letting her go. If at all possible, he wanted to keep her close to him forever.

Karan returned his brother's call. He told Varun that he had gone with Zeina on a camping trip over the weekend. Varun was not at all happy to hear that he was getting close to this girl. His tone turned cold as the conversation progressed. Karan sensed his brother's apprehensions and started to give shorter and shorter answers, but the number of questions and complexity of questions kept increasing.

"Are you out of your mind? You're going to introduce her to Mom? Are you forgetting she is a Pakistani Muslim and how you got to know her? Have you gone mad?"

There was no way he could tell his brother off. Nor could he explain to him how much in love he was with Zeina nor could he reason how important it was for his parents to meet her before they left for India for another year. Varun was like his second father. Karan had deep tolerance for his verbal abuse. He stayed silent during his brother's unreasonable rage, let him vent, and then politely said good-bye.

He remained upset for the remainder of the evening. He had never thought much of the Pakistani Muslim angle and, least of all, how he had met her. He had made the fatal mistake of telling his brother how he met her, and now the cat was out of the bag. There was not much he could do. He lay in his bed, restless.

Late at night the phone rang; it was Zeina.

"Hi, *Jaani*, sorry to have woken you up. I reached home safe. The entire ride back I thought about you and what a wonderful weekend I had. Thanks for such a special trip. I loved every bit of it."

"I did too."

He was a bit quiet and pretended that he was half-asleep in order to avoid further conversation—especially discussing anything about the talk with his brother.

"Good night. I'll call you tomorrow morning."

5. Breakup

Varun took upon himself the task of informing the family about what Karan was up to, who Zeina was, and how Karan had met her. He painted a dark picture of her. He portrayed her as a Pakistani slut who was out to get Karan. As open-minded as their parents were, their roots in India were still somewhat conservative and, even according to modern social norms in India, promiscuity was not well received. However, they were mature enough not to pick up the phone and confront their son. The family was close knit, and slight turbulences in the relationship with one family member rocked the entire boat.

"Hi, Mom, I'm looking forward to seeing you tomorrow. There is a great South Indian restaurant a few minutes from my house where I can't wait to take you," said Karan to his mother.

She responded indifferently, "Hmm, I always like *dosas*. Anyway, what am I hearing about this girl you want to introduce to us to? Have we not seen enough girls on this trip already? Your brother told us that she is Pakistani. Your father and I discussed meeting her. We don't have any problem with her religious faith or the fact that she is from Pakistan, but the rest of what we have heard does not appeal to us. Ideally, we don't want to meet her."

She had dropped a deadly bomb in his lap. She had pretty much told him that she knew more than she cared to know. She didn't think highly of Zeina. She would not like to meet her or see her son take this any further. He felt a needle pierce his heart. He felt a volcanic eruption had started that could create a crack in his family ties. He had a sinking feeling that this was not going to be easy to handle. He loved his parents but had also deeply fallen in love with Zeina. He had set himself up for a tough battle.

He phrased his words carefully. "Mom, she is a wonderful woman, and I'm simply friends with her for now. Her brother happens to live in Annapolis, which is just twenty minutes from where I live. She's visiting him next weekend anyway. How about we just meet her casually and then see how it goes? I'm not asking you for anything else. As of now, I'm not even serious about her. Only if you like her will I consider anything further."

There was deathly silence for a few seconds. Then she said, "You know what is best for you. I hope you know what is best for your family. We'll meet her and give you our opinion."

He spoke to his father and then his brother and took down their flight arrival details. Arjun was going to come as well and then take a bus to Vermont.

Karan spoke to Zeina every day that week but kept the conversations short so she would not detect the turbulence he was feeling and know how nervous he was about her meeting his parents. She could sense that something was wrong, but he remained tight-lipped. She couldn't get anything out of him, despite some subtle probing.

He received his parents and younger brother on Wednesday evening at BWI Airport. Everyone met warmly with hugs and kisses. They drove home and chatted about their road trip across America. They had seen more of the country than the majority of Americans get to see. Colonel Dev loved Las Vegas and the Grand Canyon the most.

Bobby was on his best behavior as he welcomed Karan's family. They had prepared an elaborate welcome dinner. Mom loved the small and cozy townhouse. Colonel Dev turned the gas fireplace on. It was a nice reunion that evening.

After everyone went to sleep, Karan called Zeina and told her that the plan was on for the weekend.

"I spoke to Arjun about your visit, and he told me that my parents are looking forward to seeing you," he told her, covering up the reality.

"Anything I should do or not do when I meet them? I'm a bit nervous; help me out a bit."

"Just be yourself, but dress conservatively; try not to show much cleavage or legs. My folks are not conservative, but they lean toward modest dressing."

"Do I need to touch their feet or anything like that? I see that in Bollywood movies—Indians touching elders' feet. I'm sorry to ask you such silly questions, but you know that in Pakistan no one touches anyone else's feet unless you go for a pedicure," she said, giggling.

"No, *Snuggle*, you don't have to touch anyone's feet. Touching an elder's feet is a sign of respect, and it has to come from the heart. You are not expected to do that."

"What about a *bindi* on the forehead? I'll bring *salwar kameez*. I like to wear a *bindi*, but I hope they'll not find it offensive if I wear one? It's a Hindu thing to do, right?" she asked, getting even more paranoid.

"Stop stressing so much. My parents will not judge you by your *bindi* or your *salwar kameez*. They're reasonable people and will look for what is within you. Trust me, just be yourself, and you'll win their hearts."

The part he didn't tell her was that their minds were a bit poisoned, and it would not be easy for her to win their hearts.

Friday arrived. Zoheb picked Zeina up at the train station. She told him that she had a friend in Crystal City whom she would like him to meet. The two of them drove across Arlington Bridge to Crystal City to meet Karan for a quick lunch.

For Karan it was odd meeting Zeina in her brother's presence. He couldn't give her a proper hug—and no kiss, for sure.

Zoheb was a well dressed, good-looking man. He had long, wavy hair and big brown eyes with long eyelashes. He was a few shades darker than his sister and, at first glance, the two of them didn't look related at all.

Karan was wearing a houndstooth suit with a white shirt and red-and-blue-striped tie. Zoheb greeted him warmly but formally. They went to a nearby *LahoreJees* for chicken *tikkas* and *naan*.

"How long have you known each other? How did you two meet?"

They had forgotten to prepare themselves for such queries. Karan's eyes met hers, and he knew just what to say: "We met a few months ago in New York at a party and have stayed in touch since. I go there often for work. We meet once every few weeks," he answered, creating a simple, unassuming story that would not raise any more questions.

Zeina appeared relieved by his response.

The plan for the following day was tricky. Her brother was under the impression that she was going back to New York the following morning. He planned to see her off at the train station in Baltimore and drive to BWI himself to catch a flight to Dhaka. But she was not getting on any train the next day. Karan was going to pick her up at the train station and take her home to meet his parents. The plan required coordination. After lunch, they dropped Karan off at work and drove to Annapolis.

"What do you think of him?"

"Who? Karan? He's all right. He comes across as a decent guy. Looks to me he is underutilizing his intellectual capabilities working at that hotel; he has more potential. I sense a keen drive in him to succeed. Although he didn't tell me, I doubt he will stick to being an hotelier too long."

That was indeed an accurate assessment.

"So, why exactly did we meet him? You just kind of know him, right?" he asked.

He was not convinced that this was about meeting just a friend of hers.

"He is a friend, and I like him. I wanted to see what you thought of him before I go out on a date with him," she answered with a serious face.

The speed of the car dropped from eighty miles per hour to forty miles per hour as he braked in panic. "You know that he is an Indian Hindu, right? Amma will have a freak attack. Why do you have to always take the tough path in life when you have easier options?"

"Let's keep Amma aside for a second. Do you like him? Are you going to be biased based on his country and religion?" she asked, slightly agitated at his knee-jerk reaction.

"Of course not. I'm not going to be biased based on race and religion. But damn it, we have Amma to deal with. She'll never accept it. You recall what happened the last time you were seeing that four-foot Indian loser? Amma almost exploded and took him down. Please be careful. You can do a lot of damage to our little family," he advised.

"What about you? Will you support me if I believe in him—if I truly feel he is the one?" she asked point blank.

"I'll go a certain length for you if you think there is something meaningful, but never beyond the point where it hurts Amma. Whether right or wrong, loyalty to my mother comes first, and I cannot see her in any more pain than she currently is in, suffering from cancer. You don't see most of what I see when she goes through her treatments. God has been kind and given her to us for all these years in spite of her cancer, and I will not support you at the cost of her health. I'm being fair to you and letting you know now so that you never come to me and tell me that I told you any differently."

She too had a grenade in her lap now. Her brother had made his position clear. It was obvious that fighting for Karan was going to be tough. Most likely, after a certain stage, she would be alone fighting this battle. She loved Karan too much to give up easily. She figured that with time, proper attention, and care the situation would sort itself out.

When she got home and was alone, she called Karan and diplomatically informed him of her brother's point of view. Both of them knew that they had their own set of challenges to deal with.

Zoheb took Zeina for dinner to Jake's Crab Shack, a famous seafood restaurant by the marina. They talked about their mother, childhood memories from Pakistan, and how wonderful it was for the two of them to be sitting at a pristine seaside restaurant enjoying crabs and grilled shrimps. They had come a long way in life since their father had passed away leaving them with nothing more than a house and a meager government pension. One thing they didn't talk about was Karan.

"*Butya*, your work visa is going to finish in nine months. What do you plan to do after that? Any permanent job offers on the horizon? You have to find a way to get an H1b visa," he said, a bit concerned about her long-term stay in America.

"I've no dearth of freelance jobs with top designers, but no firm wants to take me on full-time because none of them are willing to sponsor an H1b. I'm concerned about it myself, but I'm doing my best. The next best option I can think of is to enroll at FIT. That way I can secure my stay for another two years and at the same time gain more education. It'll be far cheaper than what you paid at Parsons for my undergrad degree. I hope you won't mind supporting me for two more years?" she asked lovingly.

He choked back his emotions and answered, "You and Amma are all I have. I'll support you as long as I live. You do what is best for you."

He had been the best brother ever; he had sacrificed his career and paid for her education, room, and board in New York. At the same time, he paid hefty medical bills for their mother's cancer treatments, which, for a twenty-something-year-old, were remarkable achievements.

Karan went with his family for dinner at a nearby Italian café. Later that evening, he found a quiet minute alone with his father and said, "Dad, I'll bring a friend home tomorrow so you can meet her. She'll stay over tomorrow night. I'm not sure whether Mom told you about her. She is a friend, and I do like her. I'd appreciate your opinion after you meet her. I'm requesting you to meet her with an open mind, please."

"Son, I'll be fair to her, but frankly, so far I've not heard positive things and am not feeling right about this meeting. However, I'll reserve my comments for now," said Colonel Dev. And the conversation came to an abrupt end.

Arjun interrupted and brought three chilled beers from the fridge, which broke the ice between the sons and the father and relaxed the tension. The three of them sat by the fireplace, where they enjoyed the beers and cracked jokes. Colonel Dev had a great sense of humor and could remember a boatload of jokes; he had a joke ready for any occasion.

The following morning, Zoheb dropped Zeina at the Baltimore train station, and fifteen minutes later, as prearranged, Karan picked her up. She looked nervous. While driving, he gently placed his hand on hers, giving her a subtle message that it would all be okay. He didn't want to reveal the undercurrent of complications that were brewing at home.

She was dressed perfectly. She wore khakis, a dark-brown sweater with matching makeup, and nail polish. Her hair was neatly braided, and she wore her favorite brown leather boots. Karan knew that from an appearance perspective, she would score ten out of ten with his father. He never knew how mothers react to seeing their sons with pretty women. He just couldn't predict whether his mother would be happy to see a pretty girl. Would she be competitive or act in some other unpredictable way?

It was approaching the end of September. The trees were almost bare, and the neighborhood roads were littered with leaves. As he drove into his neighborhood, he could see dry leaves dancing on the road in his rearview mirror.

"Remember, just be yourself." That is all he said to her.

She exited the car and was warmly greeted by Arjun with a hug; then Dad came out with a beaming face. He didn't quite know how to greet her—whether to extend his hand or give her a hug. She gently bowed down and touched his feet. Wow! Those were major brownie points, and indeed a smart move. Dad was more or less in the bag, thought Karan. He could sense that his father liked her appearance and disposition. He was glad that she respected Hindu culture.

Mom was in the kitchen. She walked in nonchalantly and gave Zeina a lukewarm hug. Zeina tried to reach out for her feet as well, but with the awkward hug, cheek-to-cheek kiss, and the attempt to touch her feet, it ended up being an odd greeting. Mom was reserved; she didn't display her feelings and emotions easily. Karan knew she would be a hard nut to crack. Zeina sensed that she was not totally welcome, so she also put her guard up. The battle had begun.

"So nice to meet you, Aunty; Karan has told me so much about you. He misses you a lot."

"We also miss him, but what to do. In this day and age, children are settled all over the world, and we have to run after them. It really is no different than when these boys were little. I used to run after them all the time back then as well. The only difference is that my running was from one room to another or in the backyard, but now the chase is halfway across the world."

Zeina went upstairs to the guest room to put her bag away. She changed into a *salwar kameez*, sandals, ethnic jewelry, and a *bindi*. As she walked down the staircase, Karan noticed that Dad glanced at her admiringly. He could sense his father feeling proud as the father-in-law of a beautiful girl. He also noticed a grin on Arjun's face; he seemed happy to see his elder brother with her.

Then Arjun totally screwed it up by saying, "Would you like a beer before lunch, *bhabhi* [sister-in-law]?"

Karan almost fell off the sofa when he heard that. Mom almost dropped the glass bowl she had in her hand, and Dad choked and gagged on the beer he was drinking. Karan gave Arjun a dirty stare and quickly changed the subject. "Mom, what did you make for lunch? I'm so hungry. I smell *kadi pakoda*. Zeina, have you ever had Indian *kadi*, vegetable fritters in a yogurt curry?"

Zeina also caught on to the abrupt, intentional change of subject and played along. "Of course I have had it. I love *kadi*, but in Pakistan it's made a bit differently; it's more Sindhi style than Punjabi style."

"Yes, I made *kadi*, rice, and *karela* [bitter gourd]," said Mom, in a cold monotone.

"Can I help you with anything, Aunty?" Zeina asked politely.

"No, lunch will be ready to be served in five minutes."

At the dining table, Karan put food on his plate, along with a spoonful of sliced onion salad in vinegar.

Zeina casually asked, "Can you not eat those?" pointing toward the onions, since she couldn't stand the smell of raw onions. After all, she was the one planning to kiss him later when she got a chance.

That comment generated an instant reaction from Mom. "As long as he is my son, he will eat onions," she said in a stern voice with a scornful look on her face.

Karan couldn't believe that the love of his life, someone he was madly in love with, might have to be sacrificed over an onion salad. He just didn't know what the heck to do. If he ate the onions, Zeina was not going to even come close to him, and if he didn't eat them, things could get much worse with Mom. Intimacy with Zeina could wait; he could fix that matter later. It was more important to get the relationship of the two women back on track. He winked at Zeina as a signal to drop the topic. She cooperated and didn't utter another word about the onions. Thankfully, the remainder of the meal went in peace.

"Aunty, I loved your cooking; this is the best *kadi* and *karela* I've ever had," Zeina said appreciatively, genuinely having liked the meal.

"Thank you."

Now they were getting somewhere, Karan thought. He was so tense that he had a tough time digesting his lunch.

After lunch, Zeina helped clean the kitchen, and then she went upstairs. She came back after five minutes. She had brought gifts for everyone. She gave Dad a tie; Arjun, cologne; and Mom, a set of elegantly wrapped soaps from Bergdorf Goodman. He felt like giving her a standing ovation. *Way to go, Zeina,* he thought. But of course, he had to contain his excitement. Those were instant bonus points she had just earned. Punjabis love giving and receiving gifts; it symbolizes their generosity and big hearts.

Mom melted a tad. She thanked Zeina and gave her a hug, her first proper hug. Mom's mind was playing tricks on her. She was trying to fight the poison that told her that Zeina was a girl with a loose character trying to bag her son. The gift gesture changed the ambience. Mom and Zeina sat together in front of the fireplace and discussed Pakistan, *desi* fashion, Multan, where Mom was originally from in Pakistan, and simple stories of their everyday life.

Dad was almost passing out on the couch after the heavy lunch, so he excused himself for a nap. Karan went to get some antacid to ease the indigestion caused by the luncheon conversations. Arjun, as usual, went to get some more beer from the fridge. The only forms of liquid Arjun drank ever since he had gotten to America were beer and Coke; he believed that water was strictly for bathing and washing clothes. He was young and lean and could afford a few thousand extra calories a day. After half an hour, Mom also excused herself to join Dad for an afternoon nap.

Karan grabbed Zeina's arm and took her into the finished basement.

"Thank you so much for your patience. I hope the last two hours were not overwhelming?"

"They were a bit odd, to say the least, but I could deal with them. I'm not sure what is going on in their minds, but I sense a lot of pushback. I'm not sure if they like me. I'll try my best for you, but am I doing something wrong? What's up with them?"

He just had to tell her what his brother had done, and she went absolutely red in the face with rage and shame. She couldn't believe that his whole family knew about her past. Now it was all clear to her.

"I'm really sorry, it's my mistake; I should not have told Varun."

She felt terrible and very angry about the situation. It took a lot to convince her that she shouldn't walk out and that with time and her charm, old memories would fade away. A simple "sorry" did not cut it. She was pretty ticked off at Karan.

"It's not going to be easy. You really messed it up for me," she said angrily. She knew she was up for a far bigger challenge than she had signed up for. She was ready to walk away right there and then, but her love for him was strong enough to sustain her through the harsh challenge. She got up like a brave soldier, not willing to give up.

"Well, you kind of screwed it up big-time, but I'll manage."

On the basement shelf, she noticed the red album that she had looked at the previous weekend. She picked it up, because the last time he had not let her finish looking at it. On page after page there were empty spaces in the album. Voilà! All the women with the big boobs were gone! She gave him an inquisitive look with one eyebrow higher than the other, asking for an explanation. He looked back at her with a naughty grin. He had removed and destroyed all evidence of his past. His past was his past. His experiences had made him what he was today. His present with her was what mattered now. His future was only with her.

"My life begins with you; I was nothing before that," he said and kissed her.

Arjun knocked on the door. He was bored; he wanted to watch a movie in the basement on the big TV.

"I'm glad you called me *bhabhi*, and I appreciate your acceptance and welcome, but you may have caused your folks and Karan a minor heart attack," Zeina said jokingly.

Zeina and Arjun started developing a bond of their own.

"I'm sorry for saying that. I said what came to my mind. But now that I have said it, can I keep saying it?"

"Please, no! Enough mess-up for one day for me. Any more issues today and I'll get ulcers." interrupted Karan. "Please just call her Zeina *didi* [sister] for now, until I can sort matters out."

In the evening everyone went for a drive and a stroll at a nearby public park. Mom fixed a simple salad and soup supper at home. The four of them played a card game, and the environment was becoming friendlier.

Zeina slept in the second guest room, and Karan slept with his brother in his own room. It was past midnight that Karan sneaked into Zeina's room to cuddle with her at night. Unfortunately, Mom woke up to go to the bathroom around that time; she checked on her boys. Of course, not finding Karan in his bed, she knew exactly where he was. She was now convinced that this girl was up to no good, and the whole day's work went down the drain.

Mom told Dad about their son being gone from his bed. Breakfast at the table was like a funeral gathering. They behaved as if someone had died in the house the night before.

Karan figured out that his parents knew that he had gone to Zeina's room the previous night, because they gave her the cold shoulder. Karan signaled her to meet him in the basement. He knew that it was his fault again; he should not have gone to her bedroom. He should not have taken that chance, but at that age, immaturity prevails.

"I'm so sorry. Too much has gone wrong too fast. I think they know I was in your room last night. I heard the flush go off in the bathroom after I came to your room, so one of them must have gone to the bathroom and peeked into my bedroom."

"You really should have restrained yourself. You can't take chances like this. You've messed it all up badly. What am I supposed to do now?" she asked irritably.

It was the first argument they had had. Life had seemed so beautiful and uncomplicated until family came into their relationship.

"Let's not discuss this anymore. What's done is done. I'm really sorry. Let's plan the next move. I think you need to make an early exit and take the afternoon train back," he suggested.

She packed quietly and bade the family an awkward good-bye.

Arjun gave her a hug and whispered to her, "It'll all be okay. Our parents are like artificial coal. They light up fast, but they also cool down fast. We'll see you soon, *bhabhi*."

Those words put a smile on her face.

The drive to the train station was tense.

"I'm so sorry again."

"'Sorry' really does not cut it. So, now what? I feel terrible about the way things shaped up. You should have known better than to introduce me to your folks when you were fully aware that they have such a bad impression of me. Couldn't we have waited till their next visit? What was the darn hurry? What were you thinking?"

"We could have waited, but I didn't think it all through and never imagined that my plan would fail this miserably." He was trying to justify himself.

"Who else knows? How far has the news spread? What's the damage? What am I facing in the rest of my life with you and your family? She was getting more agitated.

"I don't know. I just don't know who else my brother spoke to," he responded, in a louder voice than usual.

She gave him a mean look for raising his voice for no good reason. She couldn't believe how horrible the last day and a half had been. Now the two of them were arguing and fighting.

"I really am so sorry," he said in an apologetic tone. He pulled the car into the drop-off area at the train station.

"Please give me a chance to fix it. Let me think how to fix it. I love you far too much to just let go. Please don't leave me. I'll find a way," he pleaded.

"I love you too. I don't want our lives to get complicated. I'll be there for you every step of the way. Just don't put me in such situations without thinking them through," she requested.

He drove back to a somber environment at home. His parents were not behaving normally. They sat quietly and looked disappointed. His parents didn't like confrontations and kept their emotions between the two of them. His mother still leaked some of her feelings in a roundabout way or leaked them through an irrelevant conversation. Punjabis are masters of such communication. They say that if a Punjabi mother-in-law has to say something to the daughter-in-law, all she has to do is to scream at her own daughter. His father kept it all within himself. It was not easy to talk to them. Karan was going to be twenty-five years old in another month, and even at that age he had a hard time striking up a deep, emotional conversation with his folks.

The rest of the week dragged. The situation with Karan's parents got better with each day; they avoided speaking about Zeina. For Karan, that week's daily routine was work during the day, small conversations with Zeina, a drive to a mall in the evening, dinner at a food court, a local restaurant, or at home. At midweek, he dropped his parents in downtown Washington to explore the museums and visit the main monuments, and he picked them up after work.

It was on Thursday that Arjun came to Karan and said, "I feel for you, *bhaiya*. I'm leaving tomorrow, and you have to drive them to JFK on Sunday. I have an idea for you. Why don't you take them to Zeina *bhabhi's* apartment for lunch or tea before taking them to the airport? Maybe if they see how she lives and what her achievements are, they might perceive her differently?"

That was by far one of the best ideas Arjun had ever come up with. Zeina's personal space was sacred to her; maybe if his parents met her one more time in her space before their departure to India, they might have a positive, lasting impression. They might put her in the right perspective.

Karan called Zeina to consult with her about Arjun's suggestion.

"Just make sure you know what you are doing. I'll greet your parents warmly in my home where I'm most comfortable and confident. I'll also make sure there are no raw onions for you to eat."

"*Snuggle*, this is no time to be funny! I'm already nervous. So, the plan is that I'll try to convince them to visit you at your apartment. We can have tea with you, and I'll leave for the airport with them. I'll see if I can come back; otherwise I'll drive straight back to Columbia."

"Sounds like a plan," she said in a cheerful voice. She was feeling more optimistic, but he had not fully recovered from the previous weekend's episodes.

"The drive from here to New York is about five hours. I suggest we take a break at Zeina's apartment in Manhattan. You can freshen up before your long flight home, have something to eat, and then I'll drop you at the airport. What do you think?" Karan asked his father.

Colonel Dev had served the Indian army as a psychologist for a few years at the Service Selection Board in Bangalore, where he interviewed officer level candidates for the Indian Armed Forces. He knew where his son's thoughts were headed. He liked Zeina, but at the same time had his reservations, though not to the extent that his wife had.

After a long pause he said, "I'll discuss it with your mother. If she has objections, then we will not meet her." And he left it at that.

After dinner that night, to Karan's relief, his father informed him that both his mother and he were okay with the plan. He was glad that they were being reasonable. Later that night he updated Zeina.

Arjun departed for Vermont. Two days later, Karan drove his parents to New York. They reached Zeina's apartment in the late afternoon. He parked in the lot he had used during the previous visit. The three of them took the elevator to the tenth floor, walked down the dimly lit hallway, and rang the doorbell.

Zeina opened the door promptly. She looked stunningly beautiful. She was wearing a white *desi* outfit set off by silver jewelry and white and pearl sandals. Her nails were perfectly French manicured. The perfume Angel smelled heavenly on her. She greeted his parents warmly and welcomed them. This time, she didn't want to overdo it by touching their feet. She gave Karan a lame hug as well to avoid any unnecessary attention.

Julia was at home that afternoon. She came out of her room; she introduced herself and started chatting with Mom. He could tell that his parents were impressed with Zeina's apartment and her personality. She carried herself well and had a regal aura of self-confidence. She served a delicious, heavy tea with lots of *desi* snacks such *as chaat papdi* [appetizers], *kebabs, samosas*, cookies, pastries, and fresh fruit. Colonel Dev was simply sold on the *kebabs*; those were the best he had ever tasted. He didn't care if they were made of beef; they were just too good not to be eaten.

His mother was a bit more cautious. She carefully took account of Zeina from head to toe, examined her kitchen, bathroom, and bedroom. That was her way of seeing whether a woman was worthy of being a daughter-in-law. It seemed that she liked what she saw. Had Zeina had passed her litmus test? Karan wondered.

Colonel Dev's assessment of a woman worthy of his son was determining whether she was pretty and took care of her hands and feet, and whether she would be a patient wife and mother to his grandkids. It seemed that Zeina got his stamp of approval.

Arjun called on Zeina's cell phone to speak to everyone. Then Varun called. He was not happy that his parents were at Zeina's apartment. Karan spoke to his brother as well. He was extremely cold to Karan. After the phone call ended, Karan put the phone in his jacket pocket.

Julia was in a jovial mood. She actually sang a few Bollywood songs in front of his parents in her broken Hindi and danced around the apartment as if there were a movie being filmed. At least she added some lightness to the environment. Aarti, Karan's mother, loved her song *"Piya milan ko jaana"*—a melody from her youth.

Karan quietly told Zeina that he'd come to see her on his way back. They could have dinner together before he drove back to Columbia. She bade everyone good-bye courteously.

He drove his parents through the streets of Manhattan and Brooklyn and onto the Long Island Expressway to JFK. The traffic was heavy, as usual, and the ride to the airport became difficult and uneasy as his mother began to pour her heart out and started crying.

"This girl is not right for you. Why can't you marry someone of your own faith or at least from India? Come to Delhi, and I'll line up a hundred girls for you to pick from. After all that you have achieved in your life, you could be weighed in gold in India. I don't care about religion so much, but this girl is not right for you. I don't get the right vibes from her. She is just out to ruin your life. How can you trust her? How can we trust your life in her hands? She will not be faithful to you; your relationship will come to an unhappy end. What will happen to you?" And she went on and on.

He visualized himself standing on a balance and actually being weighed in gold. If that were true, he thought, he had better put on some weight before going to India. At the same time, it was heartbreaking for him to hear his mother. He had never seen his mother that upset. Finally she dropped the deadly emotional bomb.

"If you love me and have any respect for me, you will not go back to her today or ever again. You have to get over her. You have to! Promise me that. I want your promise now!" she demanded.

He felt as if an elephant had stepped on him. He was driving and had a massive headache just listening to her emotional blackmail. Just half an hour ago, he had thought that he had the situation under control, and now it was all messed up again. His mother would not give up. She repeated everything three or four times like a broken record. Interestingly, Colonel Dev remained quiet throughout this drama.

"Promise me; you have to promise me," she continued until he broke down. He couldn't take it anymore; all the emotional pressure and his mother's tears were more than he could handle. He made up his mind that he would not go back to Zeina.

At first, he couldn't even get the words out of his mouth. Struggling with himself, he finally said, "I promise, I won't see her again."

As he completed his words, they arrived at the airport. He silently took the luggage out, put it on a cart, touched their feet, and said good-bye to them.

His father gave him a hug and casually said, "You'll get over it."

All that his mother could say was that one day he would thank them for their advice.

He was angry at his parents and at the world. His head was hurting, and he felt dizzy and queasy. He felt that he was going to throw up. He had made a promise to his mother under terrible pressure. He loved Zeina; how could he let her go? He couldn't even focus on the road. Then he heard the ring of a Nokia phone. He discovered that it was coming from his jacket pocket. He fumbled with the seat belt to get to his pocket. It was Zeina calling from her home phone; he had forgotten to give her back her phone.

"Thank God the phone is with you. I've been looking for it all over the apartment! Come home quickly; I have dinner ready."

He was in a big fix. Just a few minutes ago, he had promised his mother he wouldn't meet Zeina ever again. Now he had no choice but to go back to her to return her phone. He recognized the signs of the *Painter Man*! He was meant to go back to her that night. He had no choice but to break his promise to his mother. He knew his promise to his mother was wrong. Larger forces were with the two of them. Their love was more powerful than his mother's desires.

He took the exit to Manhattan. He reached her apartment in twenty minutes. He picked up a single red rose from the flower vendor and ran to her arms and kissed her, hugged her, kissed her and hugged her again. She couldn't understand what caused that massive burst of love and affection, but she enjoyed being pampered. She had been a bit nervous, thinking how it must have been for Karan in the car with his parents.

"Ask me for anything I can give you, and I will give it to you," he said.

"Never leave me, and be mine forever," she asked. Of all the things she could have asked for!

She desperately wanted to ask him about his interaction in the car with his folks, but she sensed that he was not in the mood to discuss family matters, so she chose to not bring up the subject.

She had made penne with pesto sauce and garlic bread for dinner, which they enjoyed immensely with a glass of cabernet. They hung out alone for a while, and an hour later, he started his drive back home. He thought about her the entire time on his drive back. He knew that she really, truly, and deeply loved him. His family was wrong about her. But how would he ever get them to like her and get their blessings to marry her? He had a lot of questions but no answers. He was glad that he had gone back to her that night.

A few days later, his brother Varun called for a catch-up. They spoke about their parents and about Arjun's welfare. Varun had spoken to his parents before he called. He knew about his brother's promise, but just to be sure, he asked, "So, it's all over with that girl, right?"

Karan just couldn't lie to his brother.

"Actually, no. I almost did break up with her, but I couldn't."

He could almost hear an explosion at the other end. There had never been a time that he had not consulted his brother before taking any major step in his life, and his brother did the same. When Varun had made the decision to marry Simran, Karan was the first person of the family he asked her to meet. He made sure that Karan liked her and gave him the green light to proceed with the rest of the family.

"Have you completely gone insane? I'm telling you she is not good for you. Your parents, who wish you the best, are reiterating to you that she is not good for you. What part of this picture are you not getting? Do you not love and respect us? You know, I've been there for you every step of the way in your life. When I was earning a small salary as a medical resident, I still saved every penny to support your lavish lifestyle during your undergrad years. I've given to you selflessly. I need something from you. I need you to dump her now. She is like a silent cancer growing on you. What has she done to you?" The lecture went on and on, to the point where it became ugly and vindictive.

"So, you have nothing to say for yourself? Then here are my last words to you. I'm not suggesting that you leave her. For all that I have done for you, I need you to pay me back by leaving her—or you can choose to give up your family and be with her. You'll have nothing to do with us anymore," he threatened.

That simply broke Karan down; he figured he would never be able to win this battle.

"I'll leave her, just give me some time," he told his brother meekly. He just couldn't explain to his brother what she meant to him. He couldn't find the words or the courage to go on any further.

The following day he didn't go to work; he was downright depressed. It was a dark, gloomy, and rainy day. He got up late and just lay in bed thinking about how to ease the pain in his heart. He lay there for hours, just thinking about how to tell her. He knew that he couldn't face her, and it was better to just call her and end it. Finally, around noon, he called. She was at work.

"Hi, *Jaani*," she answered in a chirpy voice.

"I'm so sorry. My brother has given me an ultimatum to leave you. He's being very harsh with me. My parents are also being very unreasonable. I just can't destroy my family and leave them. I just can't do it. I love you and always will. Please forgive me, but I can't be with you anymore," he said in one breath.

He thought he would hear her scream, shout, cry, or something like that. But all she said was, *"Jaani,* I'm at work right now. I'll take the afternoon train. You'll pick me up at the train station in the evening. You are not going to break up with me on the phone. We'll discuss this face-to-face. I have to go now. See you this evening. I love you," she said firmly, calmly, and lovingly.

He was stunned! Here he was, facing the most painful situation in his life, trying to break up with her; and there she stood, strong as a pillar, ready to jump on a train in a few hours to come see him. He felt like a sissy. He pulled himself together, fixed the room, shaved, got dressed, and kept asking himself how he would be able to break up in her presence. He knew that he had to. He didn't have a choice anymore.

She met him at the train station as if nothing had happened. They met warmly. She held herself and her emotions rigidly within. He drove her home and didn't talk much on the way. He was more afraid of her than of the situation.

It had been a wet and cold day. There was mist on the car windows. It had rained all day and continued to rain on the way back home. All the beautiful dry leaves were now soaking wet as the cars drove past, crushing them. The beautiful landscape was turning ugly with dirty mulch and bare trees.

They sat by the fireplace. He made her hot chocolate. As she was sipping her beverage, silent tears flowed down her cheeks, wetting her silk blouse. Her face was glowing from the light of the fireplace. She looked beautiful.

"Our love is stronger than you think. How could you even think of breaking up with me on the phone?" she asked calmly.

He sat close to her and just remained silent. He had no answers.

"If you think you are facing this all by yourself, you are wrong. I feel your pain; we both share this pain. Have you thought about how difficult it is for me to face your family? I dread the day when my mother finds out about us; the thought gives me sleepless nights. My mother is terminally ill with cancer. You cannot imagine the trouble I'll have soon. You think I'll just call you one day and walk out on you as well when that happens? I'll never leave you. We have to stand by each other through some rough times to come in our lives, but in the end it will be just you and me. We have to live together, just you and me, not our families. We have to manage them, not let them manage us. Everyone will come around with time. They'll get busy in their lives and let us be. Will they feel the pain of our broken hearts because we let the perfect mate for ourselves go because of them?"

He pondered her words for a while and then said, "I'm sorry, *Snuggle*; I acted impulsively and like a coward. I love you so much, and I know that we are right for each other. We rushed into things with the family, and we weren't ready yet for a negative outcome. I have a tough situation, but your position with your mother is even tougher. How will we ever work out these complications?"

"So, what are you saying? This is it? Quit before it really even begins? I didn't learn to quit easily. That's not what my mother taught me. You don't come across as someone who quits. Even though my hurdle will be with Amma herself, it's her own life that stands as an example of someone who just doesn't quit when the going gets tough."

6. Amma—The Pillar of Life

She started talking about Amma. "My mother, Sahar, went from a talented housewife to a dynamic businesswoman within a course of a year after my father passed away. Most likely from stress, or God knows what, she developed breast cancer shortly after her struggles began. She's suffering from her third lapse of cancer; it's been over ten years since it all began. Few people with her medical condition have the zest and energy she has. She comes from a middle-class family in Gujranwala in Pakistan. Amma's mother used to be proud of their *Rajput* roots."

Karan broke in. "Ironically, *Rajputs* are staunch Hindus."

"I know. The ones in the northern areas of Pakistan converted to Islam under the influence of the Mughal Empire."

"Anyway, her father was not only a well-educated teacher, but also a *Maulvi Sahib*, an Islamic priest with a long beard who prayed five times a day. She was the eldest and the only daughter; she has three younger brothers. Growing up in a conservative Islamic environment made her develop an aversion to religious rules and enforcements. I would say she is deeply spiritual but not religious; she believes in and practices Islam in moderation, and that is what she taught us. She always tells us that the fundamental principle of being a Muslim, or in fact, a person who observes any religion, is to 'believe in God' and then 'to be a good human being.'"

"That's what I believe as well," he said, nodding.

"After studying fine arts in Lahore, she pleaded with her parents and succeeded in leaving home to work as an air-stewardess for Pakistan's International Airline. Back in those days, Pakistan was a relatively open country and rather Westernized—far more so than when I grew up there."

"I remember those crazy times. Russia supported India, and the Americans always sided with Pakistan," he added as he adjusted the logs in the fireplace.

"The exposure to other cultures from her travels was really what shaped her way of thinking and living. She blossomed into an elegant and beautiful woman. She still loves traveling, and she exposed us to the same desire to learn from the world. She's very different from her family; she is artistic and has great taste in everything."

"I can see that in you as well, *Snuggle*. You're a reflection of your mother. How did she end up meeting your father?"

"She met my *Abbu*, Choudhury Sikander Zaman, through university classmates they had in common. He was a handsome young man who had just graduated from government college in Lahore and was about to join the civil service. They fell in love at first sight. They courted for a few months and then one fine day, she found out from a friend that he was already engaged to his first cousin and was headed that weekend to his village in Dinga to get married!

"She was torn apart, but he, too, was in no easy position. He had no choice but to marry his cousin to keep the extended family happy and intact. He came from a *Zameendaar* family—feudal lords for whom 'family members' and 'land' are interchangeable terms. It's common in Pakistan for first and second cousins to get married. He claimed that he only loved Amma, and he would still marry her if she agreed, but he couldn't officially divorce his first wife, not only because of the land alliances imposed on him, but because their common cousins were married to his sisters. He begged for a little time to satisfy his family obligations.

"So he begrudgingly married his cousin, and our grandmother didn't leave him alone until his wife was pregnant and bore her a grandson. His first wife is a simple woman from a village, not educated and certainly not taught to stand up for herself. She knew he was not in love with her, and later when he asked her consent to marry the woman he loved, she gave it.

"Amma went through many tough months trying hard to distance herself from him, but she couldn't imagine a life without my father. Her own family was against the marriage. Her parents were devastated by her decision to marry a married man with a son; but she wouldn't give up. After many arguments, her mother agreed to meet *Abbu*. She asked him whether they would be accepted by his family and be treated well. My father couldn't lie and told her that initially he didn't expect any support at all and that no one from his family would attend his wedding. That's when my *Nani* refused to give her blessings for their wedding. Shortly after, they eloped and got married. It took many years for the families on each side to come around. She never had a proper wedding; she never even had her own wedding trousseau. That's why she made everything for my wedding probably before I reached ten. I don't know more details because this is a sad topic for her, and she doesn't like to talk about it."

"Wow! She had a love marriage and she eloped!" he exclaimed in amazement. He got up to put two new logs into the fire.

"*Abbu* continued to support his first wife and son; he provided them with what he saw as a comfortable life, but for him, Amma was his wife. My parents moved to Islamabad to start their life together. The distance from family in Lahore was helpful. My childhood memories of my parents are of two romantic people who always looked like they were in love. Everyone admired them as a couple, and when they dressed up to go to parties, they looked like movie stars.

"She stopped flying with PIA before she got married. My father wanted her to be a housewife. We grew up being close to our half brother, Aman. He spent all his holidays with us. Until he started school, he believed that everyone had two mothers! He's still attached to my mother. In fact, he calls her Ammi. Zoheb and I love him too. I wish that complications didn't exist between the two families, and we could have grown up together rather than commute between the two cities.

"My parents had just a few years of blissful marriage together. His family suffers from juvenile diabetes and heart disease. He took that threat a bit too casually. He ate poorly and rarely exercised. His physician warned him about his high cholesterol, but he thought nothing of it. He thought he was invincible. When I was seven years old, my father, who had already suffered two minor heart attacks, was given blood thinning medication to keep his arteries from clogging, but he did not take his medicine.

"He was in Cameroon for an official conference. In the lobby of the hotel where he was staying, his heart failed, and he died on the spot at the age of forty-six. I recall I was playing in my neighbor's yard, a few doors away from our home when I heard a bloodcurdling scream! A few seconds later, I realized it was my own mother screaming. She became hysterical when she got the phone call. I was too young to understand what was happening; all I knew was that something really bad had happened and my mother needed me.

"Our whole world came crashing down on us, and life as we knew it ceased to exist from that day onward. It took her several months to recover, but she gathered strength and the confidence to move on. First, the family support from his side of the family died; they took away all the land and money. Then the government support slowly died. Thank God our parents had built a house in Islamabad; otherwise we would have been without a home. Money vanished fast. Amma didn't have much to begin with, because he had never let her work, and his pension was not enough. She had to sell her car and jewelry, and still she was having a hard time making ends meet."

Karan had no words to offer; he just heard her story in amazement. The red and orange glow of the fire reflected on Zeina's face; she looked beautiful.

"At that time, a close colleague of my father's helped Amma secure a scholarship to study at the New York School of Interior Design to earn an associate degree in interior design. Most women would have taken a sewing course and set up a tailor shop, but she thought big. She knew that she had to do far better to be able to educate her two kids and get them where she envisioned. She took us to New York, where she lived on a budget, stayed with friends, and studied all day. With us in tow over the summer and then commuting while we were in school back in Islamabad, she managed to get her degree.

"Under the same friend's guidance, she started a small interior design firm in Islamabad. She worked from home so she could be there for us as well. You can't imagine what it's like for a woman to work—let alone have a business and employ and manage men—in a conservative country. She did it. She was able to set up one of the most successful interior design firms in Islamabad. Half our house became a warehouse and the other half her workshop.

"She made enough money to upgrade our education to the American School. She always says that the best investment for children is education. Soon, she became a popular figure in town. She was not only an amazing interior designer, but also the center of the social life in town. Everyone wanted to be her friend.

"Amma is very funny too. I remember something hilarious she did once: she wanted to welcome the new Indian ambassador and his family, so she put together a flower arrangement from her own garden to welcome them to Pakistan and wrote on the card, '*Welcome Mr. and Mrs. Dickshit.*' She'd heard their name and spelled it out. Their name was actually 'Dixit.' Thank God I saw the card before she sent it; that could have caused another war between India and Pakistan. We all found that incident rather amusing."

Karan could not control his laughter.

"She also has a green thumb and has the best garden in Islamabad. Each spring, she wins the first prize for her constantly evolving landscapes. And she's an amazing cook and host. She can host fifty people for sit-down dinners at home with all sorts of cuisines. She loves going to Thailand, where she walks into kitchens of small restaurants and learns to cook Thai food from local chefs. Once she brought so many Thai sauces that when one of the fish sauce bottles broke at customs in Islamabad the entire airport stank of fish. My brother and I just ran away from her! Bottom line, she is dynamic and self-made because she never gives up!"

Karan sat there looking at Zeina and listening in amazement.

"We had a few good years where she had disposable income and fewer worries and then she was diagnosed with breast cancer. She came to the States for her first chemotherapy. She lost most of her hair and energy; her business suffered. Between medical bills and loss of business, it finally came to a point where she didn't know how she was going to get the next semester's fee for my brother, who was enrolled at Brown.

"Her goal in life is to stay alive for us and get us educated and able to stand on our own two feet. She had to fight every step of the way. Somehow, she managed to put my brother through Brown. He had barely graduated when she sent me to the most expensive and finest fashion school in the world. She paid for my first semester of tuition, and my brother proudly took over the rest of the years. He left I-Banking on Wall Street and joined a power plant development company in Oklahoma. He couldn't rely on higher bonuses and lower base salaries; he needed a stable, strong base income to support my education. He sacrificed his career for me, but fortunately he succeeded in all his endeavors. Now he works for a reputable Finnish power generation company.

"As Amma is aging, my brother is taking on the role as head of the family; he supports both Amma and me. He treats her like a queen and cannot see a needle come close to her. He drops everything in his life to fulfill her every desire. We are who we are because of her; she defines us. Her last cancer relapse was last year, and so far, chemo is working well for her. Insha'Allah, her results this time around will also come back normal.

"You'll like her; she is so cuddly. She loves with a full heart, but she also hates with a full heart. She is expressive, especially verbally. No one wants to be on her bad side; she cusses people out like nobody's business. Her favorite word is *haramzada*—bastard. She learned many great words from cussing out all the male workers in her business.

"Her life story is imprinted on her face; each line on her face has a story to tell. Stress and chemo have taken a toll on her, but she never ceases to live each day to the fullest. She says that in her position, every day is a bonus and cannot be taken for granted. She does have one desire—she wants to see both of us married and to see the faces of her grandchildren. She often says that she may get a chance to see us married, but she will not be around for her grandchildren, and that is not easy to hear."

Zeina sniffled and said, "Zoheb and I can't imagine life without her. All three of us live in fear of losing her; all three of us have a different way of dealing with it. I show my stress; Amma laughs it off, and my brother just doesn't want to talk about it. He pretends that she is fine and that her cancer doesn't exist."

Karan listened with admiration; he couldn't wait to meet Zeina's mother.

Zeina took a deep breath and spoke further. "I was engaged once when I was still in high school. We never had a chance to speak about this. Amma was going through her second recurrence of cancer when we met a family friend's son during our summer visit to the States. We sort of started dating. He'd lost his parents when he was young, and on the surface was a total charmer. He totally won my mother's and brother's sympathy over the loss of his parents, and he convinced them he loved me so much that he was willing to wait till I was ready to get married.

"Ironically, he was a hotelier and worked for Hyatt Hotels in Houston. He seemed broken up over the long distance between us and played upon the family with his fear of losing me. By claiming that he had lost all he had ever loved, he convinced my mother to agree to my engagement with him. But her condition was that I finish my undergraduate studies before marriage. She warned him that, although I was mature for my age at sixteen, I might change my mind over time. He was willing to take that risk.

"She would never have accepted such an agreement ordinarily, but her own fear of dying and leaving me behind vulnerable to the world compelled her to make a wrong decision. The man she thought was right for me actually turned out to be an insecure person and a compulsive liar. To make a long story short, not only did I realize I was not ready for a commitment, but his lying made it quite easy to break off the engagement."

Karan could not understand where this story was going, so he kept quiet.

"A few years later, while I was doing my undergraduate work, I dated an Indian *Gujju* guy—Hindu, of course. Amma didn't like him and didn't appreciate his eyeing me for any kind of relationship. And now, here I am with another Indian Hindu—a Hyatt hotelier! For her, it's all her and my bad experiences packaged together. She's not going to give in easily, and she will flash all these facts in my face when she knows about you. I'll have to fight for myself. I've come a long way since the time I was engaged. I saw everything I didn't want in that person, and today I see everything I want in you. I can't let my mother or my brother pick my husband. It's the most important decision of my life. I have to make this decision myself. They have to believe in me. *Jaani*, the bottom line is that my struggle up ahead is not going to be easy, either."

It all made sense to him now. He could see both sides of the coin and knew that what she was saying was correct. He also believed their love was true and was meant to be. In the end it would just be the two of them and their children. If they had lived in India or Pakistan or a place where there was daily family interference, it would've been difficult for the two of them to be together, but all their families lived in different cities across the world.

He was still torn apart, though. He wondered how it would work in the interim. How would his family come around?

While he was engrossed in his thoughts, there was a massive burst of thunder and lightning—so sudden and loud that they jumped into each other's arms. It felt as if a bolt of lightning had fallen a few feet from the house. And in fact it had. They looked in the backyard, which opened into a small forest and there, a huge tree had fallen. Karan believed in signs, and this was a sign that he had to have faith in powers beyond his comprehension. He was meant to be with her in this lifetime, to love her and to receive her love.

"You're right. I was wrong to give up so easily under family pressure. I love you. I love you too much ever to give up on you. I'll never give up on you, ever again," he promised.

Her eyes welled up with tears. He held her tightly. They promised each other, no matter what, they wouldn't give up. Their minds were made up; their hearts were in the right place. It was a significant milestone in their lives together. She had saved their relationship. He knew that, if had she not jumped on that train, it would have been over.

He warmed up a can of Campbell's cream of tomato soup, garnished it with fresh parsley, crushed peppercorn, and a touch of shredded sharp cheddar cheese and served it with garlic bread. They opened a bottle of Wolfblass and enjoyed the warmth of the fireplace.

Zeina left early in the morning. He took another day off just to recuperate. He realized that she had lost her father at a young age and hadn't had an easy life growing up. He developed respect for Amma and Zeina from what he had heard the previous evening.

7. Beauty and the Beast

Karan's commute to work each way was between an hour and two hours. He hated leaving home in the dark every morning and returning after dark. He had grown up outdoors, but now he felt that he was always trapped indoors.

He reached his office, and the first thing he did was order flowers to be delivered to Zeina's office with a note: "*Your True Love, Now and Forever. —Jaani.*" His phone rang that afternoon; it was Zeina. She called to thank him for the beautiful flowers. He also ordered a one-year *National Geographic* subscription as a gift to her. He knew she loved reading the articles from around the world.

Zeina was back to her normal, chirpy mood. The worst was behind them, or at least it felt that way. That same day she also ordered a one-year *National Geographic* subscription for him, knowing how much he liked the photographs in the magazine. Both of them received their subscription confirmation a few days later and had a good laugh. It was a sign that they operated on the same wavelength.

"I want your twenty-fifth birthday to be a special weekend for you. Can you come to Manhattan on Friday and spend the weekend with me?"

He was tired and drained from long hours at work and the last few days of being on an emotional roller coaster. He was in no mood to drive to New York. The train ride was efficient but expensive.

"How about I take a bus this time? That way, I don't have to drive so much, either. I drive two to three hours each day of the week," he suggested.

"Amtrak would be better, but it's up to you. Just make sure you arrive no later than 6:00 p.m. It's important that you get here on time. I'll come see you at Port Authority."

He took a half day off on Friday and made it to the early afternoon bus. The bus stopped in Delaware at a rest area. He called Zeina from a pay phone and informed her that the bus was on time. Then the bus got on to the New Jersey Turnpike, which was jammed with traffic. It was 6:00 p.m. already, and the bus had not even reached the Princeton exit. He was getting anxious because he knew she would be at the bus station waiting for him. He didn't have a mobile phone from which to call her.

"Excuse me; I've someone waiting for me at Port Authority. How can I reach her? How will she know that the bus is delayed?" he politely asked the big black woman driving the bus, which was now in standstill traffic.

The woman snarled back at him. Shaking her head and her shoulders like a rapper, she said in a heavy African American accent, her voice increasing five decibels with each word, "First of all, you should not be crossing that yellow line. But since the bus is not moving, I'll let you go on that one. Second of all, I don't control the traffic. So, if we are late, we are late. Your girlfriend will just have to wait like everybody else at the station. She can *axe* the information desk, and they'll know where we are by satellite and this crappy radio. Third of all, I also want to go home to my man, who I've not seen in a week driving this piece of junk!"

He jumped back, scared by her hostile response. He quietly went back to his seat. At least he knew that Zeina would be able to find out that the bus was late. He regretted not having invested in a mobile phone. He looked at his watch; it was 7:00 p.m. The bus was just entering the Midtown Tunnel. The traffic was still moving at snail's pace. He wondered what she could have planned. Maybe it was a dinner at a fancy place that needed a reservation. *So what? We'll pick another place*, he thought optimistically.

The bus pulled into the bus station at 7:40 p.m. Through the fogged-up windows of the bus, he could see Zeina fuming. He got off the bus.

She barely greeted him and said, "Grab your bag, quick. We're so late!"

He collected his bag. She grabbed his hand, and they pushed their way out of the crowd like a bulldozer. She was out on the street hailing a yellow cab, cutting off people waiting before her. He saw the aggressive New Yorker in her for the first time. She was a tough woman. She knew how to be pushy when she wanted to.

"Broadway and Forty-Sixth, as fast as you can," she instructed the Latino driver in a stern voice.

"As fast as you can *coost extra*," said the driver in his Spanish accent, trying to be funny. But she was not in a humorous mood at all. She gave him a dirty look, and he knew not to say another word.

"I'm sorry for being late. It's not my fault. There was too much traffic. Where are we going?" he asked meekly.

"To *Beauty and the Beast* on Broadway, and now we'll not make it in time. If we're late, they won't let us in until the first act is over, which is like a quarter of the show!" she replied, sounding frustrated.

Luckily for Karan, the Latino driver also caught the hint that matters were serious. He took a right and a left followed by several sharp turns, and somehow arrived in front of the theater at 7:50 p.m., ten minutes before the show. Karan paid the cabby, along with a handsome tip for saving his ass. They rushed into the theater. The lobby was almost empty because most of the people were already seated. Some people were buying drinks at the bar. He noticed that Zeina was elegantly dressed for the occasion in a black dress. He looked like a goofball in his khakis, denim shirt, and a fleece jacket. He turned in their jackets and his travel bag at the coat check-in. The kid at the counter gave them a dirty look for bringing a suitcase to the theater, but there was no time to explain. Karan handed her a twenty-dollar bill. She accepted the bag without further questions.

They found their seats and settled into them just two minutes before the show started. He touched her hand lightly to check what kind of reaction he got. She looked at him and kissed him. Thankfully, she was relaxed now.

"Happy birthday, *Jaani*. I hope you like the show."

Karan had seen Broadway productions, but never on Broadway itself. He knew a little bit about *Beauty and the Beast*, as he had seen parts of it on Cartoon Network.

What an amazing musical it was. The set, the music, the costumes, and the amazing voices—it was just perfect. Belle was played by Tony Braxton. Karan thoroughly enjoyed the show.

"I absolutely loved it. Thanks so much for such a thoughtful birthday gift."

She was pleased that her plan had worked out.

"I would've been so upset if we had missed the show. My plan was to get you dressed up and then bring you here. Now, how about we get something to eat?"

They walked out of the theater with the intention of going to a classy sit-down restaurant, but he was so hungry that, walking past the "roach coach"—i.e., a food cart serving chicken *shawarma* and rice—he couldn't resist buying a plateful. They sat by the sidewalk and enjoyed their meal.

A winter chill was setting in, and there was steam emerging from the subway vents. She took him to a pub nearby, and they had a few martinis. Half-drunk, they found their way back to her apartment to a warm bed.

She had turned the heating on in her apartment, but it was radiator heating with no temperature control. So it was either hundred degrees or freezing. The method of controlling heat was to crack open the window. The more you opened the window, the more cold air you let in to mix with the hot air from the radiator. The size of the window opening had to be perfect. Zeina was an expert at measuring the proportional relationship between the hot and cold air, and she knew exactly how much to open the window.

Zeina had arranged for a birthday party for him the following day at her apartment. She invited only her close friends whom she wanted Karan to meet. She had thought about every minor detail. He felt that this was his first proper birthday party since he had left India. The rest of his birthdays had been about getting drunk and getting laid!

Karan called his elder brother before he could call to wish him a happy birthday. He used a calling card in order not to display his number on the caller ID, which would have disclosed his location in New York. He felt bad playing such petty tricks, but it was important to keep the peace in the family. He also called his younger brother and parents before they called looking for him.

The theme for the party was Rugrats. The decorations, plates, cups, napkins were all the same theme. Karan didn't know who these characters were.

"Let me show you the cartoon. I love the Rugrats show. They're too cute," she told him. She made him a cup of tea, put on the cartoon for him, and asked him to relax while she stepped out to run a few errands. Half an hour later, she walked in with Shiraz; they were holding twenty-five helium balloons. That many balloons on a windy cold day were not easy to handle. Goodness knows how she even got them to the apartment. The cake had the number twenty-five decorated on it. She made him feel special. All her friends met him warmly and brought him gifts. Everyone drank, sang songs, and enjoyed the wide array of snacks Zeina had prepared.

That evening, Karan met Umar, a high school classmate of Zeina's. Strangely enough, she addressed Umar as *"Baitu,"* which means "son." Apparently, Umar's mother called him by that name, and over time it just became his nickname. Baitu came across as a dear friend of hers, so Karan took some time to get to know him and speak to him. Baitu was an investment banker and worked for UBS. Karan did not know much about investment banking. All he knew was that IPOs and bond issuance were done by investment banks and that the investment bankers were extremely well paid.

Baitu invited Zeina and Karan for brunch at a restaurant the next day. Little did Karan know that Baitu was to become one of those moving forces that the *Painter Man* was going to use in the future to change his life.

After everyone departed, Shiraz helped them clean up. They did not let him lift a finger on his birthday weekend, making him feel like a king. After cleanup, the three of them sat and chatted for a while. It was almost midnight.

Zeina went downstairs to see off Shiraz and returned after ten minutes smelling of cigarette smoke.

"You smoked again?" he asked, sounding disappointed.

"Yes, I'm sorry. After a drink and spending time with Shiraz, I just end up smoking," she said with a guilty look.

"I'm being candid with you. I really don't like smokers, just like you don't like raw onions," he told her. "I'll never ask you to change anything else about yourself, but please don't smoke around me, at least."

"I'll never smoke again if it really bothers you so much."

She had really worked hard and given him an excellent birthday party. *Her feet must be aching*, he thought. He gave her a foot massage, which led to a full body massage with scented oils, which led to other exciting and pleasurable activities.

The following morning, they met Baitu for brunch at a hip restaurant near the park with high ceilings and modern decor. Karan had a great chat with him. Baitu was an interesting person. There was something pure and innocent behind his multibillion-dollar talk, of which Karan understood less than 10 percent. It was strange banking lingo comprising words like "credit swaps" and "B-pieces," which Baitu kept going on and on about.

Karan was not even sure how many zeros there were in a billion. His simple world ran in the hundreds and thousands. He was happy with those numbers. He liked Baitu for just being Baitu and not for the investment banker face he put on.

Karan excused himself to go to the washroom.

"So, what do you think of Karan?" Zeina asked Baitu.

"He comes across as a wonderful person, and I'm really happy for you. But his being Hindu will present challenges for you with your family. My advice is that you follow your heart," he replied matter-of-factly.

Baitu was her friend from a long time ago. The thought of courting had occurred to them on occasion, but never at the cost of losing their lifelong friendship. He never acted on that thought, and they always remained friends. No matter how many months or years later both of them met, as soon as they met, they instantly became the same friends who had hung out in the hallways of the American School in Islamabad.

The weekend flew by too fast. It was already time for Karan to return home. It had been a refreshing weekend, unlike the previous one. He felt alive and rejuvenated.

"Thanks so much for such an awesome weekend. I love you so much!"

"You are welcome. It was nothing. I love you too."

Karan boarded the afternoon bus back so that he could be home before dark. His savings were fast depleting. The weekend excursions were expensive. What bothered him was that he knew that the distance was not sustainable long-term. His career and green card aspirations were not getting anywhere. If he moved to Canada, he was not sure what would happen to their relationship. He wanted to speak to Zeina about these matters. The time for his move to Canada was on the horizon. Hyatt Hotels had acquired a property in downtown Toronto. Karan had put his name in the hat for a transfer through his GM. It was a perfect opportunity for him. He had nine months to move to Canada as permitted under the aegis of the immigration regulations. He had not shared these developments with her so far. He had to convince her to apply for Canadian immigration and then convince her to move to Toronto.

8. "Haramzada Hindu" (H²)

"Amma is not well again. She needs to come to Annapolis for treatment for at least a month. I've got a lot of international business travel scheduled the next few weeks. You'll have to quit your freelance assignments for a while to take care of her here. Amma and I need you," said Zoheb, sounding sad and depressed.

"Of course, I'll be there next week before she arrives." Zeina consoled her brother.

She was deeply concerned to hear about her mother being unwell. Cancer was recurring again, and Amma needed stronger therapy. This time the cancer was not localized; many parts of her body had been invaded by malignant cells. Her lungs were accumulating water rapidly, and she had difficulty breathing. Zeina called Karan and updated him on the situation.

"I'll be half an hour away from you. At least we can meet more often. I'll introduce you to Amma as a friend, and we'll take it from there. We have to be extra cautious and cannot make the mistake you made with your parents."

Karan was skeptical about her "friend only" plan, but he was in no position to suggest anything better.

Zeina quit work and arrived in Annapolis a week later. Karan drove down to Annapolis on a Saturday afternoon to meet the Zamans. As he pulled his car into the driveway, Zoheb came out to greet him followed by Zeina.

"What are those round dents on the hood of your car?" Zoheb casually asked Karan. He was a sharp and observant.

"Ah, err, hmm; I'm not sure what those are," Karan replied, looking away.

"Holy cow! Those indentations are shaped liked a girl's butt! Whose are they, and how'd they get on the hood of your car? How long have they been there?" asked Zeina, sounding irked.

"Ah, hmm; nice day today, isn't it?" Karan asked, stuttering and trying to change the topic as swiftly as possible.

As the trio walked up to the bright and airy duplex apartment, Zeina squeezed his arm, dug her nails in, and whispered to him, "You better tell me whose butt marks those are and how they got there; otherwise you're not getting any for a long time." She sounded agitated. She seemed to be angrier that she had never noticed those marks before, than about the story behind them. At least that is what Karan perceived.

The story behind the butt marks was not that exciting. Karan had long ago dated a thin, bony *Gujju* girl who wanted to make out by placing her bony butt on the warm hood of his car, which was a bad idea. Honda Civics are not meant for women to sit on them. Those Japanese delicate cars are meant for women to sit *in* them, unlike the huge, classic American cars, which are made for lovemaking on the hood, on the roof, in the backseat, in the trunk—basically everywhere.

Karan had attempted to get the dents fixed, but it would have cost him a thousand dollars. He didn't want to spend that kind of money on an old car. The marks were barely visible, so he had never gotten them fixed. Only sharp eyes like Zoheb's could have spotted them.

Zoheb had a couple from Kansas, Adam and Jane, staying with him for a day. As they walked into the apartment, Adam asked, "Hey guys, Jane and I just made some fresh lemonade. You want some?"

"I'll have some." Karan put his hand up.

Adam walked toward him and was about to pour the lemonade when Zoheb broke into a panic and made a beeline to stop him from accepting the drink.

"Let me get you a chilled Corona," he offered hastily, shaking his head, indicating to Karan not to drink the lemonade. Karan found his behavior odd, but he got the hint and accepted the beer instead.

"Hey dude, we couldn't find a jug for the lemonade. Jane fortunately found this jug in the bathroom. I hope you don't mind we used it to make the lemonade?" asked Adam innocently.

Adam had taken the potty *lota*, the water container used to wash the ass after a visit to the loo! Karan and Zeina understood what had just happened. Karan gave Zoheb grateful looks for saving him from drinking from the potty *lota*. Zeina had to leave the room to stop her gag reflex and laughter. No one could figure out how to tell their guests what they had done or even explain what that jug was really meant for. The three of them sat silently, smiling, and let the couple finish the lemonade during the course of that afternoon. A fair warning should be written on jugs that are kept in washrooms.

Adam and Jane left late evening.

Zoheb liked spending time with Karan and Zeina. He showed Karan how to fly a radio controlled airplane. He had a collection of about ten airplanes, some with powerful engines. He was a licensed pilot as well and an innovative cook. He cooked lunch and prepared *tandoori* chicken pasta. They all had a great meal and afternoon together.

"You need any help from me regarding Amma? Can I come to receive her at the airport tomorrow?" Karan asked.

"We'll be okay, but you are welcome to come to the airport," answered Zoheb.

Zeina was happy to observe her brother and the love of her life bonding. For Zoheb, Karan was the younger brother he had never had. They watched three action movies in a row that night and consumed three bottles of wine. It was late by the time they finished *Cliffhanger*, their last movie. Zoheb suggested that Karan stay over and gave him PJs and a toilet kit from Lufthansa.

Then he walked up to his sister and whispered, "Please don't even attempt to pay him a visit at night under my roof."

The more the restrictions, the more the mischief! That was true in most parts of India, Pakistan, and Middle Eastern countries where societies restrict contact between men and women. Karan slept on an air mattress upstairs in the loft. Zeina did sneak up to him at night to cuddle.

The following morning, Zeina cleaned the house thoroughly and prepared for their mother's arrival in the afternoon. It was a bright, sunny, warm day. Zoheb proposed to wash "their" cars, which meant three of his cars as well as Karan's, and then wax the cars and polish them. Apparently, Zoheb had read, understood, and implemented the classic Tom Sawyer story about tricking the neighborhood kids into whitewashing the fence.

He spent half the time on his mobile phone on conference calls while Karan slogged away—washing, waxing, and polishing the four cars! He couldn't say no to his future brother-in-law. He made a mental note not to get into a situation where they would wash their cars together again.

After the hard work, they guzzled chilled beer followed by a gourmet burger lunch on the waterfront in downtown Annapolis. Zoheb really liked Karan. He could sense amazing potential in him—more than someone who could wash cars. He was genuinely happy to see his sister with a nice guy.

Amma arrived at the BWI airport in the afternoon. She came out of immigration in a wheelchair. Zoheb freaked out. He couldn't bear to see his mother in pain or in a wheelchair like a handicapped person. He had always envisioned her as a strong woman.

"Why are you in a wheelchair? Are you all right?"

She was exhausted from her trip because she had not eaten or had anything to drink on the plane. If she drank even a sip of water, she threw up. Zoheb and Zeina hugged and kissed their mother. She was everything they had, and they dearly loved her. Amma did look unwell. Karan had seen her photographs of her as a beautiful stewardess when she was young and some recent ones of her without much hair after her first chemotherapy. In all of those photographs her face was glowing; she was smiling and happy. In person, she looked tired and weak, with dark circles under her eyes.

Zoheb introduced Karan to her. "This is our friend Karan. He lives nearby."

Sitting in her chair, Amma gave Karan a weak hug. Her eyes met his for the first time. She sensed strong vibes from him. She felt a connection she was not expecting. She looked at him again to figure out why she felt that connection, but she was too tired to analyze further. Karan felt the instant bond as well.

"Oh, you are the boy from Delhi. We spoke the last time I was in New York."

Zoheb bought her Gatorade and cookies. They drove home and settled her in. Karan went home early so the three family members could spend time with each other. He promised to come see them as often as possible, and anytime they needed him while Zoheb traveled.

Despite how sick she was, Amma always drove herself. She had an amazing talent for just getting in a car anywhere in the world, reading a paper map, and driving. Right-hand drive, left-hand drive, automatic, or stick shift, it didn't matter. She put her daughter to shame for not being able to drive.

Zoheb made all the medical appointments, arranged for insurance and cash, and left for Bangladesh for two weeks. Karan visited almost every day after work. He took Amma and Zeina grocery shopping, *desi* shopping, and for dinners. Amma and Karan hit it off well. Amma loved food and going out, and so did he. She made rapid progress the very first week. Simply being with her daughter fixed most of her aches and pains. Although there were three beds in the house, Amma slept in the same bed with Zeina.

Zeina had to go to New York for urgent work for a day, so Karan came to spend time with Amma and take care of her. He made her tea and fixed her lunch. They talked for hours. In the evening, he took her to a Bollywood movie and dinner in Silver Springs. They discussed family, movies, and food. He spent that night at the apartment to give her company.

Zeina returned the following day and noticed a new bond between her mother and Karan. Amma asked Zeina about Karan every day after that weekend—where he was, when he was coming, and what the food and entertainment plan was for each evening.

"Why don't you call him yourself? I'll dial the number for you," Zeina said to her mother with a grin on her face.

The following weekend was Christmas. Arjun came to spend the weekend in Columbia. Amma heard that Karan's brother was in town, so she invited them both for lunch. She was feeling better and wanted to cook lunch herself. She was an outstanding cook. Karan figured out where both her kids got their cooking skills. Amma was not just an amazing cook, but a brilliant designer and a businesswoman. She never sat idle. She was always painting, designing, or creating something.

She fed the brothers till they couldn't breathe anymore. The food was just too good: ethnic Pakistani dishes such as *chappli kebab, haleem, nihari, chicken kadai,* and the list went on and on.

Amma spent the afternoon bonding with the two brothers, who also enjoyed her company. She never asked whether Karan was Zoheb's friend or Zeina's, or how the two of them had met him, or how long they had known him. She connected with Karan one-on-one, and she adored him. Karan was her friend now.

The next day, the two brothers invited the Zaman family for brunch at their home in Columbia. Amma was not well enough to travel, and Zoheb had just come back from a long trip, so Karan and Arjun came over to Annapolis and cooked a stuffed *parantha* [flatbread] brunch for the whole family. They fed everyone and also cleaned up. Amma loved the cooking and was impressed by the cleaning.

Arjun gave both Amma and Zeina a hug before they left. Karan also gave Amma a hug and then hugged Zeina.

Amma noticed that the hug between Karan and Zeina expressed more than friendship. Alarm bells started ringing in her head. It occurred to her that her daughter was actually seeing Karan.

As soon as the boys left, she said in a loud voice, "Zeina, come here, sit down. Are you just friends with Karan, or is there something more going on?"

Zeina panicked! This was not the right time. Just when things were moving in the right direction, why was this happening? It was a nightmare for her to face her mother in such a situation.

"I sort of like him," she responded, carefully choosing her words, thinking that Amma liked him just a few minutes ago and might not overreact.

Barely had she said those words when Amma started screaming. "How dare you? How dare he even lay his eyes on you? That *Haramzada* [Bastard] Hindu. How can you do this to me? I'm dying, and you want to kill me faster?" she yelled at top of her lungs.

Zoheb came running down from his study as soon as he heard the screaming. Amma was hyperventilating.

"Open the windows. Get some water. Amma, calm down; nothing has happened, and nothing will happen. No need to be so dramatic. Breathe, Amma, just breathe!" he instructed.

Amma was hysterical. She thought of Zeina's last Indian Hindu boyfriend, whom she detested. Now she was stuck with another *Haramzada* Hindu! That is how she spoke of Karan from that point onward—*Haramzada* Hindu.

She calmed down after ten minutes, but she came down on Zeina full force. That was her strategy. She wanted to break Zeina down so quickly that she forgot Karan once and for all. What she forgot was that her genes ran in her daughter. Zeina was not going to give up so easily. Amma never gave up easily herself. She didn't realize that this was not just infatuation; her daughter was deeply in love. She did not foresee to what extend Zeina was willing to push matters to be with Karan. Amma spoke to Zoheb and begged him to settle this matter as soon as possible and get rid of Karan if he wanted to see her live much longer.

From that day onward, Zeina's life became misery. She was with her mother all day and couldn't even make a call to Karan. Amma was sick, she was hurt, and she was sad. There was no escape for Zeina; she had to hide in the bathroom to make calls to Karan. He consoled her as much as he could. Now it was his turn to comfort and support her. The difference was that in contrast to his situation with his family, she had a terminally ill mother and had no space even to breathe freely.

Later that month, Karan and Arjun went to Hawaii to join Varun and Simran over New Year's Eve for a short vacation. How Karan wished that Zeina could've joined them. He felt her misery every day. She was stuck in a hot apartment. Amma couldn't stand the cold weather and turned the heat up to almost ninety degrees. Zoheb was in and out, traveling for work all over the world. Every day Amma asked for confirmation from Zeina that Karan was history, and every day they argued.

"What's so special about that *Haramzada* Hindu? Why can't you find a good Muslim, Pakistani boy just like him? He'll ruin your life. What will happen to your children? What do you see so special in that bloody waiter and cook? He's just like the idiot you were engaged to who also worked for Hyatt. He doesn't even earn enough money to take care of a family. Here I am looking for a prince for you and you want to marry a pauper?" She meant to push Zeina strongly to make up her mind to leave Karan.

Zeina had no answers other than what she firmly stated, "I love him. At least, stop abusing him unnecessarily."

Each time she said that, Amma just grew angrier. So Zeina stayed quiet and figured she would give the situation more time. She badly needed a break. She needed some time just to feel free again.

Karan downplayed his Hawaii experience as much as possible whenever he spoke with Zeina because he knew of her frustrating life in Annapolis.

Varun noticed that he made calls from pay phones at odd hours. "Who do you keep calling?"

Karan had no choice but to lie. "Just checking messages and calling work," he replied with a straight face.

His brother had his doubts about Karan's response, but he didn't want to spoil anyone's vacation. Varun and Simran had worked one month in Honolulu and took one week off to enjoy Hawaii. Karan arranged for suites at Hyatt Hotels in Kauai and Maui. They explored the Hawaiian Islands and loved every part of it. They also enjoyed a helicopter ride across the waterfall in Kauai, where *Jurassic Park* had been filmed. Luau parties by the beach, cocktails, gorgeous women, beautiful mountains, and great food—Hawaii had everything. But Karan felt empty because he didn't have Zeina with him. All day long, he wished he could be with her and get her out of Annapolis for a few days. Each time he spoke to her she sounded low.

Zoheb took Zeina out on New Year's Eve to a local restaurant for dinner. Amma stayed home; she was not feeling well enough to go out in the cold. Zeina cried her heart out to her brother. He loved his little sister, but he had made his position clear to her from the day he had met Karan.

"I'm sorry to see you go through all this. I'll try to help you and speak to Amma, but when I say try, I mean that I'll only try. I can't cause her any pain and will not allow you to do that as well. If I see that she has no intention of turning around, I'll not help anymore. You'll have to give up on H-squared. Cheer up now. Bottoms up; it will be midnight in a few minutes."

"What did you call him? 'H-squared'?"

Isn't that what Amma calls him now, *Haramzada* Hindu, which is H-squared?"

They laughed together; at least some sense of humor still prevailed.

"Happy New Year, *Butya*. I love you."

Karan called a few minutes past midnight to wish Zeina a happy New Year. He was finally able to get a hold of her. He also spoke with Zoheb briefly. They all hoped that the New Year would turn things around.

It snowed that night. The whole landscape turned white. There was a strange silence. The snow had muffled all sounds, and it also muffled Zeina's pain. Her frustrations vanished; she did not feel stressed anymore. She couldn't sleep that night because, as usual, it was hot in the apartment. Amma and Zoheb were snoring. She went to the study on the second floor and opened the round attic window a little to breathe fresh air. It was snowing lightly, and on the west side of the sky, the moon was shining. Untouched white snow gleamed in the moonlight. A gentle breeze blew a snowflake on to her hand. The perfect flake glittered in the moonlight. The heat from her hand melted the snowflake. Another snowflake blew into her hand and melted away again. She noticed that each snowflake was perfect, yet different. She remembered that no two snowflakes look alike. After watching a few flakes melt in the palm of her hand, it occurred to her that no matter how bad the situation was, with each day her problem would sort itself out. Each snowflake was different, and the days to come would be different as well.

Zoheb was off work on New Year's Day. That evening when he returned home, he took it upon himself to make his mother comfortable and tried to reason with her.

"You love us. You've taught us to love and taught us to make our own decisions. Zeina truly loves Karan. He's a great guy, and he loves her too. You've friends of every religion. Some of your closest friends are Hindus. So, why have you clammed up on them?"

Nothing worked on Amma; she had made up her mind. She had a major mental block, and she could not get past the Hindu factor. She did not want to hear Karan's name or discuss this topic. She started getting angry and screaming again. It was too painful for Zoheb to handle. He calmed her down.

Zoheb approached Zeina, who was waiting in the apartment complex's gym. He put his hand on her shoulder with his head hung low. He shook it from side to side and said, "I tried, I really tried. You can't cause her any more pain. I'll speak to Karan myself. He's never to see you again, and you'll not dare have anything to do with him." His last sentence was stated firmly.

Long after her brother left, Zeina sat in the gym, numb and frozen in shock. She just couldn't believe that it was all going to end like this. Her mother, whose arms were open to the world, had closed them on someone special to her, mainly because of a difference in religion. She sat there with silent tears rolling down her cheeks for an hour. She concluded that only time would solve her problem. She would have to shift gears and start living a life of lies and pretend she was no longer with Karan until something changed.

Karan was on the plane ride back from Hawaii and had no clue what was going on in Annapolis. He reached home late evening on January 1. He called Zeina, but she had her mobile on silent. She called him back late at night, hiding in the walk-in closet, and told him everything. She sounded exhausted and drained. He heard her story quietly.

"Hang in there, *Snuggle*. We'll get past this time. I'm with you. We'll find a way out," he consoled her. "I'll handle your brother. Don't stress about it. Let him call me if he wants to."

"Be nice to him. I don't want you two to have misunderstandings."

"I promise not to argue with him. We've agreed to give the impression we are not together. It's an easy solution for now. I just have to play along."

"Amma's treatment is almost over. She is miserable with the cold weather. She wants to return to Islamabad, and get the follow-up tests done there. After she leaves next week, come to see me. I love you, *Jaani*. I missed you so much. I wish I could hold you and be with you."

As expected, Zoheb called. He was curt and official. "I like you, and I know Zeina likes you, but this will never work between the two of you. I've already warned Zeina, but she didn't listen to me. Amma is against your relationship, and I can't see her in pain. You both are causing too much tension in our family. Please don't try to meet Zeina or contact her anymore. I'm going to be tough on her, and tough on you if you disobey me. Am I making myself clear?" He sounded like a military general.

Karan politely said, "Yes, you are making yourself clear."

"Well then, it has been good knowing you. I wish you the best in your life."

Karan smiled, thinking that Zoheb had sure made himself clear, but he had never agreed that he would comply with the demands. Alas, Zoheb was not on the phone long enough to confirm that.

Karan and Zeina detested living a life of lies with their families, but it had to be done. The only family member still standing in support of them was Arjun.

Amma left healthier, walking on her feet a week later. She hugged Zeina at the airport. After two weeks of screaming at her about Karan, she kissed her and sweetly said, "I love you, *Butya*. I know what is best for you. Please don't be angry with me. You're young, beautiful, well educated, and extremely talented. There'll be a lineup of good Pakistani boys for you when you want. Forget him; smile again, please, for me?"

She smiled for her mother. At least, she didn't call him H^2 again. Deep down, Amma still liked Karan. She was just protective when it came to her daughter.

A week later, Zoheb got news from his employer that he had to relocate to the Houston office. The move was to happen within the next two or three months.

Zeina was ecstatic to be back in her apartment. Within two days, she secured an assignment at Calvin Klein. With her talent, there was no dearth of freelance jobs available. Some color came back to her cheeks, and she felt alive again. Karan visited her the following weekend. All they did that weekend was eat, kiss, hug, sleep, and watch TV. They had a lot of catching up to do from the last few weeks of stress. They didn't want to speak about family issues or the future. They just enjoyed being with each other in peace and living their present.

It was bitterly cold to venture out. They did take a walk around Rockefeller Center to enjoy the Christmas decorations, and the famous gigantic Christmas tree flickered with thousands of colorful lights.

On Sunday afternoon, Karan casually asked her, "Where are your Canadian immigration forms? Let's fill them out. You need to have a backup plan. I'll mail them for you after I check them."

She dug them out of a drawer. He spent the next hour completing the forms with her. The street-corner photo studio produced photographs to specifications within an hour. He took her forms with him and made sure they got mailed out the next day.

The following month was busy for both as they worked weekends and couldn't meet. Valentine's Day was coming up soon; Karan wanted to make their first Valentine's special. He planned a weekend getaway and reserved a room at the Hyatt in Richmond, Virginia.

"*Snuggle*, can you take the train here next weekend? We'll have a romantic time. We can go to a nice *desi* restaurant for Valentine's. There is an Indian *dhaba* [hole-in-the-wall restaurant] I know of in Crystal City that is marketing an awesome buffet dinner-dance package, a dozen red roses, and *roohafza* as a welcome drink for $19.99 per person. They'll also have live *desi* music and a *desi* DJ," he teased with a naughty grin on his face.

She knew well enough that he planned everything in detail and in style. There was no way he would take her to a *dhaba* for Valentine's, or at least, he should know not to do that if he knew what was good for him.

He welcomed her on Friday evening and announced that they were not going home at all but were headed to Richmond, Virginia, for two nights. Interestingly, he was carrying two large suitcases for a weekend trip, but he would not disclose their contents.

They checked into a beautiful suite. A dozen red roses waited for her by her bedside. He sent her to the spa for a few hours for a facial and massage so he could prepare the room for her return. He had brought red helium balloons in those big bags, and he decorated the room with balloons, confetti, and candles. He prepared a bubble bath and had champagne, chocolate-dipped strawberries, and a card waiting for her on the bed. When she walked into the room, she loved what she saw. The room looked stunning. It was a romantic afternoon, to say the least.

Zeina told him that she hadn't brought anything for him, but indeed she was lying. She was waiting for her moment later that evening to present him his gift.

Karan had made dinner reservations at Tobacco Company, a local steakhouse. She wore a beautiful burgundy dress, and he wore a black suit. She looked beautiful that night. They were happy together on their first Valentine's. The restaurant was decorated with red lanterns, and a live jazz band played in one corner. They ordered a bottle of Pinot Noir, steak with sides, and cheesecake for dessert.

After they returned to the hotel, she surprised him with a card and red cuff links. He was delighted with them.

They woke up to a terrible mess in the room. The confetti was the worst cleanup job of all. Karan left a generous tip for the housekeeper for the extra work that they caused. The poor woman must have had to vacuum for hours.

9. Canadian Work Experience

It was a bitterly cold and snowy day in early March. The roads were icy, causing accidents galore. Karan reached his office after two dreadful hours in stop-and-go traffic. He had barely arrived when he noticed that James, the meeting planner from IBM, was in the reception area of the sales office stomping his feet. He was red in the face and seemed upset. He had come to complain about the banquet staff. Apparently, the staff was late that morning. The coffee served was not hot enough; the connecting conference room door was not opened on time. The list of his trivial complaints was long.

James had probably woken up at 8:00 a.m. in his warm bed in his free luxury suite. He managed to get an upgrade because he had booked fifty rooms. Most likely, he had his free room service breakfast, since all meeting planners loved to have everything for free. They never disclosed any of these benefits to their companies. Then he must have come down and started barking orders at the poor banquet staff. Unlike James, the hotel staff had to face two-hour commutes on icy roads, risking their lives just to get to work on time.

Karan was feeling hot in his overcoat. He sighed and politely said, "Sir, let me take my coat off, and I'll look into all your problems right away."

James got even more annoyed thinking that Karan was brushing him off, and he went straight to Fred, the GM, to lodge a complaint. God knows what he said, but Karan was called into the executive boardroom that afternoon. The head of HR witnessed the meeting with Fred.

Fred was a huge black man with a strong presence and a booming voice. He announced, "I have an official complaint that you didn't coordinate

IBM's meeting properly, and you were rude to their meeting planner. IBM is a volume client of Hyatt Corporation, and we have to bend over backward to retain their business companywide. Because of you, we now risk losing their business. I've made a decision to give them a 50 percent discount on total expenses for this three-day meeting, which will cost this hotel $25,000. I'm also putting you on probation, and I'm canceling your transfer request to Toronto."

Karan couldn't believe what was happening because he had done nothing to deserve such unfair treatment. Yet he didn't say a word. There was no point defending his position. Fred was known to be an unreasonable person. Karan silently walked back to his office. He sat still for a while, digesting the punishment he was handed. The probation didn't bother him, but the destruction of his plan for moving to the Hyatt in Toronto was not easy to accept. As it was, his career with Hyatt was not going anywhere in the States. The green card was not moving forward, and he had decided to quit and further his education in the near future. This was a life-changing event. It became clear to him that this episode was orchestrated by the *Painter Man*. He sensed that it was time for him to surrender his will and give in to destiny. One door had clearly closed, but he was confident that others would open.

He called Varun and explained what had happened. "I've got to move on in life, *bhaiya*. I want to resign and move to Detroit briefly while I make my transition to Canada. I need a career change, and the only way for me to do that is by going back to school to get a master's degree."

His brother paused and then said, "You have my full support. Do what you feel is right for you. What savings do you have, and what do you need from me?"

"I have no debt other than my car loan, but I don't have much saved. I don't make much to begin with. I have enough to settle everything here and pay for a truck for a self-move."

His brother was not pleased to hear that, because he knew that Karan had been spending lavishly on women for the last two years. He could have had a good financial cushion if he had been careful with his spending.

"I'll help you with your transition into the next step of your life. How about I take over the car payments until you start earning again? I cosigned your car loan anyway. You'll have my home open to you. I'll support your expenses, and you can take your time to move to Canada smoothly." Varun comforted him with a lot of love and affection.

Next, he called Zeina and explained what had happened.

She sounded calm. "I'm sorry you have to deal with this unexpected turn. I trust you to make the right decision. I'll be with you every step of the way and do whatever I can to help. I'm sad, though. I didn't think you'd be moving so far away from me so soon. Michigan is a long way."

"I'll not be in Michigan for long. I'll fight my way through and get to Toronto to be on my own as fast as I can. I'll come get you soon to be with me forever," he said confidently.

He resigned the next day, giving his two weeks' notice to the director of sales. She had a twisted smile on her face when he handed her the letter. Karan's observation was that most of the women in the hotel sales force are unhappy and single because of the nature of work; she was no exception. She showed no emotions; neither did the head of HR or Fred. The hotel management staff hosted a farewell party at a local pub the following week.

He wrapped up his life in two days, rented a U-Haul truck, packed his belongings, and towed his car to Detroit. It snowed all the way. Varun helped unload his belongings in his enclosed garage. Simran welcomed him with open arms. He felt safe and loved in their home. He moved into the guest room. Over the next few days, he slowly moved his clothes into the guest room closet and left the remainder of his belongings in the garage. He started helping in the house with chores, cooking and cleaning to earn his keep and not behave like a guest. The first week just went by in getting settled and getting Michigan car plates and a driver's license.

One big problem with living in his brother's home was his inability to speak with Zeina whenever he desired. She called him using a calling card, which showed up on caller ID as an unknown number. Zeina only called when she was sure he was alone at home. Two weeks went by. He looked for jobs online and in local papers in Windsor and Toronto, but no one responded. He had no cash left at all, and was ashamed to ask his brother for pocket money. His brother paid for everything, but it never occurred to him that Karan had an empty wallet. Karan was getting a bit desperate for money as time went along.

One day, he was rearranging his belongings in the garage when he noticed the Peyton Manning autographed poster he had been given in

Knoxville. Just that morning, he read in the sports section of the newspaper that Peyton Manning was now a National Football Star! He put that poster up for sale on eBay, and two days later he sold it for $500 to a local Detroit buyer.

Karan was also cleaning yards and shoveling snow to make money, without the knowledge of his brother. It was a humbling experience for him. He had not had to rake leaves, clean yards, or shovel snow since his college days. His conversations with Zeina were short and flat. He was clearly depressed with his situation. She remained positive, encouraging, and chirpy. She put on a brave face for him each time they spoke.

Two weeks later, the principal of "hcareers.com"—an online platform for headhunting that focused on careers in hospitality—called Karan offering an advisory position, which paid per assignment; it was pure commission work. Karan had nothing to lose. It was work from home, and the only investment he needed was a phone, a PC, and a printer. His brother had a calling plan for unlimited calls within the United States and Canada. So the cost of running this business was almost nil. He accepted the assignment. He became a sales director with the firm, sourcing clients for job postings, and helping job seekers. He worked on this assignment for three weeks and tried to penetrate his existing contacts. It was not easy to compete with monster.com and other dot-com giants. He needed steady cash, and a commission-based job was not working out for him.

He restarted applying for jobs. Luckily, a week later, he got a call from Goodlife Fitness Center in Windsor to be their sales agent for selling gym memberships. The offer was for eight dollars an hour plus commission. He hated that place. Dealing with overweight, unmotivated people to whom he was selling empty hopes, was not his idea of progress. Karan felt that people often forget that joining a gym does not make a person lose weight, one actually has to use it.

He commuted from Detroit to Windsor every day, working ten hours a day trying to sell memberships. It was an extremely unmotivating job, and management expected miracles in days.

Every night, he studied for the GMAT exam. He was determined to get somewhere. He wanted Zeina and freedom back in his life. He felt that, despite all odds, there was a force within him making sure that he kept moving forward and did not fear the challenges ahead.

His brother and his wife had to go for a medical conference to California. He mentioned their trip to Zeina, who came up with the idea of visiting him while he was alone at home. She booked a free ticket using her airline miles. Karan was not home entirely alone, though. Gurpreet, his sister-in-law's elder sister was still at home. He spoke to Gurpreet and explained to her that he loved Zeina and wanted to see her. She knew a bit about Zeina from Simran. Gurpreet felt sorry for him and agreed not to tell anyone.

Zeina came for the weekend after Karan's brother had gone. Karan was beside himself meeting her after almost two months. Both of them felt like years had passed since they had last met. He held her tightly in his arms for a few minutes before kissing her ten times at the airport.

But something went wrong somewhere in the communication between Karan and Gurpreet. She did not keep her promise to Karan and snitched to Simran. Of course Simran told Varun. Simran called Karan and told him that she knew what was going on in their home and that what Karan had done was not right.

"Your brother will speak to you when he returns. He's disappointed in you."

Zeina flew back on Sunday evening. Varun and Simran returned on Monday afternoon.

Varun walked in, put his bags down, and blazed away at Karan. "You've disgraced me and failed me. I felt sorry and helped you, and this is what I get in return? How dare you let that whore into my house? Are you mad? You want to fuck up your life? Go for it. You'll only learn when you find out that she's fucking the milkman."

Karan couldn't take it anymore. He put his hand up and said, "Shut up! Just shut up! Enough is enough. You'll never ever insult her again; not one word against her. I'll not hear anything against her anymore. Your help is much appreciated, but not at such a heavy cost. I love her, and I love you, but you don't own me. You will not insult my love!" He fought back for the first time and stormed out of the house.

He drove aimlessly for an hour, not knowing where to go and what to do next. He felt homeless and completely alone. He drove to Vijay and Nera's home. They were good friends of his brother. He liked and trusted them. Vijay offered him a scotch on the rocks. Karan told them everything. They discussed his options. Karan was not willing to go back to his brother's home that night; he made that clear.

"I'm going to pack up and go stay with my uncle in Toronto. I know they'll host me for a few days. I'll take up a job in Toronto—any job I can get, even if it's manual labor."

It was past midnight. Varun was worried sick about his little brother. He thought that Karan would come back, but he didn't. He was about to call the police.

"Does Varun know you are here?" Vijay asked.

"No."

Vijay immediately called Varun, just before he would have dialed 911. Vijay requested that Varun calm down and leave his brother alone for a bit.

The following day, Karan went to his brother's house at a time when he knew no one would be there. He called Zeina and told her what had happened. She was worried and annoyed about how immaturely he had handled the situation. She felt that his recent choices had been hasty and harsh. Karan was still in a rage. He packed his bags, loaded up his car, and left for Toronto with no note for his brother.

At the Canadian border, his immigration papers were inspected by a pretty female officer. "Welcome home," she said with a big smile.

Those words were extremely comforting for Karan to hear. Right when he was feeling homeless and hopeless, someone had welcomed him. He was sure that no part of her training as an immigration officer had taught her to say that. Those words just came from one Canadian to another. It was so different from going in and out of the States, where immigration officers generally stare at you with the basic assumption that you are not welcome and that you are guilty of something, anything, until proven innocent.

On his way to Toronto, he stopped by Windsor and quit his work at Goodlife Fitness with no notice. He gave them his forwarding address to mail him his last pay check. He continued his drive to his *Chacha's* home in Mississauga. He was upset and disturbed with his current situation. He was angry at himself for getting into such a mess. The only positive thought that kept him going was that, once this nightmare was over, he would have Zeina in his life permanently.

He had lost almost all his material possessions. He had four hundred bucks in his pocket, a few clothes, and a car on which he hoped his brother would keep paying the monthly payments. Toronto was going to be a new beginning from scratch.

Varun came to an empty home. He called Arjun, who told him that Karan was probably on his way to Toronto and would not be returning. Varun was sad and upset, but he stayed calm. After an hour, he called *Chacha* and told him in confidentiality what had happened. He asked *Chacha* to take care of Karan. He made an arrangement to pay *Chacha* for Karan's expenses, without Karan ever knowing about it. In spite of the wound Karan had left in his heart, he still loved his little brother and cared for him.

Chacha was a reasonable and intelligent man. His wife, Sunita *Chachi* [Aunt], on the other hand, had a few loose or lost nuts. Karan could never figure out what her issue was. In fact, no one in the family ever knew what her issue was, but it was clear that she was odd. She couldn't carry on a conversation without drifting in ten different directions. At the end of any conversation, it would still not be clear what she was talking about. She came across as partly depressed and partly just crazy.

An example of a typical deep conversation with her could be something as follows: she would start speaking in whispers as if they were in a public area, although she would be sitting in the den of her house. "The weather is so cold these days, but spring is almost here. The Hindu temple I pray at has lovely flowers in the spring. You know my car broke down the other day while I was going to the temple. I had a flat tire in the middle of a snow storm. I was so scared; I was thinking of *Baghvanjee* [God] and my mother the whole time. I miss my mother. I love her so much. I love my brother so much too." And then she would start crying hysterically and mumbling.

Karan had nicknamed her Cookie *Chachi*. She was a Hindu fundamentalist who imposed her version of Hindu values and culture on everyone around her, including her two adopted children.

Chacha's house was a safe place for a start but yet another prison! Cookie *Chachi* didn't let him make any personal calls without eavesdropping. Each time a call came for him, she picked up the other line and listened to his conversations. It was extremely annoying. She would not give messages or relay the right messages to callers, including potential employers calling for Karan. It was utterly maddening to be in her presence, but he was desperate for help. He had no other support and was still thankful to his hosts for letting him stay under their roof and for the food they put in front of him. They say that even a wood splinter is enough for someone who is drowning. He was glad he had that splinter in Mississauga.

Every day Karan looked for jobs and even applied for odd jobs, with no luck at all. He had to get out of that house as fast as possible. He was down to his last $50. Zeina wired him some money from her meager savings. She herself was not in a great financial position, having taken such a long break from work while taking care of Amma. Those $200 she sent felt like $20,000 to him. He spent every penny carefully.

The first two weeks in Toronto were tough. During each interview he was called for, he was told, "Sorry, you don't have 'Canadian work experience.'"

Nothing agitated him more about those interviews than this particular comment. He was well educated, had solid work experience, spoke English well, and was highly motivated. What the heck was this "Canadian work experience"?

Karan had a hard time understanding how a fresh immigrant could have "Canadian work experience." The worst was that other immigrants who were lucky enough to have secured a job learned to say the same to newer immigrants. He swore that whenever he got to a position where he could hire people, he would never use those three awful words.

Fairmont Hotels appeared interested in him for their head office in Vancouver, but at the last minute, the executive vice president of sales hired someone else—probably someone with "Canadian work experience"!

A week later, he got a call for a senior sales manager position from the Le Meridian King Edward Hotel, also known as the King Eddy. He interviewed with several people at the hotel. Exactly two days later, HR called him to come and collect an offer letter. He drove nervously to the hotel, hoping and praying it was a decent offer. The traffic was a killer on Highway 427 that morning. It took forever to get downtown. He finally reached the hotel after an hour in traffic, parked his car, and walked over to the employee entrance. The HR manager met him warmly. The offer was 55K per annum, plus benefits and a performance bonus. He thanked his lucky stars. He signed the offer right away. Now he had five days to start work. He was ecstatic. He called Zeina from a pay phone. She was very happy and proud of him.

Karan spent the next two days looking for a safe and reasonably priced place to live in downtown. Looking through the classifieds, he circled a shared, furnished accommodation for $250 per month in the Portuguese Village area. He went to see it.

It was a Victorian home owned by a quirky old Portuguese woman. She had three rooms she rented on the first floor with one shared bathroom, and an illegal stove and sink in the basement for the tenants to cook and dine. He was a bit scared looking at the dilapidated condition of the house. She had half a dozen cats and thousands of newspapers stacked up like mountains. Luckily, the entrance to the first floor was private for the tenants, so they had nothing to do with the old woman's personal space. The staircase going down to the kitchen and laundry in the basement was in the middle of the house, which meant no interference from the landlady. The bedroom looked like a prison cell; it was nine feet by five feet with a single bed and a closet. The place was a dump.

The cheerful face of a white guy popped out from the room next door. He introduced himself as Jacob. He was a struggling window salesman from Vancouver. He spoke to Karan and convinced him to take the place while continuing his apartment search. There was no lease and no deposit required by the landlady.

"Look at it this way: you'll have a safe place to stay, kind of like a motel, for 250 bucks a month."

He had a good point. The landlady wanted an advance of two months, followed by month-to-month payments. He had only $200 left. He came home and explained his situation to his uncle, who lent him $500. Cookie *Chachi* generously spared some old rusted pots and pans, as well as chipped plates and cutlery. He had left his kitchen stuff in his brother's garage in Detroit and needed something to start with. He bought some inexpensive kitchen utensils from Honest Ed's.

He moved into the shared house and started work four days later. He had lost a lot of weight from all the stress and was looking frail and worn out. But now that he was working and earning, he was happier. He lived in a modest way, but it was temporary, he told himself. He made sure that he saved almost 60 percent of his salary. The second month, he sent a check to his brother for his car payment with a written apology and a thank-you note on his official pad, which had his name, designation, and phone number printed on it. He also personally delivered a check to his uncle for the money he had borrowed from him. Within two months, he was debt-free again.

As soon as Varun got the note, he called Karan right away. He instantly forgave Karan. He was proud of his brother for pulling through and standing up on his own feet again quickly. But he was still not happy about Karan being with Zeina. They kept that subject aside. The conversation was emotional yet restrained. After the recent series of events in Detroit, Simran had developed quite an aversion to Zeina. It was a decent start for a conversation after a long time of not speaking to each other. Slowly, they got back to talking more frequently. They had a strong bond and couldn't refrain from speaking to each other, but the conversations were just not as before. They were limited to "How are you?" and "All is well."

Karan enjoyed his work, and the staff liked him. He started getting used to life in Toronto. Spring was around the corner; flowers were blooming, and the grass looked greener. He was rapidly saving each month. His world was turning into a better place already. He opened a special education savings account at the Bank of Montreal to save for going back to university.

However, he didn't like the shared house, or the basement kitchen. He seldom ate at home. He ate cereal for breakfast, a sumptuous lunch at the employee cafeteria, and soup or salad for dinner. He enjoyed weekend entertainment in Toronto. There were lots of events throughout the year. He bought weekend travel passes on the local transit system and explored the city extensively. Karan adored the Harborfront boardwalk area, which hosted concerts, movies, and art exhibitions. He heard numerous concerts, including Zakir Husain and many Western musicians.

He made friends at work, and through them, expanded his social circle. He was often outdoors, enjoying Toronto's well-kept parks, and he took advantage of the local public library, which was like a ghost building, because hardly anyone used it. He spent a lot of time there, just reading and preparing for the GMAT. He made sure that he stayed away from his hole so as not to feel lonely and depressed. Each time he came close to experiencing loneliness, he would just go for a long walk on Bloor Street, starting from the Portuguese Village to Chinatown, through the Younge and Bloor area into Greektown and then take a streetcar back. Sometimes on cold, rainy days, he walked for hours in the underground maze from Bloor to King Street and back up to Bloor Street, using different routes. Soon, he knew the city like the back of his hand. His weekly treat was a trip to Gerrard Street, one of the many *desi* markets, to visit a restaurant called Moti Mahal, where he ate his favorite dish, *chana batura*, fried bread served with chickpea gravy.

He was adamant about not accepting any financial help from family because it came with a string attached to leave Zeina, something he was not prepared to do. He had to build a new life for himself, pay for his MBA, and get Zeina back in his life.

Zoheb moved to Houston. He flew Zeina there to help him settle into his new house, to decorate, and to give his home her professional touch. He also invited her along on a client-sponsored ski trip to a resort in Vail, Colorado.

She sent Karan postcards from Vail. She missed him so much that it hurt to be without him. Zoheb was almost sure that Karan was history and did not ask her any questions about him on that trip. Both brother and sister had an excellent time and once again bonded as family.

Spring turned to summer, giving Toronto a new face. It felt as if the population of the city suddenly quadrupled. The main streets grew crowded. Karan's favorite hangout at Harborfront was taken over by tourists. He felt as if a majority of the city went into a long hibernation during the winter, and as soon as the sun came out, everyone emerged. There were lots of tourists from around the world all summer.

Karan got sick of living in the dumpy shared accommodation. He generously bumped up his budget to $500 a month for rent and started looking for a one-bedroom or a studio. All newspapers and local advertisements were useless. Classifieds were asking for a lot more than his budget. He called a few real estate agents; some of them laughed and hung up on him, others said they would call back and never did.

One day he spoke to a kind and gentle Eastern European woman who worked for a reputable real estate agency. Her name was Vivian. She spoke to him for five minutes and asked lots of personal questions to understand who she was dealing with. At the end of the call, she said, "Come see me in my office tomorrow evening. I'll see what I can do to help you."

Vivian was in her midfifties, elegantly dressed in a light-blue business suit and a pearl necklace with a shiny rock on her finger and a Rolex on her left hand. She had a heavy eastern European accent. They formally exchanged business cards. She was a senior and highly accomplished real estate agent, who had awards and glass transaction tombstones in her office for facilitating the buying and selling millions of dollars' worth of commercial and residential real estate. She offered him coffee. Then she printed a total of ten available apartments and studios.

"I know these are slightly above the price range you're looking for, but let's view these, and try to negotiate something for you."

"Thank you so much for helping me. Your plan sounds good to me. You want me to drive us around?"

"I'll drive you in my car. It'll be easier and faster."

Vivian drove him all around the city for the next two evenings in her Mercedes, looking for a suitably priced apartment. She bought him coffee, water, and drinks along the way. He was afraid to ask what her fee was going to be, so he didn't ask. He was already embarrassed about his meager budget, but interestingly, she was not. She was happy to spend her time on him and not once made him feel that it was a waste of time.

They drove up to one of the apartments in a dubious neighborhood where there was a porn video store on the ground floor, and a studio apartment on the first floor. They looked at each other and said at the same time, "Let's not see this one." They laughed and moved on.

On the third evening, they viewed a large, brightly lit studio with high ceilings on Parliament Street, next to the Sri Lankan village area in Cabbagetown. The location was central but not safe at night. There were drug addicts and prostitutes on the streets a few blocks from the apartment. The studio itself was perfect, and the immediate block it was located on was decent. A Sri Lankan grocery store and a tailor shop resided on the ground floor of the building.

"My advice is that you take this studio. This is a large, open space with air conditioning. The back staircase conveniently serves as a private entrance, and the transit is right outside your door."

She negotiated a rent of $600 a month with the landlord and charged him half a month as her fee. She did not take a penny from Karan. She genuinely liked him and they became friends.

She was married with two children, who were a little younger than Karan.

"I helped you, just like I would've helped my own son. I see the same spark in you as I saw in myself when I came to Canada. You remind me of myself and my struggles when I first moved here. I'm sure you will go far in life. Stay in touch, and if you ever need me, call me anytime," she said, and gave him a warm hug.

Karan called Varun and organized a get-together in Detroit. He rented a U-Haul truck over Canada Day, and the July 4 weekend to bring back his belongings.

The two brothers met after almost five months. They met warmly. Varun hosted a barbecue at home for a few of his colleagues and friends, so they could meet Karan. He was happy to be with his family, but things were far from being normal. No one dared ask about Zeina. He didn't call her during those four days and requested that she not call him in Detroit.

He returned with a truckload of his belongings. His Canadian friends helped him move into the studio. Within two days, the studio looked like home. No doubt, the place had an odd location, but it was his first real home in Toronto, and it was his sanctuary. He hung family photographs, paintings, and artwork; spread small area rugs, and set up his kitchen. He started cooking healthy meals. He loved the fact that any day he didn't feel like cooking he could get Sri Lankan food from several restaurants within walking distance and eat a healthy and tasty meal.

He was happy with his new life. He was saving money and focusing on studying for GMAT. He ended up getting a decent score. He applied to the top business schools in Canada. A few weeks later, he got acceptance letters from McGill and McMaster. Then he applied for a student loan from the Ontario government (OSAP). He received a letter from OSAP rejecting his application, and explaining that he had been an Ontario resident for less than one year and thus did not qualify. Then he attempted to secure a personal loan from Canadian banks, but no bank was willing to approve his application, because he didn't have enough credit history, and no Canadian guarantor.

Not willing to give up, he drove to Montreal and met the dean at McGill. He sympathized with Karan but couldn't come up with any solutions. Then Karan went to see whether McMaster could help. Dean John, who managed the program, was kind and considerate. He came up with two solutions: the first was to delay Karan's admission for a year to help him secure a student loan, and the second was for Karan to enroll in the co-op MBA program, where he could alternate between working and studying every six months. However, the co-op work assignments couldn't be guaranteed, and the degree would take almost two and a half years versus fourteen months, as in option one. He wanted to complete an MBA as soon as possible. With a heavy heart, he delayed his admission until the following year. He had no choice but to earn and save for another nine months.

It was now almost six months since Karan and Zeina had seen each other. She received a surprise package in the mail—her Canadian immigration documents! She was not even called for an interview. The interview had been waived, given her credentials. The papers arrived in the mail, magically in less than six months. She called Karan to share the good news. She could not recognize divine signs the way he could. She was destined to be in Canada soon. Her one-year work permit was about to expire, and the only way she could continue her stay in the States was to enroll into FIT's associate degree program. Zoheb supported her decision. She applied and got accepted. She enrolled two weeks later and transferred her student visa. Now she had bought herself some more time before deciding when to move to Canada.

Zoheb was busy in his own life, and he didn't think much about her Canadian immigration.

"Zeina, hang on to those papers. Let Amma come this summer, and we'll decide what to do with them."

Karan bought Zeina a ticket on Air Canada to visit him in Toronto for the first anniversary of their meeting, a day so precious to both of them. He just had to see her. She didn't need a visa for Canada now that she had her immigration papers.

65 West 55th Street

The weather was perfect when Zeina landed in Toronto. She was shocked to see Karan so thin and frail. The last six months had been tough on him, and it showed. They held each other tightly at Pearson airport.

She liked his little studio. She brought him curtains that she had sewn herself. She put her magical touch to the place and made it look cozier. She stayed a whole week with him and cooked for him every day. They watched movies together and explored Toronto in the evenings.

Karan took her for dinner at The 360, a revolving restaurant on top of the CN tower, the tower a lot of Americans call CNN tower! They watched a superb sunset over Lake Ontario on a perfect, cloudless night. The skyline of the city looked spectacular from the beautiful, large windows of the revolving restaurant. It was the best week he had experienced in the last six months. She liked Toronto and was not apprehensive about moving there.

As the time came for her to return to the States, their hearts began to sink. The time had passed too fast.

"I'll come see you soon," he promised.

"Amma is visiting in a few weeks for about two months. She'll stay a month with me and a month in Houston. She may even come to meet her brothers in Toronto. Why don't you come see me after she leaves?" she suggested.

They didn't want to discuss long-term plans anymore until he could figure out his future. It was best to plan a few months at a time.

He got back to work and into his daily routine. She got busy with her mother. Amma was feeling much better that year. She enjoyed her stay with her *butya* and then went to Houston to spend time with her son.

At a social function in Houston, Amma met Ayesha, a twenty-something Pakistani woman who had just completed university. Her family was related to a powerful Pakistani political family. They had moved to Texas after the regime changed. Ayesha started hanging around Amma a lot and quickly made an impression on her. Amma's main goal in life was to see both her kids married before she departed this world. Amma started applying pressure on Zoheb to get married to Ayesha. He was not entirely sure about marriage, but his desire to please his mother prevailed, so he started spending time with Ayesha and her family. Although this girl was not what he envisioned for a life partner, between his mother's high opinions and Ayesha's own manipulation, he agreed to get engaged.

Zeina flew down for the engagement party in Houston. She did not like anything about the insecure girl or her strange family. She was unable to voice her opinion, given what her mother and brother had put her through over Karan. She came back after the engagement party and was informed that Zoheb's wedding was to be held in a few months in Pakistan.

After the engagement, Ayesha started spending a lot of time in Zoheb's home. She portrayed herself as an innocent airhead and played the victimized child of unhappily married parents. Amma accepted her odd mannerisms, feeling sorry for her, and reasoned that giving her love and security would help her flourish. Zoheb just played along. All he wanted was his mother's happiness and blessings.

Zoheb treated his mother and sister to a vacation in Puerto Rico. They all loved the beautiful little island. Zeina sent Karan postcards every day. She wished that he could be there beside her.

One night when Amma went to sleep early, Zoheb took Zeina out for drinks. After a few drinks, he said, "You've not been the same, *Butya*; I sense that you are sad. Are you still seeing Karan?"

"He moved to Toronto a while ago. I do not see him often, but yes, I'm still with him. I love him. I can't leave him," she admitted with wet eyes. She was in no mood to lie to her brother about her relationship.

He gently took her hand and consoled her. "Give me some time. I'll try to help you one more time. Perhaps, after my wedding, I can try to reason with Amma again."

Her spirits lifted. She was happy to have her brother's support back, but he was not ready to speak to Karan yet.

Amma visited Toronto to meet her brothers, but she didn't know that Karan was there. His name sounded like a disease to her; she didn't want to hear it. In her mind, the relationship between the H^2 and her daughter was over. Karan wished that he could have met her, or at least spoken to her. Zeina rightly advised him not even to think about it.

Amma returned to Houston for Zoheb's *Dholki and Sangeet* [singing and dancing at a pre-wedding party]. Then she flew straight to Pakistan to start planning the wedding. She was happy and excited to see her son get married. Zoheb was satisfied to see his mother's joy and excitement. He was not in love, and not sure about Ayesha, but he was hopeful and optimistic about his future with her.

Two months later, Zoheb had a grand wedding in Pakistan, followed by several parties in Lahore, Islamabad, and Karachi. The who's who of Pakistan came to the wedding. Zeina found her new sister-in-law-to-be truly slow in the head and secretly nicknamed her "Dumbo." She stayed in touch with Karan throughout the wedding period via phone and e-mail.

Zoheb took his bride for their honeymoon to Bali. Upon his return to Houston, he received an amazing opportunity to move to Singapore with a large multinational on an expat package. At first, Dumbo threw a hissy fit because all her family was located in Texas or Pakistan, but after Zoheb took her to Singapore to show her what expat life in Singapore meant, she agreed to move, simply for the luxurious life. Zoheb was now far away from Zeina and busy with a new wife and a new job.

Karan's parents were lying low all this time. They occasionally spoke to him and were aware of his situation through his brothers. Colonel Dev knew that he had trained his son to be a fighter and was not worried about his succeeding in life. Colonel Dev offered to send him money, but he was still not willing to accept financial help. They took a break from coming to North America that year since they had visited five years in a row.

Zeina was back to academics. She enjoyed being a student again, but she really missed earning. After a year of earning, it was hard for her to ask for pocket money from her brother. She detested providing details of her expenses to anyone. She loved FIT's fashion merchandizing program. She was learning a lot, but she had reached a stage in her life where she wanted to be independent. Her heart was no longer in New York; it was in Toronto. The hustle and bustle of New York didn't interest her anymore. She socialized less and stopped going out late at night. She was becoming more like Karan. With every week that passed, she felt the desire to quit and move to Canada, seek a job, and start a new life.

She started setting the stage with her family. Interestingly, her mother was glad to hear that she was thinking straight and being practical. Her brother, on the other hand, was apprehensive. He expected her to complete her degree at FIT and give the States another try to see whether she could find a teaching position or another company to sponsor her for a green card. He felt that she wanted to move only because of H^2.

Zoheb visited Houston often for business, and made it a point to route visits via New York. He discussed Zeina's desire to move to Canada in detail with her and realized that she was correct. It was better for her to move forward in life. He agreed to support her move and also take care of her financially until she could find a job and be on her own in Canada.

"My only condition is that I want you to try to find a job first and then move. Feel free to visit Toronto for interviews frequently if you have to. Try this approach for a few months, and see how it goes. I don't want your move to happen in haste. Complete this semester, and I'll help you move in December. I also have my Saab, which I've owned for over ten years, sitting in storage in Houston. You know I love that car. I don't want to sell it. Why don't you take it with you to Canada? It'll be a gift from me," he said, with a silly face.

"Zoheb, that car is ancient, and it's a stick shift! You know I'll never be able to drive it," she responded, annoyed at the preposterous proposition.

"Karan is there to help you, right? I really don't want to sell it. By the way, how is Karan?" he asked lovingly.

"He is well. You shouldn't have threatened him and fought with him, but he holds no grudges against you. He's always liked you. He understands why you did what you did. He has been accepted at several business schools, but he can't join this year. He will join McMaster next year."

Arjun moved to Stamford, Connecticut, for a nine-month internship at the Marriott. Zeina took the train to meet him on a weekend. They had lunch together, and walked around Stamford. Arjun liked his potential *bhabhi*. She brought him up to speed on the last six months of events. Arjun was the only consistent pillar of support for the two of them.

"You know Varun Bhaiya calls me and tries to find out whether Karan Bhaiya is still with you. My lips are sealed; I never say anything. My parents have a hunch that he is still with you."

They called Karan together from Stamford on speakerphone. He was happy to hear from the two of them.

"I miss you both so much," said Karan.

10. Zeina, Bienvenue au Canada!

In early autumn, Karan started the required legwork for Zeina's arrival. He introduced her to several headhunters, fashion designers, and merchandisers in Toronto. They all expressed interest in Zeina's experience but wanted to meet her in person.

She visited Toronto at the end of September for a week of interviews. But she received no offers. All potential employers informed her that once she actually moved to Canada, they would consider hiring her. The encouraging part was that traction had been established for her to feel comfortable that she could secure a job soon without going through the pain of hearing, "Sorry, you don't have Canadian experience."

Next, he had to find her a place to live. He called his old trusted friend Vivian to see whether she could help. This time, he insisted that she accept a fee.

"I'll be glad to help, but no need to offer any fee. It's easy this time because her budget is more suited to what is available in the market. I live in an apartment building at Yonge and St. Clair. I'll be glad to get you a junior one-bedroom in the same apartment building I live in. I've lived here for over twenty years. I love the area; the apartment has access to two subway stations, both less than a five-minute walk away. She'll not even need a car. Why don't you come, have a drink with us, and view the apartment tomorrow evening after work?"

She was an angel; she made it all so easy. He went to meet her and met her husband and son as well. Her daughter was teaching English in Tokyo at the time. Fortunately, a junior and a large one-bedroom were available for Zeina's targeted mid-December move. Karan called Zeina that night and described the apartment to her.

"You'll like the apartment building. It's located in a good neighborhood. You'll have excellent subway access. The junior one-bedroom is what's in your budget. The apartment is a bit small, but I think you'll manage."

She called her brother to seek his opinion, and he had no issues with it.

Karan put a deposit down the next day for a mid-December move. A Canadian citizen or a permanent resident had to cosign the lease because Zeina didn't have any credit history in Canada, so Karan cosigned.

Back in Singapore, Zoheb was not faring well with his wife. She was not only a little slow, but was actually lazy, unmotivated, and a thankless person. He traveled frequently for work, and she just complained about being bored and missing her family. She made no initiative to make new friends or try anything to settle in. Zoheb still remained hopeful and optimistic, expecting her to change and blossom into a better companion for him.

Autumn turned to winter. Zoheb drove his Saab from Houston to New York. Baitu, along with a few other friends, helped Zeina pack up and load the U-Haul truck. Zoheb hooked up the Saab to the back of the truck and drove to Canada with Zeina. They had many hours of long chats about life, Dumbo, Karan, and their mother. She called Karan before crossing the border near Niagara Falls. Karan had dinner ready and beds arranged in his studio. They arrived before nightfall.

Zoheb gave Karan a big hug. His sad eyes indicated his embarrassment and apology for the last threatening phone call he had made. Zoheb didn't have to apologize. Karan knew the pressure he had been under when he made that call. Zoheb was comfortable leaving his sister in his care. He was a bit taken aback by the neighborhood but was proud of Karan to have made it on his own. Zeina had told him the whole story about his relocation challenges.

"I'm glad to know that you'll enroll in a business program soon. Keep up the good work. I'll do whatever I can to help you both," he promised at the dinner table.

The following morning, Zeina moved into her apartment. Karan sorted out the paperwork for the Saab. Zoheb had to transfer the car to

Karan's name because Zeina didn't know how to drive. Karan was not married to her yet, but the first piece of dowry had already arrived—that is, a 1984 Saab! It was a beautiful car, but it was old and that meant expensive repairs and maintenance. Karan took a closer look at the white Saab, which he called the "White Elephant." He was skeptical about accepting responsibility for an old car, but he had to take it to please his future brother-in-law.

"*Yaar*, I'll pay for all repairs. You just take care of it for me for now. I just don't have the heart to sell it," Zoheb insisted.

Just to get the darn car inspected, install daytime running lights, new brakes, and child safety belts, which were required in Canada, cost $1,200. Karan remained nervous about maintaining the car. It drove a bit rough, but it was built solidly, and after fifteen-plus years of running, it still had massive power and hardly any rust on the body.

Zoheb flew back to Singapore two days later. Amma was going to visit him later that week. Zeina took two weeks to settle into her cozy apartment.

Karan and Zeina knew there was no way they would sleep apart. They moved her extra belongings into his studio, and he brought his clothes to her apartment. The two of them started living together. People in India and Pakistan call it "living in sin." In Canada it's called "common law." Zeina and Karan called it their "home."

It was a magical time in their relationship. They learned new things about each other by living under one roof and strengthened their belief that they were meant to be.

"I'm so happy you are here with me. I feel my world has come together. I'm completely at peace," Karan said, as she cuddled with him on the couch their first evening alone.

"I never thought I'd leave New York, but ever since you entered my life, you took my heart with you. This is where I belong."

Karan subscribed to an extra telephone line at her apartment and forwarded all his calls to that new number. The games to dodge families continued. The apartment was arranged in such a way that anyone visiting couldn't really tell that he lived there. If any family member would visit, he could be gone from the apartment with his clothes in less than ten minutes. The whole exercise was practiced and timed like *Mission Impossible*. It was unfortunate that they had to pay rent at two places, but they did it out of respect for their families.

Major Atif, Zeina's *mamoo* [uncle], surprised her with a visit one weekend, and Karan had to exit in five minutes. Major Atif was an interesting guy. He was an early retired Pakistani army major. He had fought the war at the Bangladesh border where Colonel Dev had also fought against Pakistan. Had they faced each other at the battlefield, they would have had no choice but to put a bullet in each other's head.

Mamoo had also been a prisoner at an Indian military camp for over three years. That was where he learned to make *gulab jamuns* [sweet dumplings], during his kitchen duty. Interestingly, Colonel Dev used to oversee the same camp. They had exchanged a look the day Colonel Dev's regiment captured the Pakistani prisoners. *Mamoo* later joined Pakistani intelligence and was posted in New Delhi, where he was beaten up and threatened several times by Indian intelligence. So, he had mixed feelings about Indians.

He had tea at the apartment, glanced around, carefully observed the apartment, the kitchen sink, and bathroom, and said, "Looks like two people had lunch here today. It's a bit crowded for two people to live here, I guess."

The kitchen sink had two plates. The bathroom had two bath towels. He was a sharp cookie.

"Ah yes, my friend from work slept over last night. She just left a little while ago," Zeina lied, quickly changing the topic.

A few weeks later, Zeina found work at the Amazing Clothing Company. Their offices were located far from the city center. She had to take the subway and then a bus to get to the office. It took her about forty-five minutes to an hour each way. She designed T-shirts and some other cotton garments. It was a decent start for her. She was paid enough to support herself and save a little bit of money each month.

"I'm on my own again. You don't need to send me any more money. This is thanks to the support you have given me all these years," she proudly told her brother on the phone, expressing her deep gratitude.

"I'm very proud of you."

Amma got on the phone and spoke to her for a while. She was happy and proud of her daughter. The mother-daughter connection had improved after Zoheb's wedding.

Toward the end of the conversation, Amma said, "Zoheb is off my list now. *Butya*, now we need to find you a *mahalon ka raja* [king of several palaces]."

"Not again! Please let me be! I'm just starting my life," she begged, hoping that her mother would not start sending Pakistani boys her way, which Amma and her friends often did.

Zeina recalled that a year before she met Karan, a guy called her speaking heavily broken English, and, in a thick Pakistani Punjabi accent, said, "Hello, Zeina *jee*. *Billo aunty*, your mother's friend, gave me your mobile number to speak about marriage. Me, I'm a *dactar* in Edison, New Jersey. Its *bery* nice place *jee*; lots of Pakistani community living here. I *habe* a *bery* big house, big swimming pool, but no wife. Tell me about yourself; do you like cooking and cleaning? You're not the fast type, I hope. I mean, you don't drink and smoke?"

Annoyed as hell, Zeina said, "I love to cook and clean for my boyfriend. I only smoke when I drink. I don't think I am suitable for what you're looking for. You need a maid, not a wife. Please don't call me again!" and she hung up.

That was her way of dealing with references from Amma, aunts, and uncles. It was not easy to ward off weirdos, but she always had her ways.

"*Snuggle*, you know if you start driving, your life will be so much easier. Imagine your commute in a nice car, listening to music. Canadian winters are harsh. You'll be miserable waiting for buses."

Both the Honda and the Saab had manual transmission. She had a phobia about stick-shift cars. Apparently, Zoheb had tried to teach her to drive in Islamabad, but he was not the most patient teacher. She ended up crashing the car, and it left her traumatized.

Karan convinced her to try driving once again. They went to an empty neighborhood in early morning on a weekend. She started the Saab and got the car moving after a few attempts. The car was going up a slight hill in second gear just when an SUV came zipping across the street in front of her. She panicked, put the car in neutral, and let everything go. She closed her eyes and started sobbing! The car started rolling backward downhill and scared the heck out of an old couple out on their morning walk. Karan pulled on the handbrake to stop the car.

"I can't do it, I just can't do it!" she screamed, hitting him on his hand.

"Calm down, *Snuggle*. It's all right. We'll try another time on an automatic car."

They found new meaning in their relationship now that they were living together. Their personal space in the tiny apartment was reduced to nil. They fought a bit like little children but then quickly made up as well. A little bit of bickering was good for their relationship. He woke up at 6:00 a.m. every day to prepare her lunches because she didn't have the option of eating near the office.

He visited his studio once a week to collect mail and check for ants, rodents, or cockroaches.

For Karan, life was beautiful. He was with the woman he loved, work was good, and she was happy. Both of them were enjoying their independence and exploring a new city together. They made new friends, and their social circle grew. They had friends from everywhere—local Canadians, Portuguese, Italians, and Sri Lankans. However, they remained careful about socializing with Indians and Pakistanis, especially Pakistanis. Pakistani educated society is so small that everyone knows everyone, and they could not afford having people gossip about them.

Zeina put together an elaborate dinner for Vivian and her husband during Canadian Thanksgiving as a thank-you for helping find apartments. They laid out a traditional spread. Zeina bought large pumpkins, which they carved and lit, from a farm outside Toronto. She also bought rustic decorations from Pottery Barn to go with the theme. Her apartment looked beautiful. The four of them sat in her tiny living and dining room for hours just drinking wine and chatting away. Vivian was glad to see them well settled into Toronto. She was impressed with Zeina's hospitality and personality.

That year for New Year's Eve, Karan and Zeina went to a medieval dinner and show at the Exhibition Place. The costumes, sets, and ambience reflected the era. There were no electrical lights in the amphitheater, just lanterns. The show was about knights fighting on horses, trying to win the princess's heart. They ate a meal of fire-roasted chicken and potatoes with their hands, as no forks and knives were provided.

As the winter progressed, Canada got colder—cold to a point that in February the temperature reached minus fifty Celsius with the wind chill! To stay alive, Zeina had to purchase heavier winter clothes made for such severe weather. She hated waiting for the bus in the freezing cold. The temperature between the subway trains and outside could vary fifty to sixty degrees. There were days where she walked into her office and had to thaw herself for an hour and then come home to do the same again.

"I've got to get a car, and I've got to learn to drive. If I have to do this commute one more winter on public transport, I'll just die!"

"This spring, we'll work on it, *Snuggle*. I wish I could help you now, but I cannot do much for you."

No one from her extended family came to visit her that winter. She was not close to any of them. One of her uncles who lived nearby was a successful dentist. He had about ten kids from two different wives. He was too busy and had no time for Zeina. She was glad about that.

Chacha and his wife were absorbed in their own lives. Cookie *Chachi* never liked Karan anyway, so she never once called to see whether he was dead or alive all this time. *Chacha* was a caring man. He regularly spoke to Karan but never asked anything about his personal life.

Varun called his brother once a week but didn't ask any personal questions, either. He had no idea that Zeina was now living in Toronto. He thought that Zeina was history now that Karan was in Toronto and she lived in New York.

Spring came along. The city thawed out a bit, and so did Zeina. Slowly, the layers of clothing came off; winter clothes got packed, and out came the summer clothes.

Zeina got a job offer to join a local famous Canadian designer, Ann Lundvorm. Karan couldn't stop laughing when he heard the name; it had the word *lund* [penis in Hindi] in it. Interestingly, Ann's father's name was Dick Lundvorm—thankfully that man never visited India! She was a well-known and well-respected personality in Canada. She was one of the most positive people they had ever met. She believed that there is good in every human being. Ann took a liking to Zeina—both her talent and her professionalism.

Zeina was now working in a far better environment and doing some real design and merchandizing work. She was a lot happier than before. Ann became friends with the two of them over time, and she invited them to her cottage on a lake in northern Ontario on weekends.

As spring came into full bloom, Karan and Zeina started traveling in Canada. They drove to Ottawa, Montreal, and Quebec City. They stayed at small, quaint bed and breakfasts and enjoyed romantic weekend getaways.

11. Taliban May Have a New Assignment

As Zeina and Karan's social circle grew, they started getting invited to parties and social gatherings. At one of the parties, they met a whole bunch of Pakistanis who recognized Zeina. The word spread like wildfire within the Pakistani community that Zeina was dating an Indian Hindu! That was a major topic of gossip. It was sensational news. It didn't take long for the word to reach Islamabad. A few days later, Amma heard at a gathering in Islamabad that her daughter was dating an Indian Hindu. She went red in the face with anger and embarrassment. She came back home and called Zeina right away.

"I just heard from Rabia, who heard it from her daughter that you are seeing an Indian?"

Zeina was stunned! She didn't know how to react. She paused, thought for a second, and said, "That Indian is Karan."

Amma was in shock. She howled, screamed, yelled, and cussed Zeina out for half an hour. She could not believe that H^2 was in Toronto.

"I thought he was long gone. I can't believe that I have to hear his name again. Why don't you just kill me? All of Islamabad is laughing at me. What will people say? What will all your relatives say? What have you done! Is this the day I was living for? I wish I was dead by now. I hate you for doing this to me."

The conversation was harsh—the worst ever.

"I love him. I'll not marry him if you don't want me to, but I'll also not marry anyone else. I know what I'm doing. You raised me to be independent and to make my own choices," Zeina screamed back at Amma.

Once Amma started getting upset, she lost her temper completely. She threatened to bring Zeina back to Pakistan, and moreover, she threatened to get Karan picked up by the Taliban!

She yelled, "I'll have him kidnapped and out of your life for good. No one will even know where he went!"

Amma hung up to call her faithful son.

Zeina was crying hysterically after her mother hung up. Her own mother had never insulted her so badly.

Zoheb heard everything. He pretended that he didn't know that Karan lived in Toronto. Amma started hyperventilating while talking to him and really scared him. He was worried, because her immune system was low, and she needed rest and peace. The stress of dealing with Zeina was too much for her.

Once again, Zoheb had to make an ugly call. "Karan, this is it. You cannot cause any more stress to my mother. You and Zeina just have to go your separate ways now. I'm not kidding this time. I don't want to hear your name anymore or see you around my sister anymore. This is it; this has to end here."

He was calm, sad, and stern. It was obvious that he saw no possibility of a turnaround with Amma, and he did not want to deal with the situation anymore.

Then he called his sister. "This is your last time to come clean. No more dramas, and no more Karan. If anything happens to Amma, I'll not spare you. If I hear one more time that you've not broken off from him, I'll personally come on the next flight and drag your sorry ass to Pakistan for good."

That same evening, Karan got a call from his parents, and later from Varun. After a long time of leaving him alone, they reopened the subject of Zeina. Everyone came down on him as well. His mother shed a few tears on the phone, and Varun kept telling him to move on.

It had been a rough day. As Karan and Zeina sat on the couch looking at each other's sad faces, they recognized that the pressure had become too much to handle. They caved under the threats for the first time. The threats sounded serious and real.

"We should talk to someone to know our rights, in case someone in the family tries to drag you away or something dramatic happens to me," he suggested.

They were shaken and afraid. She had never heard Zoheb growl like a ferocious lion in that way ever before. At 10:00 p.m. they decided to go to the nearest police station at Yonge and Eglington to discuss their situation.

"What can I do for you?" asked Officer Roody.

"My name is Karan Dev. This is my girlfriend, Zeina Zaman. We're both Canadian immigrants. I'm a Hindu from India, and she's a Muslim from Pakistan. Her family overseas is threatening her. They say if we don't separate, they'll forcibly drag her back and also get me kidnapped. We wish to know our options and rights so that no one can ever take such actions against us. Also, we want to see if we can restrict her brother's entry into Canada."

The officer had an amused look on his face. He understood the gravity of the situation and sensed the panic in Karan's voice, but he had a long line of other real emergencies such as rape, murder, and theft cases to take care of first. He asked them to take a seat in the waiting area. Judging by the number of rough-looking people sitting in the waiting room at the police station, it was obvious that it was going to be a long night. They held hands and sat and waited for their turn. Zeina was exhausted from the stress.

Out of nowhere, Karan got on his knees and said, "Will you marry me? Please marry me. Let's legally get married now. We'll wait for our families to come around to get married properly later. I'll always love you and protect you. I've loved you from the minute I met you. I wanted to marry you from the time our eyes met the first time. I'm sorry I don't have a ring on me. I didn't plan to propose to you like this. I'll buy a ring tomorrow morning."

She looked at him kneeling on the dirty floor, thought for a second, smiled, and said, "Yes, I'll marry you. You can give me a ring anytime tomorrow, or the day after, or the week after!"

There were a few thugs, prostitutes, and scary-looking people in the waiting room who clapped and cheered for them, including a few police officers guarding the waiting room.

Officer Roody came back after two hours and told them, "Here is what I can do for you. I'll make a report on your story and document it. We can't do anything about your brother or restrict his legal entry into

Canada. Had he been in Canada and threatened you, we could have done something. No one can force you to leave; you have rights here."

The two of them departed the police station with a false sense of security and peace.

The next few days were surreal. They had never wanted to get married without their families' blessings. Zeina was torn apart between love for Karan and her family. She pondered for hours on end but could not decide whether getting married in court was the right decision. In her wildest dreams she had never imagined that she would have to elope and wed in a court. After a lot of internal struggle, they decided that a court wedding was necessary as a backup. She was marrying Karan for love. Amma had gone though the same emotions when she got married. She had also eloped to marry someone she loved. History was repeating itself.

Once the decision had been made, both of them took a day off and applied for a marriage license at Toronto City Hall. Karan made an appointment for the upcoming weekend to get married by a nondenominational priest. Zeina asked her close friend and coworker, a Sri Lankan woman and her boyfriend to be their witnesses.

On the day of the court wedding, she wore a black pant suit with a hot-pink and orange tank top. He wore a blue shirt and black pants. In the presence of their two friends, who knew no one from their families, they got married. The four of them went out for lunch at Baton Rouge near Eatons Center to celebrate.

No one could separate them now. They promised each other never to disclose their legal marriage to anyone. Neither of them wanted to hurt their families' feelings. Whether it took their families one year or ten years, they were determined to give all family members time to accept them. Both prayed they would have a proper wedding someday. Now, if either of their families were to pull off an ultimate threat, their last resort would be to present their marriage certificate and put an end to the fights and arguments.

Their marriage certificate was nothing more than a safety net. Mentally, they had been married to each other for a long time. A marriage ceremony was for society to recognize them as a legal couple. They were already living together under "common law," which is considered being more or less a married couple. Their hearts and souls had united since the first day when they met. Their marriage had been planned and destined long ago by the *Painter Man* in the stars.

Zeina felt nothing had changed; they still lived together and shared bank accounts as before. Their future together was more secure, and that was it. Both felt more confident and better prepared for future family dramas.

Zoheb flew Amma to Singapore for a visit as well as checkups. He informed her that H² was history. He convinced her and himself that they would never hear his name again. She was relieved to hear this and happy to be in Singapore, driving herself around and discovering new places.

Meanwhile, Zoheb's own problems with Dumbo were increasing steadily, but he was trying to ignore them. Amma noticed the issues with Dumbo as well but did not say anything to Zoheb. Sadly, on Amma's first visit to the cancer specialist, he detected a recurrence of the cancer. This time, it was in the stomach lining. She needed chemotherapy again.

Zeina, despite all the issues with family, flew to Singapore immediately to be with her mother. She was taken aback by Dumbo's bad attitude. Instead of sympathizing and supporting her husband, Dumbo threw a fit that her mother-in-law would have to stay for more time than expected, due to medical treatments. Zoheb was unhappy just being around her. She slept all day and didn't take care of his mother at all. In fact, at times, she tried to be rude to Amma—and no one dared to mistreat Amma. Amma could eat rude people alive! Zoheb's house was ignored, and nothing about his marriage felt right. He was not in love with Dumbo; he had never loved her. In his heart, he knew that he had married for the wrong reasons.

Zoheb's work travel continued to increase. Matters deteriorated fast at home. Dumbo's relationship with the two of them grew bitter. One night, Amma overheard Dumbo on the phone saying bad things about Zoheb and herself. On the telephone, she told her parents that she was being mistreated and was unhappy with Zoheb. When Dumbo saw that Amma was standing behind her listening to her conversation, she screamed at Amma out of guilt. She knew that she had never been poorly treated or had any restrictions in that house. The sorry life that she had created for herself was a result of her own bad attitude. Amma didn't say anything to her, but she did tell Zoheb what was going on. Zoheb couldn't stand Dumbo anymore. He asked her to pack her bags and dropped her at a relative's place. He instructed her to stay there a few days and told her he would buy a ticket for her to Houston within a few days. He also told her that he didn't want to be with her until she fixed her attitude.

Dumbo took this gesture to another level. Under her parents' influence, she asked Zoheb for a divorce. Amma was heartbroken. She didn't want to see her son unhappy and divorced. She confessed that it was a bad decision for him to have married Dumbo. Zoheb heard her out; he struggled with himself. He attempted reconciliation with Dumbo; he also tried to convince himself his marriage could work, and to uphold the sanctity of marriage, but he finally concluded that Dumbo was not going to change. He couldn't see her being the mother of his children. He had never loved her and could not get himself to love her. He agreed with Amma and decided to proceed with a divorce.

Amma spent several hours talking to Zeina, seeking guidance and consolation for all her son was going through. Even Zoheb constantly called Zeina for advice. He was shaken by what he thought a marriage should be, and what it turned out to be. Keeping the issue of H^2 aside, the family grew closer due to frequent interaction and support needed to deal with the divorce.

The divorce took a few months to resolve. It was not ugly, but of course, as with all *desi* divorces, there were petty arguments over some "gold bangles" and some "earrings." Punjabis indeed have their priorities correct.

Everyone was relieved to have Dumbo gone. They were also aware that a huge mistake had been made. It was as if their mental system internally was all shaken up; they had been given a wake-up call to understand that the foundation of marriage should only be love, respect, and trust.

Varun called Karan out of nowhere, sounding excited. "Hey, Buddy! I've ten days off, and was supposed to go to India with Simran for her sister's marriage, but my J1 waiver is still stuck somewhere in the INS system. She's still going to India, but I can't go. I have all these days off and nothing to do. Can I come and spend time with you?"

It had been over a year since the two of them had spoken so lovingly to each other.

"Of course you can. I'd love to have you with me."

Karan was excited to have his brother to himself for ten days, but that meant a move back to the Parliament studio, which was easy to do.

Varun arrived a week later. He was ecstatic to meet his Karan. The first night they went out for spicy Thai food on King Street. Then they went to a nearby lounge for cocktails.

"If I may ask, where is Zeina? Are you still in touch with her?" he asked cautiously, after a few whiskeys.

Karan did not expect this question. His mind raced back to how badly his brother had insulted her. He put his guards up immediately, preparing for the worst.

"I'm still dating her. She actually lives here in Toronto. She immigrated six months ago," he answered, with a stern look on his face. He was not sure what his brother's reaction would be. He didn't want his brother's visit to end the very first day. The next thing that came out of his brother's mouth surprised him.

"Can I meet her?" he asked Karan politely.

"I can ask her how she feels about it and let you know," he replied, with a big smile.

He called Zeina to explain what had happened, and how his brother wished to meet her. She was as much taken aback as he has been.

"I'll be glad to meet him as long as you are sure this is a good idea," she said. "We've got to start somewhere, with someone in the family."

"Well, he wants to meet you of his own accord. God knows what image he has of you. Let him at least put a face to the name."

"All right, invite him on my behalf for tea at my apartment tomorrow after work."

Varun met Zeina formally with a handshake. She wore a yellow cotton *salwar kameez*. She had laid out an elaborate tea. They hit it off instantly. Varun found her to be charming, genuine, and friendly. He loved her well-decorated, cozy apartment. He loved the food she served him, and most of all, he loved the fact that she welcomed him with open arms, well knowing how merciless he had been.

Karan sat back in the hanging cane swing on the balcony with eyes wide open, watching the two of them interact and thanking his lucky stars that at least one opposing person in his family was giving his beloved a chance.

In the car, Varun apologized and almost made Karan cry.

"I'm sorry for judging her before even meeting her. She is a wonderful person. I'm happy to see you with her. You chose well. I'm glad you stuck by her."

Karan felt as though he had just been presented with an Oscar. He was deeply gratified.

Zeina and Varun spent each one of the remaining eight days together. She cooked all kinds of dishes for him. He even ate lunch with her without Karan one afternoon. The more time Varun spent with her, the more he liked her. He knew that he was wrong to have judged her. He also knew that it was time to fix things. He was going to get his own wife on board and then work on his parents.

That was the first victory for Karan and Zeina.

Varun said a warm good-bye and drove back to Detroit the next day. He called them the following day. "It's almost fifty Celsius in Delhi right now. I'm going to send our parents tickets to visit us for a few weeks, so they can take a break from the sweltering heat."

"I'm also going to speak to them about Zeina. I'll help you both. She is the one for you; definitely a keeper."

He persisted with his wife and managed to open her up to opening up to Zeina. He slowly stirred the topic up with the parents, but they were not ready to give in that easily. They still had their reservations. Mom particularly still believed that the Pakistani was a *churail*, a witch, who had done some black magic on her son.

Varun found an Air Canada direct flight that flew over the Arctic from Delhi to Toronto. He gave his parents these tickets and informed them if they didn't use them, the tickets would be wasted by the end of the summer. They were to fly into Toronto, spend a week with Karan, and drive to Detroit for three weeks before heading back to India.

As planned, his parents arrived three weeks later. Karan, of course, moved back to his studio. Surinder *Chacha* came to the airport to meet his older brother. Cookie *Chachi* didn't show any interest in entertaining any of his in-laws unless forced to.

Karan dedicated all his spare time to his parents. After two days of enjoying the city, Colonel Dev said, "Son, your brother told us that Zeina lives here. Are you still friends with her? I think we should meet her."

Varun obviously had done a good job of preparing his parents and turning things around with them.

Mom shot Dad a hostile glare. She did not look ready for such a meeting. Zeina's *churail* status had not changed, even though Varun hammered away at her praises every day on the phone.

Zeina was nervous about meeting his parents, but since the meeting was specifically requested, she agreed and remained positive. Karan arranged for a brunch, followed by a drive to a lovely town called Niagara-on-the-Lake.

Once again Karan's parents met Zeina. They greeted her warmly with a hug. The four of them eased into simple conversation and warmed up to each other as the brunch finished. They had a fantastic day together; it seemed that the ice had been broken. Zeina was too adorable to be mad at for long, and for no good reason—not raw onions, for sure!

It was a splendid Canadian summer day. The falls looked majestic as always; flowers were in full bloom; Niagara-on-the-Lake was picture-perfect.

On the drive back, Mom asked Zeina, "What do your parents think of our son? How do they feel about you going around with him?"

Karan smiled as he heard this. He had not heard her mother be so open to anyone he had dated previously. "Going around" is a popular term for dating in India, maybe because boys and girls mostly just go 'round and 'round each other and finally get married to someone else the family picks.

It was apparent that Mom didn't know that Zeina's father had passed away long ago. She told them about her late father, and about her mother being terminally ill with cancer. She told them about her mother usually being open-minded but so far not accepting her relationship with Karan. She tried to convince them that she was working on her mother, but the fact was that her brother Zoheb too had been swinging like a pendulum. She wanted only to tell the truth because she saw no point in sugarcoating the facts.

After her response, there was deathly silence in the car. Karan's parents were a bit too quiet. They went from warming up to her all afternoon, to a sudden cold stop. After they dropped Zeina at her apartment, Mom started doubting again.

"She is a nice girl. I may have been unnecessarily judgmental about her."

All right, that makes sense, and it was nice to hear, but where is this going? Karan thought.

"But why do you want to be with a girl whose family hates you? Why do you want to do that to yourself? Marriage is between two families, and what she is telling us is that you will only have us, and no one from her side of the family to support you both. What kind of wedding will that be? What kind of family will that be?"

And then she continued on and on about the lineup of nice Hindu girls waiting for Karan in India with wedding garlands in their hands.

Colonel Dev was practical. "Son, I want you to first complete an MBA. I advise you to keep putting pressure on her to ensure that her family accepts you and treats you and us respectfully. I'll be glad to welcome her as our daughter-in-law."

Crap, this had turned into a pissing contest. "We like them if they like us!" How does that help anyone? Matters just got more complicated as egos came into the picture. His parents started their walk on a new path of resistance. They decided that they would accept Zeina only if all her family accepted Karan with open arms. Anyway, he had won his folks halfway, at least.

They didn't want to meet her again on that trip. That was their brilliant way of putting pressure. She was already under a lot of stress from Amma and didn't want to tackle anymore, so she ignored his parents as well.

He drove his parents to Detroit the following weekend. He returned on Sunday and moved back in with Zeina.

Amma was feeling slightly better but had frequent accumulation of water in her lungs, which had to be drained every few days.

Zoheb was living it up as a bachelor and a free man in Singapore. He had to detoxify from his short, ugly marriage. He was a man on a mission and wanted to dump all of his frustrations before he got married again. Singapore was a perfect spot to have fun. His only daily worry was his mother and her health.

12. Atrial Myxoma

"Mom, you look a bit weak; are you feeling all right?" asked Varun.

She was sitting in the porch at sunset, enjoying a cup of tea.

"I have a strange, sinking sensation and feel a bit dizzy, but I get that often; it's nothing unusual. It's probably just general weakness. I think I need those vitamin injections I get once every few years in India."

His mother had barely finished her sentence when he noticed a stream of tea flowing from the left side of her lower lip, down her chin, and onto her chest. She had no sensation that tea was running down her face. Varun didn't want to create panic. He knew that her face was partially paralyzed. Being an ER physician, his hunch was that she was having a stroke or had already had a minor stroke and didn't even know it. He checked her blood pressure and pulse, and it was clear that he had to take her to the emergency room immediately. He told Simran quietly and then calmly asked his mother to get into the car.

"Let's go to the ER and get some tests done to make sure that everything is all right."

Dad came down and saw what was going on. "Everything all right?" he asked with concern.

"Yeah, she is feeling a bit weak and out of breath. We'll take her to the ER and have her checked out."

"Hang on, I'm coming too," he said, and rushed into pants and shoes. He could sense that something was off.

The ER team ran numerous tests but couldn't find anything grossly abnormal. Varun's mother continued to have low blood pressure. The doctors confirmed that she had numbness on one side of her face. Varun recalled that about twenty years ago, while the family lived in Bangalore, she had returned home from her morning walk with left facial paralysis and had been diagnosed with Bell's palsy. As simple-minded as she was, she believed that going from the warm indoors to the cold wind outside had paralyzed her face. The Indian army physicians treated with all sorts of neuro-injections and got her back to normal in a week's time—or at least everyone thought that she was diagnosed and treated correctly.

Varun crossed checked his online medical library to confirm facts: Bell's palsy is a form of facial paralysis. Several other conditions can cause facial paralysis, including brain tumor, stroke, and Lyme disease.

"I have noticed that she has signs of weakness and dizziness, especially when she stands for long hours in the kitchen," said Colonel Dev to Varun.

Could it be Bell's palsy again? Varun wondered.

He refused to sign off on his mother's release from the ER. He was not convinced that the doctors understood her medical condition correctly. He called physicians at surrounding hospitals and got second and third opinions. He asked his neurologist and cardiologist friends to see her and give him their professional opinions, as a favor to him. He sat by her bedside, both as a physician and as a son, all night thinking and researching medical archives, books, and articles on his laptop.

The next morning, his mother's heart rate had dropped even further, and she was not breathing well anymore. It was clear they were losing her, and no one could understand why. She was given intravenous antibiotics, but she got worse. The cardiologist came back and did an ultrasound of her heart. What they found out after a few hours of research was just mind-boggling: inside one of the four chambers of her heart, there was a tumor the size of a golf ball that had many tentacles, like an octopus. One of the tentacles of the tumor was blocking the valve between the two chambers of her heart, which separated the oxygenated blood from deoxygenated blood. Thus, the oxygen level in her blood stream was low. Her heart was trying harder and harder to pump more blood and was getting tired. The tumor had been growing inside her heart for over twenty-five years. That explained why she used to feel dizzy and weak.

The physician told Mrs. Aarti Dev that one in a million people suffer from such heart disease. In medical terms, such a tumor is known as an atrial myxoma. An atrial myxoma is a benign tumor found in the heart, commonly in the upper left or right side. It grows on the atrial septum—the wall that separates the two sides of the heart. The only way to fix it, in this case, was open-heart surgery, which had to be done within a few days.

Mrs. Aarti Dev became a celebrity in the greater Detroit area because such cases are rare. Cardiology students were sent from other hospitals to observe and learn from this case.

Varun called both his brothers and told them about their mother's surgery. Karan left work immediately; he called Zeina, who was at work. Then he quickly packed and started driving to Michigan. Arjun got on a flight from Boston to Detroit within the hour. They arrived at the hospital in less than five hours.

During those five hours, Aarti was prepared for the surgery. She was shown an educational video about open-heart surgery. She had to sign countless forms declaring that if she died on the operating table, the physicians and the hospital were not liable. The forms mentioned that there was a fifty-fifty chance of her surviving this surgery. Even if she survived, there were risks of her having a stroke or paralysis; nothing could be guaranteed. She threw up after seeing the graphic video, where they demonstrated how they cut the ribcage open, took the heart out and placed it in a bowl, made the heartbeat stop, cut it open, fixed it, stitched it, and put it back in the body. Then they jump started the heartbeat again with electric shocks, like recharging the dead battery of a car.

Varun felt that sometimes, such information is far too much for a patient to see. But alas, in the States, given the threat of lawsuits, full disclosure is a necessity. For the same surgery in India, the doctors tell the patient that they'll do a minor procedure, and later, the patient discovers that his chest has been cut open and his heart taken out and then put back in.

At first, Mom trembled with fear. Colonel Dev held her hand throughout the video, fearful of what would happen to his beloved. They had spent over forty grand years of their lives together. He couldn't imagine a life without her, but he also didn't want to see her in pain or incapacitated after the surgery.

"Just have faith. You're in God's hands and have the best surgeons in the world," he said, comforting her.

She gathered herself and put a smile on her face as she saw her two sons walk in. She was already prepped for the surgery and ready to proceed to the operating room.

"I want five minutes with my family," she said to the nurses. "I'd like to see you one by one—alone, please."

First, she spent a few minutes with her husband and told him she dearly loved him, something she rarely did in so many words. She thanked him for being a wonderful friend, husband, and father to her children, and told him mundane things like how much jewelry she had in the bank locker, and what should be done with it. She had saved a bunch of cash in her locker for a rainy day, which he had never known about.

"If I don't make it, make sure you get the children married off in a manner that I would've liked."

He hugged her and held her tightly.

Then she met with Varun. "You're my *Sharvankumar*. The day you were born was the happiest day of my life. When I held you in my arms for the first time, the happiness I felt at that time, I've never felt again. When you were a small child, I used to tell you the story of *Sharvankumar*, a young boy who carried both his blind parents on his shoulders to safety. When I used to ask if you'd do the same for us, you always said, 'First you become blind and then I'll carry you.' You've been a wonderful son to me. Take care of our family and your family-to-be. You've married a nice girl. God gave me three sons, and I always wanted my daughters-in-law to be like my daughters. So now I have one daughter, and I hope to see the day when I get two more. I love you."

Varun had to control his tears.

"Nothing will happen to you. I'll watch every move the surgeons make."

Next was the "black sheep" of the family, the middle child, Karan.

She held his hand and said with a big smile on her face, "Did you know you insisted on being breast-fed for four years, until Arjun was born? You're my cutest, naughtiest, and most handsome son. You've always excelled in everything you've done in life. There is a special spark in you. You did mischief that your brothers never did. I love you."

Karan couldn't contain himself and burst out crying like a little baby.

The final meeting was with Arjun, her baby. She hugged him and kissed him. "You're my baby and always will be. You're a faithful son and always dear to my heart. Work hard in life. Listen to your elder brothers; both of them are wise like your father. Respect and follow their advice. Varun and Karan are both almost settled; I want you to settle soon as well. I'll seek a wife for you if I come out alive."

She was almost sure that she would not survive, but if God would be kind and give her another life, she wanted to do many things differently. The nurses rolled her away into the operating room. Her family stood in a row, holding hands and restraining their tears, looking at her, not knowing what condition she would be in when they saw her next.

The following seven hours felt like seven years. Varun was not permitted to be in the operating room, but he watched from the observation deck. He watched the monitors and the surgery like a hawk, ready to barge into the room if anyone made the slightest error. He came out after the sixth hour and told everyone that her heart was back in her body and had started pumping again. Now they were putting the ribcage back into place and stitching her chest.

Another hour later, she was taken into the recovery room. She was unconscious, but her heartbeat was normal. She regained consciousness after an hour. There were no signs of stroke, and her reflexes and eyesight were okay. Then the hospital staff let the family see her for a few minutes. She was weak and frail from the surgery.

As soon as Karan walked into the recovery room, she asked in a groggy voice, "How is Zeina? I'd like to meet with her when I get home. Can you bring her to me?"

The Painter Man had granted Karan and Zeina's love its second (albeit major) win!

Her heart had to stop and start again in order to accept Zeina, but the *Painter Man* has mysterious ways.

"Varun *Beta*, I gave you life, and today, you gave me life. As I see it, I was dead on that table, my heart had stopped beating," she said with a faint smile.

She took another five days to recover. Varun didn't sleep for those five days; he made sure she recovered under his observation. He knew that a lot could go wrong during the recovery period. She left the hospital in stable condition but had to stay in Detroit for another month to recover fully before traveling to India.

Zeina traveled to Detroit the following weekend. Everyone welcomed her with open arms. No matter what transpired from that point on, it was given that his family was going to support her and Karan's union. It was a happy weekend. Zeina cooked for everyone. They had a lot to drink and celebrated the successful surgery and Zeina's welcome into the family. Mom gave Zeina a beautiful gold ring and some money as a token of her acceptance and love. Colonel Dev gave them his home garden's herbs, including a large bag of dried basil leaves to take back to Canada.

At the border, as always, a friendly Canadian immigration and customs officer welcomed them.

"Anything to declare?" asked the friendly officer.

"No, we bought nothing over the weekend and have nothing to declare."

The customs dog started sniffing, getting excited, and scratching on their car's trunk. The officer's attitude changed entirely; he became unfriendly and curt.

"Could you slowly step out of the car and pop the trunk open? Don't remove anything from the car," he warned sternly.

Two more officers joined the drama. They opened the suitcases and noticed a huge bag with dried green stuff and jumped back in surprise.

"What is this, sir?" asked one the officers in a loud voice.

"It's just dried basil, not marijuana!" shrieked Zeina, all freaked out.

The officer opened the plastic bag, poked his nose inside the bag, and burst out laughing. "It sure smells like spaghetti sauce."

All three officers started laughing and waved them off.

Summer was soon coming to an end. Karan's parents went back to India. Karan resigned to start his first semester at McMaster shortly. He celebrated this new beginning with Zeina at the famous King Eddy Sunday brunch before he resigned. The King Eddy hotel had been good to him. He was granted a handsome bonus because he had achieved all his sales targets. He had saved up enough money and had no need for a student loan, but, since the OSAP loan was interest-free, he still applied for it. He kept his savings in a bank to arbitrage on interest. This time his loan was approved in a week. He wrapped up his apartment, donated most of his belongings to charity, and squeezed the rest into a storage locker in Zeina's apartment building.

He rented a room in a shared student house with eight students near the campus; there were five girls and three other guys in that huge house. With the exception of him, they were all undergraduate students. He was seven years older than the oldest undergraduate in that house, and he had a hard time relating to them. He was there for serious studies, and the rest were there only to party. This was not undergraduate study; this degree was supposed to change his life.

He had a tough time in the first few weeks. He chose to major in finance without realizing that he had not studied math for many years. He was totally out of touch with complex math and calculus. He had to spend four times the effort of the other students to nail down the basic concepts. However, his learning curve was steep and he caught up fast.

A normal day during the first semester entailed walking into a classroom of forty Asians students, mostly Chinese, and a Chinese finance professor, who would fill a gigantic board with strange mathematical symbols and solve the Black–Scholes formula in half an hour, leaving Karan dizzy. The professor would barely leave the room for a water break, and the room would turn into a Chinese fish market. Apparently, all the Chinese students were arguing about whether the sigma or the integration symbol in the corner of the board was correct or not; if it was not correct, who would challenge the professor? Meanwhile, Karan just sat there fretting about how many hours it would take him to understand what that board full of data actually meant.

The first three months were rough; after that, classroom sessions slowly became easier. The Chinese were so darn competitive that they never helped their peers. During the second semester the tables turned on the Chinese students. The second semester was all about teamwork, presentation skills, and writing skills. Almost none of the Chinese students knew what "teamwork" meant. Culturally, they had been taught to think only about themselves. They could not present or write a paper to save their lives. Karan and the other Canadians helped them as much as possible, hoping that they would learn the lesson that being selfish and working in isolation is not how the corporate Western world operates.

Karan came home to Zeina on weekends. He spent most of the weekend studying and a small portion of the time with her. She was considerate and was just glad to have him home. Each week, she prepared ten boxes of delicious meals for him—lunch and dinner for every day of the week. So all he had to do was microwave the food. Since she gave him a wide variety of dishes, he was spared from eating bland food at the university café. She also gave him a hundred dollars a week for pocket money so that he didn't have to dip into his savings account. She took care of him and made sure he had enough time to study. She was the anchor of his life and the lighthouse of his ship.

Amma visited Zeina for two weeks in Toronto. This time, all traces of Karan had to be removed, which was tough, but it got done in time. Of course Karan did not come near the city during that time. Mother and daughter had a lot to talk about and catch up on. Unfortunately, Amma again started putting pressure on Zeina to move on with her life and find a good Muslim boy. She politely told her mother to back off and not bother her with marriage.

Her mother was sad to see her *Butya* so upset. Ultimately, all she wanted was Zeina's happiness. Zeina was happy, but with a guy her mother thought would not be suitable for a long-term relationship. Although Amma liked Karan, she worried that the religious and cultural differences could cause issues down the road. She didn't want her daughter ever to be divorced or to have her grandchildren not know what religious faith they belonged to. Peering into her beloved daughter's sad eyes made her rethink whether what she was doing to Zeina was right. She felt that she had been harsh with her. She questioned herself and wondered whether she actually knew what was best for her daughter. What if Zeina was right in her choice? She was scared of facing the whole of Pakistan and was concerned about what Pakistani society would say.

Amma's own brother had married a German woman and had three children with her. Then, after thirty years of marriage, he turned into a Muslim fanatic and he divorced his loving and dutiful wife. His own half-German kids didn't want to see their father's face. They hated him for trying to impose Muslim fundamentalism on them. She knew many others who married into different cultures and religions whose marriages hadn't worked out. Her mind was playing tricks on her because she also knew of many mixed marriages that did work out, and she also knew of arranged marriages that had not worked out. So what was right, a love, or an arranged marriage with all the right ingredients that society dictates? Her judgment was clouded, but at least she had started reasoning with her conscience. She herself had eloped with a married man she was madly in love with. His existing marriage did not matter at that time; "love" was all that mattered to her, and her decision to marry was based on it. So is it love that matters the most when it comes to deciding who you marry?

Her own son had had an arranged marriage. She had chosen the girl for him, and that hadn't worked out. Long ago, she had also agreed to get her daughter engaged to someone she had chosen and that had turned out to be the wrong choice as well. The more she thought about it, the more she felt she had to do something about it, but she was not ready to give in yet. Each day, she struggled with herself and couldn't come up with the right answer. There were too many mental and social barriers that kept her heart from taking over her thoughts and enabling her to make the right decision.

During the remainder of her stay, she didn't bring up any of these issues. She left her daughter alone and departed on a happy note.

Zeina found the spacious ground floor and basement of a house in the Greentown area for slightly more than what she was paying for her present apartment. This place was almost three times the space she currently lived in. The house was a bit old and run-down, but her wall painting techniques and decorating touches made the place look great in just a week. The house had a small backyard and a broken garage. She loved her new living space. Old Chinatown was just a five-minute walk from the house. She and Karan bought fresh vegetables and fruits there and enjoyed dim-sum every Sunday morning; it became a weekend ritual. The Greektown High Street was just a five-minute walk on the Danforth. It is full of Greek restaurants, bars, pubs, clubs, and grocery stores.

"You know, it is common to hear plates break on weekends when Greeks get together for family dinners. Of course, the restaurant owners are smart enough to keep the plates for breaking separate from the regular dinner plates. Restaurants actually have a plate-break and cleanup charge on the menu," Karan told Zeina.

"You are kidding me!"

Whenever Karan had time on the weekends, he would go out for a movie or a drive with Zeina. Karan discovered that Don Valley Parkway located in the middle of Toronto is one of most beautiful places to experience Torontonian autumn. They used to go on nature walks on the trails in the valley.

One morning, while Zeina was at work and Karan was busy studying, he heard a lot of commotion on the TV in the background—something about a plane crashing into a building. He walked over to the TV in the living room, and his jaw dropped! He saw live coverage of the two planes crashing into the Twin Towers in Manhattan. In the days that followed, the financial markets crashed, which quickly affected Canada as well. "If the States sneezes, Canada catches a cold" is what the world says. Karan would soon be seeking an internship and a job in the financial sector, and he knew that after such financial turmoil, it would be difficult to find decent work.

Zeina made it a point to speak to Karan's family often.
"How is Karan doing?" asked Varun.
"He has everything under control. He is managing well."
"I'm amazed that he is paying for tuition, room, and board all by himself. I recall when he moved to Canada, he had nothing on him. How did he do it? I know after past incidents, he will not reach out to me for financial help. But please, if he has problems or either of you has any financial difficulty, promise me you will let me know."
"I promise. I will let you know, but really, we are both managing well," she told him proudly.

By luck, Zeina found a senior designer position at Outdoor Designs, at a far better salary, but the job entailed designing sports and outdoor clothing, which was new to her.
The hiring manager smiled and told Zeina as she handed her the offer letter, "There is an interesting saying in Canada: 'There is no such thing as bad weather; there is only bad clothing.' Canadians are always out and about in nature throughout the year, so we as outdoor clothing company, do well. We look forward to working with you."
Her new workplace was in Mississauga, which meant that there was no way she could ever take public transport without spending half her life just

commuting and changing trains, streetcars, and buses. Her procrastination came back to bite her. This time, she had to learn to drive, get a license, and buy a car with automatic transmission; and she had to do it within thirty days!

She found a Chinese driving instructor who ran a licensed and authorized driving school. He taught her how to drive an automatic car in two weeks. She passed the written test and then the driving test in one shot. Voilà! When she wanted to do something, she got it done!

Karan scouted the market for a car for her, and after two weeks of browsing, he decided to buy her a Honda CRV. He sold the Saab for a decent price. They dipped into their savings and bought their first car together all in cash. She was proud of her dark-blue CRV. They went to the dealership to sign the purchase papers. He made her drive around the block twice and then left for Hamilton for his evening class. She was frightened of going onto the Gardiner Expressway on her own, but somehow she managed to get over her fears and drove home.

She resigned her current job and had two weeks to practice driving before assuming her new duties. They drove to Mississauga on the weekends so that she could be confident with directions. A few days later, she started her new job, learning to design outerwear and sportswear. Three weeks into the job, the managing director threw a curveball at her. He asked her to go to the factory once every few weeks to meet the production staff. The factory for the company was located in Foymount, Ontario, which really is in the middle of nowhere. The hotel nearest to the factory was forty-five minutes away. She freaked out when she heard that news, but she did not have a choice. A few weeks later, she found herself driving on her own to a village in Ontario, a place most Torontonians would not be able to point out on a map.

She learned fast and progressed well with the organization. She was earning more and was happy with the work environment. The long commute bothered her, but that was a part of life in a big city.

Karan desperately started looking for a three-month internship in the States or Canada, but both economies went down fast after the events of 9/11. Banks laid off staff by the hundreds and thousands. He felt that it is sad that even at multimillion-dollar organizations, the first cuts usually are the free coffee and the summer interns. If they simply laid off one or two unproductive white-haired executives making several million dollars a year, that would take care of free coffee and two dozen summer interns for several decades.

The Ford Motor Company offered Karan an internship in their automotive research department in Oshawa. When he asked about the job description, he was told that he would be evaluating car prototypes to check whether the FM radio button was in the right place or the reading map light was directed properly—something crazy, to that effect. It was deeply depressing to hear such job descriptions. He had not left a decent job and cracked his brains to go through a rigorous MBA in finance only to figure out whether car interiors were designed properly.

He reached out to his network to seek a better option for an internship, but no one provided any real help. It is in such times that one finds out who one's true friends are and what distinguishes them from people who offer only lip service.

One afternoon Baitu called Zeina, informing her that he was going to be visiting Toronto for a day and would like to meet them. Karan also spoke to him and during the conversation told him that he needed an internship.

"Would you like to do an internship with UBS at the Toronto office? I'm almost sure I can arrange something for you, but it might be unpaid."

Karan's heart skipped a beat. It would be a dream come true to enter an investment bank of that caliber—paid or unpaid; it didn't matter.

The following week, he interviewed with UBS, and a week later, he joined the bank as an intern. The group CEO in Canada was a woman. She was kind enough to pay him eighteen dollars an hour, plus time and a half for overtime, which was a tiny drop in her budget, but good financial help for him. He put his heart into his work. His colleagues appreciated his efforts and dedications, and he became good friends with them. Some days he worked sixteen hours. Only a small group of fifteen people worked in that office, and almost every Friday afternoon, the office doors were closed for business at five. The staff bought several cases of beer and drank. They chatted and discussed business and then went home drunk.

After three months, his internship was extended in perpetuity. He committed a minimum of thirty hours a week to work and shifted all his classes to evenings and weekends. He was now working almost full-time and simultaneously attending university full-time. On top of all that, he was commuting between Hamilton and Toronto. His life was tough but rewarding, and it was moving in the right direction. He knew it was imperative to secure a full-time position with UBS; otherwise, upon graduation, judging by the gloomy economic forecast, he might end up at the Ford factory.

Time flew by. Zeina continued to support him every step of the way. He spent quality time with her whenever possible. They went for a cup of coffee or for a drink at a pub on the Danforth in Greektown. Both of them continued to surprise each other with small gifts, cards, and love letters, even though they lived under the same roof and shared the same bed most of the time. They didn't let their busy lives, education, family pressure, or anything else get in the way of their relationship.

13. "Hamara Haramzada Hindu" (H³)

Amma's dear friends Junaid and Alia moved back to Islamabad after living in various countries during his thirty-five years with the Pakistan Foreign Service. Junaid was a prominent Pakistani diplomat. After retirement, they moved temporarily to Islamabad, with plans to move to Toronto where their extended family resided.

Amma held them in deep regard and respected their opinion. She used to visit them in various places across the world. She had special memories of her visit to them in Katmandu, Nepal. Alia was a perfect diplomat's wife and a fine host. Amma found herself spending a lot of time with them. Their only daughter had grown up all over the world and had completed her higher education in the States. While studying for a master's degree, she had met a Caucasian American, had fallen in love with him, and had recently married him with her parents' blessings.

"You're both Pakistani Muslims, yet you handed over your only daughter to a white Christian boy. What made you agree to her marriage? How can you be sure that you made the right decision? Are you certain that she made the right decision for herself?"

Junaid was a mature and intelligent man. He knew where Amma was coming from and what she was trying to address.

"We brought Sofia up to follow her heart and make her own decisions in life. Alia and I provided her the tools to make the right choices. We sent her to the best schools possible. We provided her exposure to all cultures and religions. We gave her our love unconditionally and taught her to love. When she met Adam, instead of questioning her, we actually supported her and reminded her that whatever decision she made must come from her heart and that she should believe in it. She told us time and again that she loved him dearly and couldn't see a life without him. At that time, religion, race, color—nothing mattered to us. We wanted to see our daughter happy, and we knew that she would be happy with the man she loved. As for being sure if this was right for her, we could never be sure. No one can ever be sure. Look around yourself in Islamabad. You'll observe numerous arranged marriages that don't work out. Why is that? Most likely, the marriage lacks true love between the couple. I've been married to Alia for forty years now. I have loved her every day of my life. We have been through significant ups and downs during my diplomatic career. What kept us together is our love for each other."

He smiled and continued, "I know why you are asking all these questions. This is not about Sofia, it's about Zeina. We've known your daughter from the time she was born. You've given her the values, education, and the right tools to make her own decisions. You sent her to Parsons and to live alone in New York. Then, you let her immigrate to Canada. And now you expect her to revert back to you to make the most important decision of her life? My dear Sahar, you can never be sure whether she will make the right choice. Even she can never be sure. Life comes with no guarantees. If she loves someone with her whole heart, and that person loves her the same way, then chances are that they'll make a good life together."

"You're right, this is about Zeina. I'm worried sick about her. I'm confiding in you because I have no one else to turn to and trust for advice. She met an Indian Punjabi boy in New York who now lives in Toronto. I've met him and spent time with him. He is a good boy. I like him, but he is Hindu. There are too many religious differences. What will people say if I let her marry a Hindu? What will happen to my grandchildren's religion? I've already made the mistake of choosing the wrong girl for my son, and now he is divorced. I can't see my *Butya* divorced. God forbid she should have children and then get divorced. I'll never be able to forgive myself."

"You can ask him to convert to Islam if that is really important to you, but I can tell you that will only facilitate the *Nikkah* [Muslim wedding]. Converting will not mean that he will embrace and follow Islam like a born and raised Muslim. That should not matter much to you. All of us are open-minded Muslims. Our son-in-law converted to Islam to satisfy our society, and we were able to keep our head up amongst our peers. But for a minute, put Pakistani society aside; you need to look at it from your daughter's perspective. All your questions and concerns are valid. If her love for this boy is strong, and he loves her just as much, they'll fare well together, and you don't have to be concerned about anything. They'll figure out what to do with their children and their lives during their journey together. All they need is your support and blessings to be happy. The boy is a Hindu Punjabi and your family is Muslim Punjabi; culturally there is not much difference. Sahar, put your mind at ease and think of your daughter's happiness. What's the boy's name, by the way?" he asked.

"Karan, but I call him *Haramzada* Hindu," she responded with a naughty grin and upturned nose.

"*Mashallah* [God has willed it], lovely name, Karan, not *Haramzada* Hindu, that is to be precise. Only you could have come up with that," he said, laughing.

Amma spent a lot of time thinking and analyzing her daughter's situation. She recalled precious memories from the time Zeina was born to the time she left home. She had always trusted Zeina. She had faith in her daughter's choices and maturity. When Amma went on business trips and Zoheb was a teenager, she left the car and liquor cabinet keys with Zeina and not him. She trusted her daughter with bank locker keys and financial papers. She admired her daughter's intelligence, beauty, and talent. She desired to marry Zeina into a comfortable life, but at the same time, she also wanted her to marry a tall, handsome, self-made man. She knew that Karan was almost everything she wanted for her daughter, except that he was an Indian Hindu. What if he converted to Islam? She kept imagining her daughter's tearful, sad eyes and remembered how Zeina had asked her to be left alone and not be bothered with suggestions of other men. She spent countless hours and days putting her thoughts together.

Her own life danced in her thoughts. She had married for love. She had eloped and fought her parents tooth and nail. She had never had a proper wedding and a wedding dress. She wanted to shower her blessings on Zeina and wanted to host a grand wedding and design a most beautiful wedding dress for her daughter. She had started collecting things for her daughter's wedding from the day she was born. She had trunks full of fine fabrics, lots of jewelry, and all sorts of beautiful household things to fill Zeina's home.

Amma tried to open up to her brother Atif without divulging any details about Zeina. All she told him was that Zeina was dating an Indian Hindu. The response she got back was not from her brother, but the Major Atif within him. He retaliated and reminded her. "Baaji [elder sister], are you forgetting what the Hindus did to me while I was their prisoner? I forbid you to let Zeina make such a mistake. Zeina should not even go near him."

As a surprise, Zoheb came from Singapore to visit his mother for a weekend. They went out for dinner together. It was just the two of them dining at the Islamabad Club. They sat on the patio enjoying a candle-lit dinner.

"I'm heartbroken about Zeina. I can't see her being sad anymore. I want to help her, but I'm not able to decide what to do. My heart tells me to believe in her decision. You've been an excellent son to me. I trust your advice. I made a mistake by choosing the wrong girl for you, and now I doubt my own judgment. What would you do if you were in my place?"

Zoheb was taken aback. He never thought that she would relent on H^2. He grinned at her and could see through it all; his divorce from Dumbo had caused Amma to rethink this Muslim boy wedding plan for Zeina.

"I would let her marry him if I were you. I like him. He will keep her happy and take care of her. He has the making of a good friend, a good husband, and a good father," he told her straight out without any hesitation.

There was an awkward silence for a few seconds as they sat looking at each other, deep in their own thoughts. They smiled at the same time.

"I'm ready to speak to her then," she said.

Amma had made her decision. She was convinced that the only thing that mattered to her was her daughter's happiness, and she trusted that Zeina had made the right choice. From that point onward she did not care one bit about what her society or what anyone else thought.

Zoheb extended his phone to her with the number displayed on it, ready for dialing.

Karan and Zeina were in Michigan for the weekend. Zeina answered her phone expecting to hear her brother's voice, but was surprised to hear her mother on the line instead.

"Hi, Mommy, is Zoheb with you? All well?"

"Yes, he surprised me this weekend. We're at the Club and missing you. *Butya*, I have been thinking and thinking and thinking. I've raised you to make good choices in life. If you love Karan and have stuck by him for so long, then he is the right one for you; you know best. I'd like to speak to him and also to his parents about your marriage. Why waste any more time? I've lived on borrowed time for fourteen years, and each day is a gift to me from Allah. If everyone can agree, the wedding should take place this very year." She said all that happily and without any hesitation.

Zeina dropped to her knees. She hadn't thought this day would come so easily. Her mother had come around just as she had wished and dreamed.

"Thank you, Mama," she whispered.

Zoheb put the speakerphone on. "You can thank me as well. I'd like to say that I had something to do with this good news!"

"What about the Haramzada part? Are you still going to call him H-squared?" Zoheb asked his mother jokingly.

She went a bit red in the face. "I never said that."

"Yes, you did!" said Zoheb and Zeina together.

"Well, I was just angry then. Now he is *Hamara Haramzada* [Our Bastard] Hindu!" She laughed.

"Awesome. So, now he has moved on from H^2 to H^3." Zoheb giggled.

In an instant, all the anger and anguish of several years had transformed into love and acceptance. Karan was a part of their family from that point on.

"Will he convert for the *Nikkah*?" Amma asked politely.

"He is a reasonable person. He told me long ago that he would."

"When can I speak to him and his parents?"

"You can speak to him tomorrow morning. I'll ask him to call you. He will arrange for a conference call with his parents."

"How is he? Is he still fond of his *chaat papdi, tikkis,* and *gol gappas*?" she asked affectionately.

"Oh, yes he is. His taste buds will never change, just like yours. He is working at UBS and wrapping up the final semester of his MBA," she told Amma proudly.

"Tell him to get ready for some pampering soon. We have to make up for lost time."

That was Karan and Zeina's final victory!

Zeina went down to the living room and shared the news with Karan. They were beyond happy and stood silently gazing at each other for a few minutes with beaming faces. It all seemed unreal. It was a dream that had come true. Karan was stunned by how smoothly and miraculously Amma had accepted them.

The next morning Karan called Amma.

"*Salaam alaikum* [Peace be unto you], Amma," he said, sounding formal.

"*Wa-Alaikum Salam beta*; may God bless you." After a pause, she said, "Zeina told you about my conversation with her? Please don't hold anything against me, *beta*. I did what a mother had to do, but you both passed the test. I'm willing to hand my beloved daughter to you. How are you? I miss you."

That was the happiest he had ever heard her. She sounded totally at ease and content with her decision. They joked around a bit. She teased him for having long arms and how difficult it would be to find clothes and suits to fit him for the wedding.

"I'd really like the wedding to take place this year in Toronto. September will be perfect weather for it, and it gives me enough time for the preparations. If possible, later we can host receptions in both India and Pakistan. When can I speak to your parents? Are your parents happy with Zeina?"

"I'll arrange for a call tomorrow. My parents have accepted her wholeheartedly. I had my own challenges with them, but all that is in the past. I am sure they'll have no problem with a wedding in Canada."

Karan spoke to Amma for a long time. He held nothing against her, because he knew that she had done her duty as a mother and was making sure that her daughter was doing what was right.

The parents spoke for the first time on a conference call the following day. Everyone was courteous and formal. His parents reiterated to Amma that in their hearts, Zeina was their daughter-in-law already. After debating a little about the wedding venue, they mutually consented to host the wedding in Toronto. At that time, it was almost impossible for Indians to go to Pakistan and vice versa. The two countries were on the brink of a nuclear war. Military troops were deployed on the Himalayan border near Kashmir and live firing occurred daily, keeping the tension high. Toronto presented itself as a safe common ground for the guests from all parts of the world.

Karan started researching what being a Muslim really meant. He read a few books and researched articles online. The more he read, the more he got confused. He had taken theology classes in college, and none of them made any sense. This was the case with every religion he had ever tried to understand. He simplified what he read and wrote down what he believed in:

1. He believed there is one supreme power, that is, one God. He feared only one thing, which was God.
2. He believed that it was important to be a good human being and to love and respect others, no matter how different they were, or what they believed in.
3. He believed that God has empowered humans to use common sense and distinguish between right and wrong actions. Thus, it was up to all people to use that skill to live their lives.

It dawned on him that these three principles were common to all religions. The fundamental principles of Islam focused on the same ideas. So that is where religion began and ended for him. Based on these simple beliefs, technically he was already a Muslim. So how do you convert when you already believe in one God?

Then, he called a dozen mosques, and only one, a Turkish mosque, returned his call. The Imam asked him to bring a Muslim man as a witness, repeat the *Kalma* [Islamic prayer] three times with the right intent, and he could become a Muslim.

Karan spoke to a Muslim colleague at work who was most grateful for this honor. Apparently, facilitating a Muslim conversion gave him a guaranteed premium ticket to heaven.

"*Snuggle*, I've decided to convert to appease everyone. I know your mother has not forced me to, but I want to do this for your family. This way, we can have a Muslim ceremony, and a Hindu ceremony, and everyone can be pleased. I did a lot of thinking and research, and I'm fine with the conversion."

"Thank you, *Jaani*. Thanks for being so accommodating," she said, kissing him.

She called her brother, and his first question was, "Is he really going to convert, like in getting circumcised as well?"

Karan heard him on the speakerphone and said, "Don't push your luck, Zoheb!"

Then they called Amma to discuss the conversion and *Nikkah*.

"So, are you considering adopting a Muslim name?" she asked. She was happy that he was going to help keep her head up in the Pakistani society.

"Sure, I'll add a Muslim twist to my name as a middle name, but I won't change it officially. I was thinking about Qutubuddin," he said, suggesting a ridiculous historic name to her with a serious tone in his voice.

"No way. You are better off not taking a Muslim name rather than such a boring name."

"How about Aurengzeb?" he asked, trying to pull her leg a bit more. Then he said in a serious tone, "It will be Ibrahim."

"A bit boring, but it works," she said. She seemed happy.

Karan visited the Turkish mosque with his colleague and half an hour later returned with an actual certificate. His colleague gave him a white prayer bead, a prayer rug, and the Imam gave him a Quran as a gift.

"Amma just called; she wanted to know if you converted at a Sunni Mosque or a Shia Mosque," Zeina said in frenzy.

"I have no idea. The certificate says I am a Muslim; it says nothing about Sunni or Shia. I believe in one God. Is that not good enough? Life is too complicated anyway. Why do we human beings make it even more complicated? Well, I declare I'm a Sunni Muslim, or whatever that means, to appease all."

Amma had new life blown into her! She was like the Energizer Bunny, running around taking care of wedding preparations. She started designing a wedding dress, jewelry, and gifts for people. She came up with unique decoration ideas for the evening events, designing the wedding invitations, creating guest lists, and so on. Her daily life was all about wedding planning.

She called often to ask questions about what Zeina wanted and liked and then most of the time chose something that she herself liked. Zeina let her mother have the pleasure of taking matters in her own hands, and of doing all these things the way she wanted. Her mother slowly started telling close friends and closest family about her daughter's upcoming wedding in September. Some of her friends were happy and others were jealous because they had unmarried daughters ten years older than Zeina still looking for "good Muslim boys." Then there were others who were plain curious about how she had accepted an Indian Hindu.

She cared only about people who supported her decisions. She couldn't care less about the remainder of society anymore. She had lived her life to the fullest and made a place for herself in a society, which ordinarily would not let a widow live in peace, let alone progress professionally and prosper. She had proven everyone wrong. This was her time to be happy, and she wanted to include people around her who were truly happy for her.

She spent hours going through Zeina's trousseau, which she had collected for years, rummaging through huge steel trunks and closets full of clothes, fabrics, bedsheets, and kitchen sets. She used to sit in her favorite chair and order around the house help to open suitcases and trunks, arrange things, and then rearrange them again to perfection.

She kept humming Punjabi wedding songs and loved to hear one song in particular, "*Mahalon ka rajah mila, ke raani beti raaj karaygee* [Found a king with palaces; my lovely daughter will now rule as a queen]."

14. "Amma Wins"— "Cancer Loses"

It was early April, and Toronto was still freezing cold.
"Where is Zeina? She is not answering her phone!" Zoheb asked Karan, sounding stressed and upset.

"She's probably in a meeting with her phone on silent. Is everything all right?"

"Amma is unwell. She has a lot of fluids accumulation in her lungs; too soon after all that chemo she just received. I'm flying to Islamabad to bring her to Singapore. Please tell Zeina not to worry. I'll call you later today." He hung up in a rush.

Cancer was taking over Amma's body. Her immune system was becoming weaker, and chemo was not helping anymore. She was visiting the cancer clinic every other day to have fluids drained from her lungs, and each time the physicians extracted a few liters. She patiently waited for her son to arrive.

Zoheb was surprised to see her so calm. She was in pain and yet had a smile on her face. She looked happy, peaceful, and beautiful. He discovered that her daughter's upcoming wedding was the best medicine God could have given her. He also noticed that the house looked different. She had covered all the furniture with old bedsheets and packed all her clothes in suitcases and metal trunks. She had a lot of papers scattered on her study table, including a handwritten will.

"What's all this?" he asked.

"I'll not be around forever. I'm living on bonus time. You and I both know that. I'm making sure that everything is in order in case something does happen to me. You need to know about the house, car, bank locker, jewelry, and everything I own. You need to know what to do after I'm gone." She said all that pleasantly.

He didn't want to look at anything or discuss anything with her about such a horrifying subject. He simply didn't want to even think in that direction.

That evening, she called all her dear friends. One by one, she met everyone. They all brought small gifts. She also had a surprise gift for everyone. She had a lot of unfinished tasks for Zeina's wedding, which she assigned to her trusted friends. The wedding dress was still at the designer's, and the jeweler had a few things that he was still working on. She paid the household helpers two months' salary in advance and asked her driver to fill up the car with a full tank of petrol. Her behavior seemed odd, but Zoheb didn't question anything.

The following morning, they flew to Singapore. Zoheb flew her business class so that she would be as comfortable as possible. The physicians in Singapore conducted many tests. The results showed that the cancer had spread to her vital organs. The physicians called Zoheb into the room and told him that, although they could try some intense chemo that could have some serious side effects, it was estimated that she had at best three to six months to live. In their opinion, chemo could not help anymore.

Zoheb became angry with them. He yelled and said, "Try something else! I'm sure there is a way. Is there an alternative treatment? We are willing to try anything."

The chemotherapist sympathized with him, and, upon Zoheb's insistence, he started a higher dosage of chemo. The chemo was so strong that Amma threw up immediately after each treatment and was constantly in pain. After all, chemo is poison that was being pumped into her to kill fast-growing cells. The physicians prescribed heavy painkillers to reduce her pain, and those made her drowsy and dizzy.

"Amma has little time left with us now. I'm trying everything I can. You need to come as soon as possible," Zoheb told Zeina, choking back tears.

Their worst nightmare was becoming a reality. Her cancer had been a constant threat all their lives.

"She wants to witness your wedding. I suggest you speak to Karan and his family. I suggest that all of you come to Singapore, and we can arrange for a wedding in her presence. Most likely, she is not going to make it till September."

Zeina became hysterical, crying and screaming incoherently.

"Stay calm. Just like she has been our pillar for all these years, we have to be her pillar now. She needs to see your happy and smiling face. You'll be surprised that in spite of all the pain, she seems to be happy and at peace. Your marriage has a lot to do with it."

Zeina put on a brave face and spoke to Amma for several hours that day and kept the conversation as pleasant as possible and kept Amma's excitement going for the wedding.

Karan immediately had a word with his parents and siblings. His parents called Amma right away.

"We'll arrange for the wedding in Singapore as soon as possible. I'll look into visas and travel arrangements right away," promised Colonel Dev.

Everyone agreed to pick a wedding date as soon as visas and tickets could be arranged. All family members started working on the logistics of how best to arrange for a last-minute wedding. Karan figured that he could leave for Singapore right after his final exams, which were coming up in another week. The next morning, Zeina gave a heads-up at work that she would leave work for an extended period as soon as she got a Singapore visa to take care of her terminally ill mother.

The following day, Friday, Zoheb called again. "Amma is deteriorating fast. I need your help here; just come and spend time with her."

Zeina decided to take a sabbatical from work immediately. She decided to tell her boss after the weekend when the office opened. She had decided simply to quit if her employer gave her any grief at all about taking time off.

Karan started looking into arranging a visa and airline ticket for Zeina. He found out that, with a Pakistani passport, a Singapore visa took at least a week. Only after the visa was issued could an airline ticket be purchased.

Zeina was nervous and extremely sad. Karan didn't leave her alone for a minute and comforted her all weekend.

On Sunday afternoon, Zoheb called again. "Amma had to be hospitalized. Her body is not responding to medications, and she is having difficulty breathing. I need you to get on the next plane." He was crying on the phone.

"I need a week to even get a visa, and only then I can buy a ticket. How can I get on the next plane?" Zeina asked, sobbing hysterically.

"The Pakistani ambassador in Singapore is Amma's old friend. He'll arrange for a visa on arrival for you."

"But I need a visa before I can even board a plane. That is what we were told by a travel agent this morning."

"In that case, I'll expedite a visa and fax a copy of it to you. Just show the fax to the agent to buy a ticket. I've got to go for now. You look into a ticket right away, and I'll look into the visa. Let's speak in half an hour."

Karan frantically started calling agents. All travel agencies were closed for the weekend, and post-9/11, online tickets for international flights couldn't be bought less than forty-eight hours in advance, especially if the ticket was one way. He tried every travel website and all airline websites. The only solution was to purchase a ticket by using frequent flier miles, since that booking process had some flexibility in bookings for emergencies. Neither Karan nor Zeina had enough miles, not even combined between the two of them. Karan called Varun to see if he had enough miles even for a one-way flight. Varun didn't have enough miles for an international fight either, but between him and Simran they had enough miles for a one-way flight. All family members started calling frequent flier customer service to see if miles could be combined, but it was Sunday, and even the Continental Airlines customer service call center was closed. It was a hopeless situation.

Karan suggested that they drive to the airport and inquire directly at airline ticketing counters to see whether a ticket could be purchased right there. Meanwhile, Zeina started packing. Just as they were about to leave the house, Zoheb called back. Karan explained the complications with airlines and bookings. Zoheb had accumulated enough miles with his frequent international travel. He gave Karan his miles details and his online password. Within minutes, Karan was able to secure a ticket for an 11:00 p.m. flight that night.

"What number should I fax the visa to?" asked Zoheb.

"Send it to the Novotel in Mississauga; my classmate is the executive chef there, and it's located next to the airport. I'll pick up the visa and then drop Zeina off at the airport."

Karan quickly looked up the fax number on his PalmPilot.

Time flew by that afternoon. They drove to the Novotel. Thankfully, the visa was waiting at the front desk of the Novotel.

Karan dropped her at the airport. He gave her a big hug and a kiss and asked her to be brave. "I love you, *Snuggle*. I'll be there right after my exam next week."

Zeina had cried all afternoon, and her eyes were red and swollen. She gave her mobile phone to him because it would be of no use on the trip. She didn't have an international roaming plan. Zoheb needed to reach Karan often in Toronto, so it was better for him to keep it.

He waved good-bye to her and kept looking at her through the thick, double-paned glass doors until she vanished into the crowd of travelers.

Karan drove home feeling completely empty and helpless. He wished that he could do something more for Zeina. She had a tough flight schedule. The flight was from Toronto to Newark; Newark to Tokyo, with an eight-hour stopover in Tokyo; and then Tokyo to Singapore. She would be traveling thirty-plus hours. Karan called Zoheb to let him know that she was on her way.

On Monday morning, Karan went to work as usual. After work he went for a haircut. While he was in the barber's chair, Zoheb called. He sounded broken and devastated.

"Amma is on life support. She won't make it. She's just hanging on for Zeina to arrive, and then the physicians will take her off the ventilator. She's peacefully asleep in front of me, and she is in no pain."

Tears rolled down Karan's cheeks. Johnny, the barber, stopped and stepped away to fetch him a glass of water. Johnny had been cutting Karan's hair for three years and knew something serious had just happened in Karan's life.

"I'm so sorry, Zoheb. May God give you the strength to get past this difficult time. I wish I was with you."

"Where do you think Zeina has reached?"

"She should be about to land in Tokyo or already in Tokyo."

"Don't tell her anything if she calls you."

"I promise I won't."

Karan took a few minutes to recover from the shocking news. He skipped his evening classes. He called his parents in India and brothers and informed them. Everyone was extremely sad, and they prayed to God to help both brother and sister get past what was about to come their way with the least possible pain.

Zeina called Karan from the Tokyo airport. She sounded exhausted and tense. He didn't utter a word about Amma.

"I'll call Zoheb and let him know that you are in Tokyo. You don't need to call him. He is attending to Amma and cannot take calls right now. He calls me every few hours to keep me posted. He told me that airport services will receive you right at the gate when you come out of the aircraft and will help fast-track your exit."

Zeina took a shower at the Tokyo airport and changed her clothes. The stopover was too long for her. She was anxious to get to Singapore.

Zoheb came to meet her at the airport. They shared a tearful, tight hug. Both had red and puffy eyes from long hours of crying and no sleep. He held her hand tightly and told her that their mother was waiting for her, and that she was going to have only a few moments with her. After that, the physicians would take her off the ventilator. He was essentially letting her know in the simplest and most gentle way possible to be prepared to witness their mother's death.

"Amma is in deep sleep and on a ventilator. She's hanging on and waiting for you. The physicians are not sure whether she can hear or will open her eyes when you see her, but I know that she can hear us. I've been talking to her for the past several hours."

Zeina almost fainted when she heard what her brother told her. She felt that the earth below her feet had moved. She could not believe what was happening. It was a living nightmare. She had come prepared to spend several weeks with her mother, and now she realized that she would only have a few moments with her. She was not ready for this. She had been dreading this event all her life, and now it was right in front of her. She held herself together. Zoheb helped her walk to the car as fast as she could. She wanted to get to her mother as soon possible and not waste another second.

The two of them entered a large, cold, dimly lit room with many small red and green LED lights and medical gadgets. Zeina saw Amma lying covered under blankets on a bed. In the background was the regular beeping of machines and the sound of Amma's mechanical breathing though the ventilator.

She sat by Amma and gently held her hand with the IV drip in it. She poured her heart out to her mother. She told her how much she loved her. She told her how much she meant to her. She told Amma not to worry about her and that she would be all right. She promised that she would take care of Zoheb.

She thanked her for being the perfect mother and for giving them such a wonderful upbringing. She hoped to make her proud always. She asked for forgiveness for any pain she had caused her and spoke to her about how special her mother had made her feel all her life and how lucky she was to have her in her life. She told her how many special memories she had with her.

After talking to Amma for an hour, Zeina became quiet for a second to catch her breath. Amma took a deep breath. She opened her eyes gently. She looked at Zeina and then at Zoheb and closed her eyes forever. The heart monitor indicated that her heart had stopped.

Zoheb and Zeina looked at each other and slowly laid their heads on their mother's chest. The physicians and nurses rushed in to see what was going on. Recognizing that the patient had passed away, and her two children were resting on her, the staff quietly left them. After ten minutes, Zoheb and Zeina got up to walk away from her body.

Amma had not let the physicians stop the ventilator. She departed when she was ready. She left her body after she had met and touched her *Butya*, and heard her. They knew that Amma was not in that body anymore, but she was in that room. They felt the strong and happy presence of her soul—a laughing, giggly presence. They knew that she was relieved of the body that had given her so much pain and agony for so many years. They knew that she was in a better place. Both were sure that she knew they loved her, and both also knew that her aura would always be around them to love and protect them.

Fourteen years ago, it had been disclosed to Amma that she did not have much of a chance to live long. Zeina was thirteen years old then, and Zoheb had just turned eighteen. She had fought cancer for fourteen years. She brought up her children as a single mother. She gave them the best education at Brown and Parsons. She did better than any set of parents could have done for their children. She never let cancer get the better of her. She lived every day to the fullest, traveled all over the world, ate what she wanted, and did what she wanted.

Amma beat cancer to death every day.

After an intense, internal struggle, she had overcome reservations about her daughter marrying an Indian Hindu, a major victory for her. Her last wish of attending their wedding in person couldn't be completely fulfilled, but her blessings were with them.

We are all born free of biases and prejudice. Somewhere along the way we embrace religion and social norms, and we gather prejudice against others. Blessed are the ones who are able to free themselves of all such biases before their life's journey comes to an end. Amma was one of those fortunate ones. As she freed herself from all prejudice, she felt a mountain of pressure lift off her shoulders, and she left this world as pure as she had come into it.

Amma had won; cancer had lost.

Zoheb and Zeina came back to the apartment and let the physicians complete what they had to do with the body.

Zeina found Amma's handbag in the bedroom. Amma never, ever left the house without her handbag. She had been hospitalized many times before, but she had always taken her handbag with her. This was the first time she hadn't taken it along. She knew that this was going to be her last visit to a hospital.

Zeina examined the contents of the handbag. Each item reminded her of her mother's peculiarities. The bag had a sweet smell of *paan* and *supari*, something that Amma loved munching on. The *paanwalla* in Islamabad had her *paans* prepared for her every day sharp at 9:00 p.m. He looked forward to Amma coming to pick up the *paans*. Amma had stuffed various currencies in her bag. There were Pakistani rupees, Singapore dollars, and US dollars. In the side pocket was her favorite, small, brown notebook with telephone numbers and addresses. Zeina couldn't help but hug the bag and lie down with it on the bed, going over precious memories of her mother. It would take her a lifetime to accept that their mother was gone.

Zoheb poured himself a tall glass of whiskey with ice to calm his nerves. He rested for a few minutes to gather his thoughts and called Karan. To Karan's surprise, both of them were calm and stable on the phone, and they felt strong, positive, and ready to face the world. They had their emotional times, though—times when both of them felt feeble, vulnerable, and completely broken apart.

Zoheb then called their nearest and dearest family and friends.

Amma's body had to be transported to Islamabad for the burial. She wanted to be buried next to her husband, and she had reserved her spot long ago. Their friends in Singapore got to work on taking care of all formalities for the coffin to be transported by air. Other family members in Islamabad arranged for the coffin's arrival and other burial arrangements.

"I have to be with you in Pakistan. I want to be with you for the burial. How can I get a Pakistani visa?" pleaded Karan.

"Uncle Junaid will arrange an emergency visa for you. We're leaving tomorrow morning for Islamabad. I don't think you can make it in time for the burial, but whatever day you get there, we need you with us."

Karan told his parents and brothers that Amma had passed away, and all of them called to offer condolences.

The Pakistani consulate in Toronto approved a visitor visa within twenty-four hours, which was unheard of, since it normally takes six months for an Indian to get a Pakistani visa. Uncle Junaid personally called the Pakistani ambassador in Ottawa for this favor. The visa clerk was a jerk, though; he was shocked that this Indian was granted a visitor visa within one day because he had a special drawer where he kept all visa applications from Indian citizens to rot for eight weeks before faxing them to Pakistan for a security clearance. He made sure Karan waited for at least eight hours, although the approved visa papers were sitting right in front of him. During the waiting period, Karan arranged for tickets on the phone with a Sri Lankan travel agent whom he knew.

Only a few days ago when Amma had departed Islamabad, in her heart she was sure that she was not coming back there alive. That is why she had said her last good-byes to all her friends and given them parting gifts. She had filled the car with a full tank of petrol because she knew her children would have far too many things to do arranging her burial. She even had white *salwar kameez* washed and ironed, waiting for her children in their closets, because she knew they would need them for her funeral.

Zoheb and Zeina saw the white clothes hanging and waiting for them and couldn't contain themselves in missing their mother. They loved her so much.

Amma's funeral was attended by hundreds of people: foreign diplomats, Pakistani diplomats, politicians, Amma's friends, family from across the country, tradesmen, workers, and domestic help. Every person she had met in her life, whose heart she had touched, came to pay their last respects. She was buried next to her husband as she desired.

For the first three days after the funeral, the house was full of people. On the fourth day, the majority of the people left. By the time Karan arrived, almost all the people had gone. Zoheb and Zeina met him at the Islamabad airport with hugs, kisses, and tears. Karan held back his emotions.

65 West 55th Street

Zoheb drove him to the graveyard, where Karan had a few minutes alone with Amma. He had never had a chance to say good-bye to her. She came into his life like a sandstorm and left like a gentle breeze. His interaction in person with her was pleasant for the few days they spent together in Annapolis. After that, she grew angry with him about dating Zeina. Near the end of her life, Karan spoke to Amma every day for a few days. She had left him her daughter, her most precious possession, to take care of. He swore at her grave that he would always love Zeina, protect her, and take care of her and treat her like a princess, just as she wanted her daughter to be treated.

"I'll miss you," said Karan.

He walked back to the car in silence. They drove home in complete silence. As soon as Karan was in the guest bedroom, he cried like a baby. He was consoled by Zoheb, who heard him weeping. Karan felt Amma's presence all around him. He was sad that she was not able to see her daughter as a bride and him as a groom.

Zoheb took Karan to the nearest police station to get him registered, because Karan had a police reporting visa. He was supposed to show up to the police station every day, and then get a final exit stamp on his last day in Pakistan. That was going to be a major pain, but a hundred rupees to the clerk who registers foreigners was enough to enter his hypothetical presence each day. So he just had to show up on the last day for an exit stamp. It was nice to see that the British had left equal corruption in all the nations they ruled. The process in India is similar for Pakistanis with reporting visas.

The second day in Islamabad, Karan requested the house helper to give him a white *salwar kameez* to wear. They found an old one of Zoheb's, which was washed and ironed. It was old and had a tear on the right pocket. One of Amma's dear friends noticed the tear and felt embarrassed. For her, Karan was not just her friend's son-in-law-to-be, he was Pakistan's son-in-law-to-be, and he was wearing torn clothes!

The word spread that Karan was wearing old, torn clothes. That evening, and the following morning every hour or so, a car pulled up the driveway with a driver or one of Amma's friends who came with a brand-new *salwar kameez* for Karan. By the end of the day, he had almost two dozen of them.

The next two days, the trio was invited for breakfast, lunch, and dinner by extended family and friends. They were never left alone. They didn't get much time to be sad or to think much.

Karan noted some interesting facts about Pakistanis. They generally kept cleaner and better-decorated homes than Indians. Most Indians live a simple life and do not believe in decorating their homes with expensive carpets and paintings. One thing Pakistanis didn't have a clue about was how to cook vegetables, though they did serve the most amazing meat dishes.

Pakistanis were curious to meet Karan.

"*Hai*, he's such a nice person. He's just like us! He speaks like us, and he behaves like us," said some of the aunties. They behaved as though they expected Karan to have two horns on his head or a spring in his neck like the typical image of an Indian who nods his head and one cannot tell if that head nod means "yes," "no," or "maybe."

"Of course he is like us," Zeina said. "He's a Punjabi as well. His mother is from Deragazi Khan, and his father and grandfather were both born and raised in Pindi."

Karan was treated well in Islamabad and welcomed by everyone with open arms. Never once did anyone ask about his religion or discuss politics or cricket. He was made to feel at home.

Kamran aunty, popularly known as "Kammo," originally from Lucknow in India, could not stop her show-off session. Apparently, her husband had accumulated enough wealth for the next six generations, but she would not stop talking about all they had left behind in India at the time of the partition between the two countries.

"*Beta*, we have had to make a new life for ourselves in Pakistan when we moved after the partition. We live modestly here, but back in India we used to have acres of '*Pudhinay ke baagh*' [mint gardens], and many other agricultural businesses."

Karan kept a straight face during the name-dropping and show-off session of Kammo aunty. He was used to such petty conversations from dealing with his extended Punjabi family in India, where the only one measure of success is "prosperity."

After leaving Kammo aunty's "minipalace," Karan could not stop laughing.

"You know that mint grows almost wild in India. Why the heck was she bragging about acres of mint gardens?"

"Oh, let her be—in one ear, out the other. She used to say crap like that to Amma as well. Wish you could've heard some of Amma's insults about her mint garden bragging. She never cared about her name-dropping and her wealth. Amma just cared for her friendship."

A lot had to be done to make arrangements for Amma's home, belongings, and bank accounts. Zoheb and Zeina were not ready for such tasks.

Karan and Zeina wanted to buy a townhouse or a house soon in Toronto. They didn't want to sell the family's classic solid wood furniture. Uncle Junaid was moving to Canada in a few months, and he was going to import his furniture. So, instead of one container, he offered to send two containers and move all their furniture as well.

Zoheb sold Amma's car and also found a buyer for the house. Both brother and sister had to appear in court for her to grant permission to Zoheb to sell the house. What a drama that was. The judge wanted to make sure that Zeina had not been coerced into giving permission to Zoheb to sell the house.

The issue was that the judge spoke hardcore Urdu and somewhat mumbled in his mouth. He first asked for Zeina's name. Then he asked, "*Zaat* [caste]?"

"Muslim," Zeina said confidently.

The judge had an amused look on his face and repeated his question, speaking slowly to make sure Zeina understood his question.

Zeina asked, "*Choudhury* [feudal lords]?"

He shook his head in utter dismay and disbelief.

Zoheb tried to prompt, but the judge shot him a harsh look, warning him not to interfere.

After a few attempts, Zeina finally came up with, "*Gujjar* [shepherds]," which seemed to satisfy the judge.

Then he asked her about her father's name and some more details, to which Zeina kept saying, "What?" and "*Pher se boleyae* [Say that again, please]," making him go red in the face with anger because he had to repeat each question two or three times.

The judge finally gave up on Zeina and just asked in broken English in a thick Pakistani accent, pointing to Zoheb, "You give, permission brother, sell house, your will? No pressure?"

"No pressure at all, Your Highness. I give him the power of attorney of my own free will," Zeina told him. And that settled the matter.

All matters got resolved, and they had one day before the flight to Singapore. Karan and Zeina had agreed to spend a week with Zoheb in Singapore so he didn't feel lonely, and that time would also give the three of them a chance to bond as a family.

On the last day in Islamabad, Zoheb drove them up in the hills to show Karan some more of Pakistan. He first stopped at Faisal Mosque and then drove up to Muree and Bhurban, beautiful hill stations near Islamabad. They stopped at a roadside restaurant in Bhurban and had the best *kadai chicken* ever! The cook put juliennes of ginger, blanched tomatoes, and sliced lemons in the *kadai*.

Karan took lots of photographs as they walked around in the beautiful mountains. The cold weather and low-lying clouds of Muree reminded him of Shimla and Mussorrie in India. These were all hill stations established by the British during their rule; thus the overall look, feel, and structure of these small villages and towns in the mountains were similar.

On their way back they stopped by to say good-bye to Amma at her grave.

15. Healing

On the flight home, Zoheb asked Zeina, "Can you sleep in separate rooms in my house?"

They promised to honor his simple request.

The next few days provided excellent bonding time for the three of them. There were times when the brother and sister broke down, but then they had Karan to console them.

The three of them tried to keep themselves occupied. They did some sightseeing. They visited the Singapore Zoo, the Botanical Gardens, the Night Safari, Santosa Island, Little India, Chinatown, and much else the beautiful island had to offer.

Zoheb went back to work the fourth day. Zeina and Karan still had three more days in Singapore. When the time came for them to go back to Toronto, Zoheb was sad to see them go.

"Amma's last wish was that you get married this year. It's my desire to see that her last wish is fulfilled. I want the marriage to happen in Toronto as planned in September," requested Zoheb.

Zeina was far removed from the thought of her wedding at the moment. It really didn't matter anymore. It would not be the same. She thought a lot about it, and she knew that their mother would have wanted her properly married that year. She agreed to discuss it with Karan's family, and to continue with the plans after she settled back in Toronto. The responsibility of the wedding planning was now up to Karan and Zeina.

They returned to Toronto and got back into their daily routines.

Zeina wanted to begin working on the wedding planning, but her heart was just not in it. Karan tried to help by setting up an outline of what was to be done, and by putting a timeline together to get her excited. But it was not helping.

She began suffering from mild depression after the loss of her mother. She was not able to express her grief fully. She got upset for no apparent reason. She did not like to meet anyone for days. She went to work because she had to, but she was not able to perform well.

Karan was worried about her mental state. There was so much to do before the wedding. He still had one more semester before graduation. They had to buy a house and plan for a Punjabi wedding, which meant a five-day affair where hundreds of people were expected from around the world. Karan couldn't get Zeina motivated. In fact, they started arguing and fighting about petty matters.

"*Snuggle*, you need to seek professional help."

She got even angrier. "Are you suggesting that I'm mad or gone crazy?"

"No, honey. God, no! I love you, and I do not mean that at all. All I'm suggesting is that you are not able to speak to me about what you are going through. So how about you speak to someone who can help you with your current circumstances and guide you. I feel helpless myself. I want to help you, but I'm not trained to aid in such matters."

Finally, after weeks of Karan's pleading with her, Zeina visited a psychiatric social worker. She didn't want to be treated as a clinical patient by a psychiatrist.

What came out of the discussions was rather interesting: Zeina just needed to grieve. She couldn't really understand why life was so unfair, and why her mother had to die.

The social worker patiently listened and let Zeina grieve. She helped Zeina to reexamine life in an optimistic way, and to count her blessings. That helped her be positive about the present. She guided Zeina in shifting her negative energy, channeling her positive energy, and focusing on her upcoming marriage, and mainly fixing her relationship with Karan.

In just two weeks of meeting with the social worker, Zeina was able to overcome her mild depression. She felt that she had renewed positive energy. She was ready to face the world again and take on new challenges in life.

In spite of the professional help, Zeina did go through a roller-coaster ride of emotions for the first eight weeks. She felt Amma's presence often.

One night, Karan was sitting with her at the dining table, and she was silently weeping, missing her mother.

"How will I know she is all right? How will I know that she is in a better place? Amma's life wasn't complete without attending our wedding."

Right then, there was a flash of blue light that zipped across the room, followed by a gentle breeze from nowhere that made the dining room curtain move!

Karan rushed to examine what happened. The stove knobs were shut tight, there was no smell of gas, and no windows open to let in any breeze. The blue light and the breeze were extremely mysterious. He looked at Zeina, and she smiled. They knew that it was indeed Amma in spirit, trying to respond to her apprehensions and questions.

Another unique incident occurred a few weeks later. While sitting on the living room couch, Zeina was craving her mother's touch, and terribly missing her. Karan pointed to Amma's battery-operated teddy bear key ring. The key ring hanging on the door knob was flashing its colorful lights! Normally it flashed its lights only if shaken vigorously. No one had touched it or moved the door, and the lights were flashing.

Zeina squeezed Karan's hand. They were convinced that Amma was with them in spirit again, trying desperately to convince them that she was all right.

Finally, Zeina was ready to move on and plan her wedding, just as Amma had wanted.

Karan and Zeina explored established and new housing communities to buy a home.

They also looked at numerous venues for the *Mehndi* [henna] and wedding reception. It was obvious that finalizing the venues and purchasing a home were not going to be easy decisions.

After weeks of searching, the two of them were able to choose a townhome near the DVP and Eglington in a new development called the English Lane. They put a deposit down and signed a purchase contract. The townhouse was to be ready for delivery by November after the wedding, which was well timed with the furniture arriving from Pakistan.

16. Rabba Rabba Mee Barsa

Six months later ...

The wedding was going to consist of a week's worth of events including a *Dholki*, a *Mehndi*, a Hindu wedding ceremony, a Muslim wedding ceremony, and a final reception. The *Dholki* is a small kickoff party with drinks, singing, and dancing, which could be held in Zeina's home.

The Hindu wedding ceremony had to be at a Hindu temple. The Muslim wedding had to be at a mosque, unless they could find an Imam to come to their home. It would be preferable to host it at home. Now, all they had to do was to find large venues for 150 people for the *Mehndi,* the henna ceremony, and the main reception.

Then there was the long list of the nitty-gritty details of food for each event, flowers, decorations, live music, DJ, lights, photographer, and videographer. The list was endless. Zeina wished they could afford to hire a professional wedding planner, but other than cost, they doubted that a local wedding planner would know about a Punjabi wedding. Bottom line was that they had to do most of the work themselves.

Karan opened a new spreadsheet in Excel to plan the wedding. The sheet had a tab for guest list, wedding invites, cost, wedding gifts, gift registry, and many other things. The sheet was, of course, color coded. It was a spreadsheet that could be sold for a million bucks to a professional wedding planner.

After looking at numerous halls and hotels, Zeina stumbled upon a unique concert hall with high, vaulted ceilings called the Great Hall. It had originally been a church and was now was rented only for special occasions. The place was perfect for the *Mehndi*, since that event was mainly about music and dance, and the entire floor of the Great Hall was a dance floor. Zeina envisioned decorating the hall with henna-inspired colors, draping bright, colorful *dupattas* [ethnic scarves], and swagging yellow and orange fabric around the orchestra rails and over the huge windows. She planned to light up the huge hall with hundreds of candles and *diyas*, traditional earthen pots with wicks dipped in oil. She designed a stage where the two of them could sit for the ceremony, and have pictures taken with their family and friends. It would look like a maharaja's gazebo, adorned with Rajasthani furniture and sheer, colorful drapes.

A *Mehndi* is not complete without *dhol* players, *desi* drummers. After a few calls, Karan found a DJ who had *dhol* players working for him. Together, they created the perfect mix for the evening to progress from the bride's traditional entrance to a late night of crazy *bhangra* dancing. The Great Hall did not permit outside caterers, but their Canadian catering team was willing and able to offer a *desi* buffet. A florist was arranged to provide traditional marigold and gardenia garlands for the event. The *Mehndi* plan sounded perfect—Zeina's dream decor, an open bar, *desi* food, *paan*, *Kashmiri chai*, and dance-till-you-drop Punjabi music.

The Hindu wedding was easy to organize. There are plenty of Hindu temples in the greater Toronto area. So many Hindus get married throughout the year that all the priests have the whole wedding ceremony down to a science. The priests gave Karan and Zeina a brochure about what to do, what to wear, who to bring, and what to bring along, with a price list for a regular wedding, a middle-budget wedding, and a VIP package. The temple even had a banquet hall in the basement of the temple where five hundred people could feast. The temple had agreements with two or three caterers the temple's management trusted to provide excellent food and service. Karan picked a date and signed a contract and paid a small deposit. They walked out of the temple impressed with the arrangements and level of organization.

The next task was rather challenging, and Zeina conveniently assigned it to Karan. He had to find a mosque for the *Nikkah* [Islamic wedding] or find an Imam who would be willing to come to their home. Zeina left all such uninteresting assignments for him, and kept the fun part of the wedding planning—such as choosing the flowers, decorations, plate settings, and center pieces—for herself.

Karan called a dozen mosques; he left voice mails and personal messages but couldn't get anyone to call him back. Until one day, someone from the mosque near Eaton Centre called back.

"Hi, my name is Imam Benny Rockbridge. You left a message about a *Nikkah*. I'd like to meet you and the bride-to-be tomorrow, if possible before I can agree to marry you. I own and run the clothing store in front of the mosque at Eaton Center. Come there and see me at 4:00 p.m. tomorrow. I'll be at the store."

Karan couldn't get over his cool name, but since he was the only one who had returned his call, they drove to Eaton Center. They got to the mosque but couldn't figure out which store the Imam meant, because there were three or four clothing stores next to the mosque. Karan went to the mosque to ask where he could find the Imam. A group of young men about to go for prayers pointed to a hip-hop clothing store across the street, blaring loud rap music.

Karan and Zeina entered the store and walked right past a middle-aged man all dressed in black.

"Excuse me, where can I find Imam Benny Rockbridge?" Karan asked one of the sales girls dressed in a miniskirt. He noticed that she sure had a lot of piercing on her body.

"I am Imam Rockbridge," said the cool dude!

The Imam was in his midforties, dressed in a black muscle T-shirt and black jeans. A thick, silver chain and key ring hung across his back pocket.

"You must be Karen, and she must be the bride-to-be."

"My name is Zeina, and his name is Karan, not Karen." Zeina smiled at the Imam and extended her hand.

"Pleased to meet you, sister. Please don't mind, but I don't shake hands with women," he replied with a serious face.

Karan gave Zeina a look to see whether that was their clue to run away or stick around for a few more minutes.

"Follow me to the mosque, and let us speak in my office there."

The office was full of books and videotapes on Islam. Apparently, he was a popular Islamic figure in Toronto. His office walls were decorated with photographs of him dressed in ornate Arabic cloaks along with prominent Muslim leaders of the world. He even spoke on national TV in Canada on the Muslim channel every Friday.

The Imam took a seat behind his desk and offered them tea. Then he said, "I take this seriously. I'll ask you questions, and if I'm not satisfied that you are ready for marriage or right for each other, I'll not do the *Nikkah* for you and not advise you to unite. You can get it done somewhere else. Not a single marriage contract gone through me has ended up in a divorce. You'll have to have five or six sessions with me in my office before we pick a date to get you married."

Karan was ready to get up and leave, but Zeina held him back. First, the Imam interrogated them. After one hour of interrogation, he was convinced that they were mature enough and ready to be married. Then his one-hour lecture started. Parts of the lecture were not that bad. They were about the virtues of marriage—how to remain attractive to each other; personal hygiene (something like, smell nice for each other); act as an umbrella for each other; and other interesting stuff.

Then came the killer boring part. The Imam made them watch one hour of videotapes on Islam. Karan almost passed out with exhaustion. He had almost given up when the Imam came back and said, "You are an unusual couple. I feel that you are right for each other. I'll give you some books to read and some tapes to watch. You don't need any more sessions with me. Let me know the date, time, and location, and I'll be there."

Karan almost jumped with joy! The thought of a few more such sessions was simply depressing.

"What will you charge?" asked Karan. He was holding the budget, and the Excel sheet, and a certain number had to go in cell C14.

"I don't charge anything. You are free to donate what you like to the mosque."

They walked out with a dozen books and tapes on Islam. What an experience that was.

"*Snuggle*, when you are done reading and watching these, just let me know the summary in case he decides to quiz me before the wedding," Karan said with a laugh.

Driving around one Sunday afternoon, Zeina noticed a sign for the Old Mill. Karan took a U-turn to discover an English Tudor–style inn with sprawling, manicured lawns. The ambience was perfect for their wedding. The wedding garden was excellent for the cocktail reception and the indoor hall was large, yet cozy. Zeina fell in love with the inn, so they reserved a date and paid a deposit.

Zeina's mind began working overtime coming up with great ideas she had once discussed with Amma. She came up with the theme for the decor, colors, dance floor, music, and food, just as her mother would have liked.

A week later, while Karan was waiting for the subway at the Bay and Bloor station, he heard two Mexican musicians singing "Unchained Melody." He almost froze listening to their beautiful voices. A few trains passed by as he stood there listening to them. The last four years of his life flashed by in his mind while the pair sang the melody in their heavy Spanish accents. He asked them whether they performed at special events. The lead guitarist told him that the two of them were a part of a professional mariachi band and charged $500 per hour. He asked for a $200 deposit if Karan wanted them to play at the cocktail reception. The trick was that there was no contract, no receipt, and no guarantee that these guys were going to show up. Karan looked into their eyes and sensed sincerity. He gave them the deposit and exchanged mobile numbers to coordinate for the event.

The last difficult task was finding a good photographer. The ones who were well-known charged an exorbitant amount. The ones who were lesser known charged less but were booked solid. Karan found a Russian photographer who was fondly nicknamed the Photo Nazi during the wedding. If the guests moved even an inch from where he expected them to be, he would actually yell at them. He was tough, but he did decent photography. Karan signed a contract with the Photo Nazi for the *Mehndi* and the reception.

Numerous hours were spent in planning, organizing, and collecting special ethnic items to make it a fun wedding. Between wedding planning and work, the summer just flew by. The only thing Karan and Zeina did not get to plan was their honeymoon. Other than that, the tiniest detail was planned.

They organized a few furnished apartments where close family could stay during the wedding and arranged three meals a day for a week with different caterers. Lots of friends offered their homes for guests and helped cook meals. Countdown for the wedding week began.

Family and friends started pouring in from the States, Europe, Pakistan, and India. The wedding started with the *Dholki,* where Simran and Gurpreet stole the show and outperformed everyone in singing and dancing. Karan was the official *Dhol* player for that evening. The event was held in the apartment's backyard, which was decorated with candles, lights, and bright, colorful fabrics. There were about fifty guests who sang, drank, and danced till late at night.

The Hindu wedding ceremony was scheduled for the next morning. Only immediate family and nearest and dearest friends were invited. The priest was fully prepared when they arrived at the temple. The fire pit was located in an enclosed glass patio, with huge industrial exhausts in compliance with strict local fire codes. Zeina wore a fuchsia and purple flowing skirt known as a *lengha* with jewelry that Karan's mother had given her. Karan wore a long ornate white jacket known as a *sherwani*. He looked like a *maharaja* in his turban. The wedding was an emotional event for his parents because this was the first Hindu wedding in the family. Varun had been married in a Sikh ceremony. Karan's grandmother was from a Sikh family, and his grandfather was a Hindu. It was normal for the family to observe two forms of worship in the same house.

Surinder *Chacha* witnessed the wedding, but Cookie *Chachi* opted out of all the events and did not let her children attend any of the events, either. She did send a basket of fruit and homemade sweets. Reluctantly, Karan threw away the sweets, as he was not sure of Cookie *Chachi's* intentions.

For all the Hindus in the wedding procession, Karan and Zeina were married that day. All of them congratulated him on the wedding. The Muslims at the temple put on polite smiles but were not willing to accept that they were married yet. For the temple itself this was the first time ever that Hindus, Sikhs, Muslims, Jews, and Christians had attended a wedding ceremony.

Next was the exciting day for the Muslims in the family. It was the day of the *Nikkah*. The bridegroom wore a black *sherwani*, and the bride wore a burgundy silk *salwar kameez*, one of Amma's many gifts to Zeina.

Karan paced up and down the driveway waiting for the Imam. He was not sure that he would show up. Precisely at 11:00 a.m., the time given to the Imam, he showed up in a crisp brown and gold robe, a beautiful ornate cap, and a Quran and prayer beads in hand.

The Imam noticed that the room was filled with Muslims and non-Muslims, including Sikhs, Christians, and Jews. He did not once question the presence of such a diverse crowd. He conducted most of the *Nikkah* in English. Anything the Imam recited in Arabic, he explained in English. Not for a minute did he make any non-Muslim in the room feel uncomfortable. He completed the whole ceremony in an hour and left. He couldn't stay for lunch. Barely had he left when all the Muslims congratulated everyone in the room.

Arjun popped open champagne, beer, and wine for the guests.

The doorbell rang. It was the Imam! He had forgotten his mobile phone. Everyone panicked and hid their drinks. As soon as he left, the bottles and glasses reappeared.

It was a sunny afternoon. Brunch was laid out in the backyard. All the guests basked in the sun, drank all afternoon, sang songs, and danced.

Almost all *desi* weddings are affiliated with a particular song. It is usually a Bollywood song that is most popular at the time of the wedding. For Karan and Zeina, it was a song known as, "*Rabba rabba mee barsa* [Lord, let it rain]," a vibrant Punjabi song with great *dhol* beats, and it is perfect for *bhangra, a* typical Punjabi dance.

The following night was the *Mehndi* at the Great Hall. The hall looked gorgeous. It was lit with hundreds of candles, and the glow against the yellow, red, and green fabrics looked regal. The event was attended by over a hundred guests. All people who were near and dear to the bride and groom showed up.

Major Atif, Zeina's *mamoo*, also surprised everyone. He came all the way from Pakistan. He came in memory of his beloved sister and to honor her last wish. He met everyone warmly. As he approached Colonel Dev to give him a hug, they made eye contact. Both of them felt a chill run down their spine as they looked into each other's eyes. They recognized each other from their encounter on the battlefield in 1971. They had a flashback to that horrible night. They looked around themselves. There was music playing, people dancing, and they thought about Karan and Zeina. They forgot all about 1971 and embraced each other, communicating with their eyes that no one needed to know or ever to speak of their past on the battlefield.

Zeina walked into the room under a yellow canopy held by six married women. Several other women brought the henna in platters decorated with yellow flowers, glitter, and candles. She walked in with all the women singing traditional *Mehndi* songs followed by a well-known movie song, "*Mehndi hai rachnai walee,*" from the movie *Zubeidaa*. As the dynamic *Dhol* players strolled into the room, they brought with them the rhythm that defines a Mehndi ceremony. No Punjabi can resist dancing to a live *Dhol*. Men and women danced for half an hour as the drummers played nonstop.

The DJ then took over, and people danced for hours. They took short breaks for dinner and drinks but kept dancing. Zoheb and Simran danced to "*Rabba Rabba Mee Barsa,*" and swirled around like whirling dervishes, testing and challenging each other to see who would drop to the floor first. After about fifty turns, Zoheb gave up and Simran kept on going and won.

The grand finale of the reception day finally came. It was by the far the most perfect autumn day ever. Zeina personally looked over all the details and discussed every little part with the banquet manager. Only after she was convinced that everything was in order, did she go to dress.

The Photo Nazi took lots of family photos with the bride and groom around the lovely gardens and fountains of the Old Mill. He didn't like the videographer because he brought his super bright light everywhere and spoiled his exposures.

The mariachi band showed up at 4:00 p.m. The three guys were dressed in traditional, ornate Mexican attire, complete with sombreros. Karan was delighted to see them. He hadn't expected them to show up at all, let alone show up perfectly dressed.

Zeina was a beautiful bride. Amma had created a masterpiece wedding gown. It was deep red with delicate antique gold embroidery. Her *lengha*, a long flowing skirt, weighed a ton because of the gold work. Her jewelry was exquisite: a gold set embedded with hand-cut diamonds, and trimmed with tassels of rubies. She looked at herself in the mirror, put on the final touches of her *teeka* and *jhoomer*, one worn in the mane with a pendant dangling on the forehead and the other, shaped like a fan, worn to the side of the hair. It was always her mother's dream to see her daughter in those two pieces of jewelry. Something she herself had never gotten for her wedding due to circumstances. In the mirror, Zeina saw Amma's dream girl, and she felt at peace.

About 150 people attended the reception. People still talk about that wedding to this day. The cocktail hour was mesmerizing with live music, delicious hors d'oeuvres, and perfect weather.

The bride elegantly entered the patio on her brother's arm. Karan and Zeina exchanged vows and rings in front of all their guests because most of the guests had witnessed neither the Hindu nor the Muslim ceremony. After dancing to the mariachi band and consuming a few cocktails and appetizers, the wedding party moved indoors. Zoheb opened the evening with a speech that went something like this:

"Thank you all for being here and sharing this special occasion. Zeina, my beautiful sister, as she sits there dressed as a bride, is everything to me: my little sister, sometimes my big sister, my best friend, and my soul mate. In our South Asian culture, today is the day Zeina leaves her home and enters that of her husband's. While it is indeed a very happy day for me, seeing Zeina start a new life with Karan, I should feel a certain sadness as she leaves my life, but instead I rather feel that Karan is entering mine. I wish to thank Karan's parents for giving Zeina the ideal husband, and to me the best son-in-law, brother, brother-in-law, and friend. Lastly, I'd like to say a few words about our mother, who is no longer with us. More than anything else in her life; today was the most important day for her. Today was the day that she waited for and meticulously planned. Today would have been and still is the happiest day of her life. She is around here somewhere, beaming cheek to cheek. I would like to share a few glimpses of our mother as a token of her presence here tonight."

With that, he turned on a slide show of about a hundred photographs of Amma, from her very first picture in life to her last one, synchronized with an extremely emotional song by Amy Sky called "I Will Take Care of You."

Zeina had found that song accidentally one day driving back from work. The lyrics instantly touched her heart. The song was perfect for how she felt about her mother. While at several moments people sniffled, they also couldn't help but smile and cheer Amma for the uniqueness exhibited in her photos, such as her making funny faces, getting pedicures, eating waffles loaded with whipped cream, and parasailing during the days of her chemo.

Colonel Dev, Varun, and Uncle Junaid also said a few words. Colonel Dev came up with an interesting line in his speech. He said, "My son Karan reminds me a lot of myself. He does look a bit like me and also behaves like me. About forty years ago, I fell in love with my wife, who was my neighbor, and now I see Karan also getting married to a neighbor, a girl from a neighboring country."

Varun gave a funny speech about Karan being a "neat freak," and "organizer" from an early age.

After dinner and cake cutting, the bride and groom had the first dance to "Unchained Melody." Their lives had come around a full circle. It had all started with the song "Unchained Melody" and happily ended with the same song, but in between it had taken one death, one open-heart surgery, one divorce, and countless painful events to get to that happy ending.

The bride and groom looked into each other's eyes, mesmerized by the beauty of the moment. Both were in a daze, remembering what they had to go through and experience to be dressed as a bride and a groom, and dance to this song in front of all those people.

Their guests represented a wide range of religions, races, languages, and cultures. They were all present to support them. However, the deeper question was how many of the guests present that night would support someone from their family who crossed lines and fell in love with someone different from them.

"I love you," Karan said to Zeina and kissed her in front of 150 people.

"I love you too," she said, as she kissed him back.

"We've been so busy with our wedding planning that we never planned our honeymoon. Not that I have any remaining time off, anyway," Zeina said with a sad face.

"Maybe I took care of that for us," Karan said with a mysterious smile on his face.

The second dance was to "In the Arms of an Angel." Zeina danced with her brother, who was so emotional that he was crying while he danced.

The DJ and the crowd took over after that, and the guests danced for hours. At one point, every single wedding guest danced in complete synchronization to the "Macarena."

At midnight, Zeina and Karan bid farewell to their guests, as Amma's favorite song played in the background—*"Mehlon ka rajah mila, ke raani beti raaj karygee."*

Zeina then stepped into a *palki* [carriage for a bride] adorned with flowers, which Zoheb and his three other friends, who were like her brothers, carried to the end of the hallway. From there, Karan and Zeina went to their honeymoon suite.

Zoheb bade her a tearful farewell. He was handing his sister over to Karan forever that day.

At last, they were officially alone under one roof, married in the eyes of the Hindus, the Muslims, and the courts of Canada.

"First time I read your palm, I could see that you were to be married twice, but now you are married to me three times already!" Zeina laughed.

Shiraz had left a special negligee and candles for Zeina in the room.

"*Snuggle*, I asked for a week off for you from your boss as a wedding gift. I also packed your bags, which are in this room. Tomorrow morning, we are going to Disney for a week! Whatever I did not pack, I'll buy for you in Orlando."

She jumped with joy to hear that! It was her dream-come-true honeymoon.

And finally, there they were, holding hands under a moonlit sky with the Disney castle in the background, looking over the fireworks and the Disney parade. It was all worth it. They were together forever.

17. And Now …

Karan and Zeina's first son was born a year and a half later. Karan was relocated to New York, where he worked for an international bank on Wall Street and Zeina worked as a designer for one of the largest global retailers. They all became permanent US residents; they bought and renovated an old Victorian home from the late 1800s in Jersey City, and the greater New York City area became home. Three years later they were blessed with another boy who was born in New Jersey.

Karan's work later took them to various destinations around the globe. Zeina took a few years off to raise their two boys. Karan remains a successful banker and continues to enjoy traveling, photography, and, yes, he still sings songs to her and their children. She keeps a lovely home. She has become an even better cook and dedicates her time to her family. She hopes to return to work as the children become more independent.

They visit both India and Pakistan frequently to meet relatives. No one ever questions their religion, their nationality, or how they raise their children. They are raising their children to believe in God, to be good human beings, and to develop their own beliefs without prejudice and biases. Their children will have the opportunity to be whoever they wish to be.

With time, religion, culture, and political boundaries have all faded away for them and what is left is their nuclear family and the love between them.

Once a year, Karan and Zeina take a stroll down 55th street. They take a moment together under that awning of building number 65 and share a kiss like no other, reminding them how precious their bond is and how it came to be …

Love goes beyond boundaries. To all those who go against convention and dare to love someone of a different religion, culture, or country, believe in yourself, and stay firm in your belief. All forces against you will gradually wither away and what will remain is true love. It is important to have faith and recognize the signs given by the *Painter Man*. Sometimes when you feel helpless, listen to your heart, do your best, and then let destiny take over.

We all are sent to this world equal and empty-handed. All that we take back with us is our experiences and what we have learned. We gather biases and prejudice along the way. Blessed are the ones who leave the world just as pure they come into it.

The End